ACCLAIM FOR AWARD WINNING AUTHOR BARRY FINLAY

SHADOWS OF TRUTH (BOOK FOUR)

"Finlay excels in creating a vivid setting, immersing readers in the luxurious yet perilous world of a cruise ship. The storm scenes are particularly well crafted, evoking a palpable sense of danger and urgency." – **Readers' Favorite**

THE SECRET TRUTH: A JAKE SCOTT MYSTERY (BOOK THREE)

"As a former journalist, I have an appreciation for how effectively the author has developed Jake's character. Not only does he have an appealing sense of humor, but he's genuinely a good person." - **Novels Alive**

THE GUARDIANS OF TRUTH: A JAKE SCOTT MYSTERY (BOOK TWO)

"Perfectly executed, well written, thoroughly and utterly enjoyable; I really do hope Jake doesn't stop scratching that journalistic itch, because I'd love to spend another few hundred pages in his company." – **Cath 'N' Kindle Book Reviews**

SEARCHING FOR TRUTH: A JAKE SCOTT MYSTERY (BOOK ONE)

"Searching For Truth is an intriguing whodunit that embraces much more psychological depth than most mysteries and will have readers both guessing and involved to the end." – **D. Donovan, Senior Reviewer, Midwest Book Review**

Shadows of Truth

A Jake Scott Mystery

Barry Finlay

Keep On Climbing Publishing

ACKNOWLEDGMENTS

My wife, Evelyn, and I have been fortunate to travel the world alongside family and friends. These experiences offered times to enjoy each other's company and share some laughs while we explored new places and were introduced to new cultures. I appreciate each of our fellow wanderers more than they will ever know for the part they played in making our travels memorable.

The opportunity to connect with new cultures is a gift I wish everyone could experience. Some of our journeys took place aboard cruise ships—including one memorable voyage from Vancouver to Alaska. That's where the seed for *Shadows of Truth* was planted.

The idea of being trapped on a manmade luxury liner, caught in one of Mother Nature's worst temper tantrums while a killer prowls the corridors, struck me as both terrifying and captivating. Jake Scott, Dani Perez, and her daughter, Emilie, are the unfortunate souls navigating this nightmare. I'm happy to report that our cruises have never involved murder or mayhem—though we were once chased out of Da Nang, Vietnam, by the tail end of a hurricane, and we've ridden through towering waves in the Caribbean. Thankfully, real life seldom mirrors fiction. But imagining the chaos was undeniably thrilling.

Writing a murder mystery set on a cruise ship presented unique challenges. I needed to understand the ship's inner workings, and for that, I'm deeply indebted to Jennifer Weaver. Her years of firsthand experience at sea, paired with her generous willingness to answer countless questions—no matter how minor—were invaluable. Any errors or liberties taken with cruise ship life are mine alone.

Mirna Gilman from Books Go Social once again transformed my minimal cover concept into something vibrant and compelling. This marks her fourth Jake Scott cover, and my gratitude hasn't wavered since the first. A heartfelt thank-you also goes to Sigrid Macdonald, whose eagle-eyed edits caught what my own repeated readings could not. Her expertise elevates every page.

To my readers—you are the heartbeat of this journey. Your enthusiasm, feedback, and encouragement are what keep me going. I write for the love of storytelling but knowing that these stories resonate with you makes the process even more rewarding. I'm especially thankful to my team of early readers, who offer their support before each book officially launches.

And to Evelyn: thank you for always reading the earliest, roughest drafts and offering suggestions. Your unwavering support, whether it's travelling, writing, or just life, means everything.

Finally, a word to everyone—please continue to support indie creators. Whether authors, musicians, or artists, they pour their souls into their craft. Your support keeps their dreams alive.

Now, follow Jake, Dani, and Emilie on their latest adventure—and most importantly, enjoy the ride.

Cataloguing data available at Library and Archives Canada.

ISBN: 978-1-0688371-6-6 Paperback

ISBN: 978-1-0688371-7-3 eBook

The story, all names, characters, and incidents portrayed in this production are fictitious. No identification with actual persons (living or deceased), places, buildings, and products is intended or should be inferred.

Chapter One

The extended blast of the ship's horn announced they were about to be on their way. Jake Scott couldn't believe he was doing this. How had Dani talked him into a cruise? He decided when the ship started moving, there was nothing to do but embrace it. What else would he do? Jump overboard? Since the thought of drowning appealed to him even less than being stuck in a floating city surrounded by nothing but water and thousands of other brave souls, he promised himself to make the best of it.

As the ship edged away from the dock, Jake sat on the balcony of the stateroom he shared with Dani and her daughter, Emilie, who had an adjoining room. Jake had never been on a ship before, so he didn't know what to expect. Never a fan of water except for showering, drinking, and filling the dishwasher and washing machine, he didn't know how much motion to expect or how much he could withstand. Dani assured him she had packed sufficient motion sickness pills for all three in the event things didn't turn out as well as they hoped. She had been on a cruise, and she convinced Jake they would be fed and pampered beyond his wildest dreams and that the motion would be minimal. He hoped she was right. Seventeen-year-old Emilie vibrated with excitement as the ship's air horn announced to everyone within a mile or two that the journey had started.

The threesome watched without speaking as the city of Vancouver grew smaller. Buildings that towered over them minutes earlier could now be measured between a thumb and a forefinger. Jake and Dani sat on either side of a table big enough for a couple of drinks on the balcony while Emilie leaned over the railing, her shoulders twisting from right to left as she tried to capture every picture-worthy sight with her cellphone. The lack of movement impressed Jake as the ship effortlessly glided through the water, and he had to peer down at the bow to convince himself they were moving. He realized the buildings and trees offered protection from the wind and that things could be different when they arrived in the ocean's expanse, but while the ship departed, he relaxed and enjoyed the scenery. Little did he realize that the ship's movement would be the least of his problems on this journey.

After watching the departure, they returned inside to their stateroom. It wasn't large, but it was functional. Like a motor home, the designers used every conceivable space. At about 180 square feet, it barely left room to walk between the wall and the bed, but suitcases slid conveniently underneath the box spring. A sofa suitable for two sat against one wall while the one opposite featured a storage unit with a mirror, safe, minibar, and drawers. A 45-inch TV hung on the wall. The utilitarian bathroom on the same side as the sofa contained a shower unit barely large enough for one. On the ceiling was a speaker from which the captain's or a senior officer's unintelligible words came. *That part needs work,* Jake thought.

They changed from shorts and T-shirts into casual clothes for dinner, then collected Emilie from her room and wandered down a corridor whose walls could almost be reached if you stretched out both arms. A bell dinged, announcing the elevator's arrival on the eighth floor, the location of their home away from home. A man in a multicoloured top and shorts and two women in dazzling white shorts and identical purple T-shirts with the logo of a dancing lion on the front moved to the back of the elevator as Jake, Dani, and Emilie stepped on. The first thing Jake noticed was a rectangular plaque on the floor at the front of the elevator with "Sunday" engraved on it. "They change the plaque every night at midnight," Dani said. From the back of the elevator came the woman's voice in a southern drawl. "Believe me, by about Wednesday, you'll need it. It's easy to lose track of time on a cruise."

A smiling Filipino woman in a flowered white shirt and black pants danced to music only she could hear and greeted them at the door to the dining room with a gigantic bottle of hand sanitizer. "Don't forget to wash your hands," she said through smiling lips, her hips swaying as she squirted a liberal amount of cleanser for each of them. "I have enough for three people," Jake griped as he rubbed his hands together multiple times. Emilie held out her hand as if offering to take some of Jake's but applied more to his hands with a laugh. They proceeded past the front entrance, where a maître d' led them to Table 144.

The dining room was immense, with a waterfall as its centrepiece and a wide staircase at the front. The staircase split into two sections that led to more dining on the fifth deck. Hundreds of white cloth-covered tables with sparkling silverware that would accommodate various group sizes were spread throughout the room. José and Maria introduced themselves as their waiters for the cruise.

José stood about five feet seven inches tall with a slim build. He had a round, pleasant face that smiled easily and jet-black hair. Maria could have been his sister. She had the same round face and pleasant demeanour. They wore the standard uniform of black pants and a vest with red piping, a red tie, and a white shirt. Badges on their lapels helped passengers remember their names.

When they placed the menus on the table, Jake's eyes widened at the nine appetizers, six mains, and seven dessert options available. Narrowing the choices took time for Jake and Dani. Emilie had already chosen from her phone app before she arrived at the dining room and suggested the other two might want to do the same after rolling her eyes with a deep sigh at the time it took them to decide.

They joked with the waiters throughout the meal and chatted with the people at the neighbouring table. Despite the size of the room and the number of people, there was a calm, efficient approach to taking orders and delivering meals that could have been run by a drill sergeant. When they finished, they found a spacious theatre to watch a stage production. By the end of the performance, the day's activities had worn Jake and Dani out, but Emilie was ready to go. She veered off to explore when Jake and Dani headed to their room. The thought of Emilie wandering around by herself on the ship bothered Dani, but she had prepared herself before they arrived with a reminder that it wasn't much different from going downtown with her friends in Ottawa. In fact, it might be safer as there were staff and cameras everywhere on the ship. No way would Emilie want to stay with her and Jake throughout the entire trip, she told herself. Dani told her daughter to be back in her adjoining room by eleven and to knock on the door between the rooms to let her know she had arrived.

Jake and Dani put on their pyjamas and the plush robes provided by the cruise line and opened the door to the balcony. Jake poured a glass of Pinot Grigio for each of them from the beverage package they had ordered and handed one to Dani before depositing the bottle back into the compact refrigerator. The tepid outside air hummed from the water lapping against the side of the ship and the laughter and music from the pool deck. It reminded Jake of the activity in any slightly populated city, except for the soothing sound of the waves. He decided he could get used to this without difficulty.

They raised their drinks in a toast and clinked glasses. "Such a beautiful night," Dani murmured as she leaned back in her chair. "So calm and relaxing. Look at the moon. Doesn't it look mysterious just hanging there? And such a nice, fresh breeze blowing off the ocean. It feels like paradise right now." As if on cue, a wisp of her hair waved in the soft wind. "I love the nights at sea, but I'm looking forward to Alaska. It seems like such a unique place." They got up and leaned on the railing the same way Emilie had earlier. Rows and rows of lights from another cruise ship twinkled in the distance behind them. In the darkness, each row seemed suspended in the air with nothing between. "I wonder if that ship will follow us all the way to Alaska," she mused as she turned her head toward Jake. "Is that port or starboard?"

"All I know is we're *on*board, and I hope the captain keeps the shiny side up for the entire trip," Jake said. "I wonder how far away the ship is. They say the water distorts distances. Maybe we'll learn something about sailing in the next seven days."

Jake pulled her close but noticed her gaze directed past him into the balcony next door. The look evaporated as quickly as it arrived, so Jake let it go. Neither of them said anything as they embraced. They returned to their seats and enjoyed each other's company, the music from the pool area, and the warm air. Quiet murmurs drifted from the balcony two cabins to their left. Looming shadows in the distance and the occasional house lights that faded in and out like fireflies as they passed wooded areas assured Jake that they weren't far from land. They finished their wine and wandered back inside around 10 o'clock. They got ready for bed, and Dani read her thriller novel while Jake flipped through the limited TV channels as they waited for a tap on the door, announcing Emilie's return.

It came around 10:40. Emilie opened the door between their rooms, and words tumbled out of her mouth about an acoustic guitarist she had watched in one of the many lounge areas. "The ship is huge!" she said. "Oh, and I found cookies in a restaurant on the deck a couple of floors above us. It's a place called The Mainmast, all one word, and we can go there for hamburgers and stuff at lunch or snacks anytime." She held out a napkin with four chocolate cookies stacked on it. "One for each of you and two for me," she declared with a laugh before Jake and Dani had a chance to touch them. "I'm going to get ready for bed and figure out what to do tomorrow. See you in the morning." Dani hugged her daughter. They discussed a plan for meeting at breakfast and said their good nights before she closed the door between the rooms.

"How is she going to figure out what to do tomorrow?" Jake asked.

Dani patted Jake's knee, and her voice grew bubbly. "Well, we have a daily planner. See?" She held up a four-page brochure highlighting the next day's activities, the weather forecast, and other essential information. "She also has the ship app. You know the one we had to download before we arrived? You should access it." Her relaxed smile displayed a level of comfort and contentment that filled Jake's heart.

Jake regarded Dani as she grunted while edging the hefty balcony door open and went back outside. He assumed she wanted a final bit of fresh air, but she leaned over the railing and peered to her right into the balcony next door. The corners of her mouth turned down again, but this time, more pronounced. She returned inside, closed the door, and said, "We need to call a doctor. The man next door hasn't moved in his chair for more than an hour. I thought he was sleeping with his head at an odd angle, that he would wake up with a stiff neck, but his colour isn't good. I think he might be dead."

Chapter Two

Dani planned the cruise nine months before the launch date. When she first proposed the possibility to Jake, he responded with a resounding, "No." She knew that would be his reaction. It was his first response to anything new. She had snickered to herself. She planned to throw it out there and let it simmer for a while. Then, she would launch a second offensive with a more detailed explanation of how much fun and safe it would be. It was a matter of wearing him down day by day until he agreed.

Dani had sold her condo and Jake his house, and they purchased a new home in the same Westboro neighbourhood in Ottawa, the capital of Canada, where they had both lived for several years. They loved the neighbourhood, and, as a bonus, it was still close enough to walk to Brew and Buns, the restaurant where they met their friends for breakfast every Saturday morning. Dani would have been comfortable moving into Jake's home, where he had lived with his wife, Mia, until her death from an aneurysm five years prior, but he insisted they should have a fresh start.

They settled on a thirty-year-old three-bedroom bungalow with oak hardwood floors, a porch on the front, and a narrow yard. It had a two-car garage that would accommodate Jake's Subaru and Dani's Tucson. Ceramic floors, granite counter surfaces, and pot lights everywhere modernized the house. The backyard had low-maintenance shrubs while mature trees draped like an awning over the street at the front. In fact, the new place bore a significant resemblance to Jake's previous house. The only thing missing was the water feature in the backyard, but the two-car garage easily compensated for that.

The new place thrilled Emilie. She had applied to universities, so it was undecided where she would live after being accepted. In the meantime, Emilie had declared the bedroom in the finished basement and the separate bathroom just outside her door "sick," which Jake interpreted as perfect.

Oliver, Jake's temperamental cat, wandered around checking things out in the new place for about two days, but realizing he could still watch the birds in the backyard from his perch, he settled in comfortably. He meowed contentedly when a squirrel bounced along the fence surrounding the yard.

Jake had rented a truck, and their three friends from their Saturday breakfast group, Pierre Chevrier, Eric Jacobson, and Ryan Cambridge, had helped them move. It had been an opportunity for Jake and Dani to downsize, but it wasn't a simple task. They both discovered that memories collected over the years were difficult to part with. They helped each other decide.

Dani hadn't had a vacation from her job as a homicide detective for months. She and Jake had visited Toronto a few times to see his daughter, Avery, and her husband, Nick, and especially to get to know his new granddaughter, Ava. Jake loved spending time with Ava, and that was one excuse he used for not wanting to go on a cruise. "We'll only be away for two weeks," Dani argued. Jake came back with, "Two weeks is a lifetime for a baby." When Dani replied he usually went four weeks without spending time with Ava, Jake said, "What about Oliver? Who'll take care of him?" Dani said she was sure they could find a nice kennel to handle the belligerent cat. "Maybe he'll learn some manners."

The negotiation continued, but Jake ran out of excuses.

He had also observed how tired Dani was. The murder rate had increased in the city over the previous year, and some went unsolved. Many nights she came home, ate dinner, and collapsed into bed, only to awaken early in the morning to start the routine over again. It didn't help that the department had a staff shortage. Jake knew the best thing would be for her to get away from everything for a couple of weeks. Maybe he could convince her to go to Portugal in the winter, and he suggested it twice. She met the suggestion each time with a wry smile and a glance toward a brochure under the coffee table.

One Friday evening in November, Dani snuggled close to Jake on the sofa in the sunroom with the table lamp's light shining off the brochure in her hand. The drapes hung open, and ice pellets ricocheted off the glass doors, driven by a wind that made the house creak. The ever-changing flames in the gas fireplace warmed them and offset the winter raging outside. Jake put his arm around her as she pulled her bare feet up on the sofa and leaned back against his chest. She innocently flipped the pages of the brochure to the back, which displayed a room schematic. "What do you think of this?"

"What am I looking at?" Jake asked as he peered over her shoulder at the open page. It described connected rooms, each with two twin beds that converted to a king, a sofa, a balcony, and a private bathroom. "They look comfortable. Is that in Portugal?"

Then the words "ocean view" jumped off the page. Uh oh.

A blast of wind smacking another batch of ice pellets off the windows and a blender grinding in the kitchen interrupted the conversation. When the grinding stopped, Emilie yelled, "Does anyone want a smoothie?" Jake and Dani both declined. Dani had kept her finger on the page but closed the brochure, so the cover faced Jake. It displayed a photo of a huge cruise ship framed by palm trees, its polished hull gleaming in the sunlight, with the name "Ocean Wanderer" painted in gigantic black lettering on the bow. Joyous faces caught in a moment in time waved from the ship, and the sun trailed rays across the rich, navy-blue water, beckoning like a candle to a moth for the readers to join in the fun. She said, "It's an Alaska cruise leaving from Vancouver. There are only a few dates available. There's one in July that still has connected rooms. It would be a wonderful way to spend time with Em before she goes to university. The agent said we would have to book soon because the dates go fast. She said the water through the inside passage is smooth because it's sheltered. It's only when it gets into the Gulf of Alaska before the ship turns to come back that the waves could get higher, but it's rare in the summer months. You would love it, and I know Em would."

Jake knew Dani had trouble sleeping, and the dark shadows and puffiness under her eyes confirmed it. He kissed the top of her head. "Okay," he whispered.

Dani pushed her feet off the sofa and whirled around. "What did you say?"

"I said, okay." Jake chuckled as she threw her arms around him. His face pressing into her shoulder muffled his voice, but he squeaked, "Let's get our spots booked. Shall we tell Emilie now, or should we wait?'

"Let's wait until we've booked our rooms. It's so exciting. I love you, Jake Scott!"

"I love you, too, Daniela Perez. Now, we should have a drink so I can calm my nerves. You said it's rare that the ocean gets rough. That means it *could* get rough." He laughed as he got up to retrieve glasses of wine for them.

Emilie wandered into the sunroom in checkered pants and a navy shirt Jake thought belonged in the bedroom rather than outside, but it was the trend. She sipped her pinkish-green smoothie. "What's all the yelling about? Did we finally win the lottery?"

"No, we're going on a cruise to Alaska," Dani blurted.

"So much for keeping it quiet," Jake laughed as he carried the glasses of wine back to the sofa.

The excitement in the room didn't die down for an hour as they pored over the online brochure on Dani's laptop. It alarmed Jake to learn the ship held 2,800 people, had an immense dining room with two sittings, countless bars, and a choice of excursions that included helicopter rides and the possibility of seeing bears. Still, he couldn't help but get caught up in the excitement as Dani and Emilie scanned the website and ran through the endless possibilities of things to do throughout the week of sailing.

Jake visited his granddaughter four more times before their departure date, but before they knew it, the time had arrived, and they were on their way across the country to Vancouver. They had whiled the next day away, relaxing in Stanley Park. Emilie spent her time sunning and swimming at Second Beach Pool, while Jake and Emilie had walked along the seawall and taken a relaxing, narrated, and enchanting horse-drawn carriage ride.

The next day, they took an Uber to Canada Place, had their photo taken, and wound their way through registration. They received the cruise pass that would give them cashless access to everything onboard, as well as allow them to disembark and return for their excursions. The walk through the registration line and up the ramp to board the ship seemed like miles to Jake. Although he had prepared himself, the immensity of the vessel still startled him. He couldn't get over the towering decks with sparkling glass doors opening onto balconies that promised breathtaking panoramic views. Dock workers scurried about, completing final tasks before the ship departed. There was a hint of salt water and fresh paint, and the faint hum of the gigantic engines vibrating somewhere deep in the bowels of the ship. Between where the rows of portholes ended, and the balconies began, hung lifeboats with orange tarps covering them. A combination of excitement and trepidation overcame Jake as they arrived at their assigned muster station for a safety briefing. It reminded him something could go wrong.

He didn't want to think about it.

Chapter Three

J ake dialled the Medical Centre on the ship while Dani leaned over the edge of the balcony, waving and yelling at the passenger next door, but to no avail. As Jake watched her calling to the man, her body language told him she knew it was too late. When someone picked up at the Medical Centre, he said, "I'm in Room 8835, and we believe the man on the balcony in the next room is in trouble. He hasn't moved in his chair during the time we've been here. It's been over an hour now. Please send someone as soon as possible."

Dani rushed past Jake to the corridor, and he heard her banging on the door to the next cabin and calling out for someone to answer. Jake said into the phone, "Just a minute. I'm not sure if the numbers go up or down. I'll check." Jake set the phone receiver on the bedside table and hurried to the door.

Dani looked at him before he could speak. "I can't get any response."

Jake checked the number on the door and hurried back inside the cabin. The steward rushed down the hall to check on the commotion. Jake said into the phone, "It's 8834. Please hurry. The man isn't responding."

Jake propped the door open to their cabin as Dani came back inside. The steward knocked next door and was about to use his master key when another man arrived. Jake and Dani returned to the corridor and introduced themselves to the tall, blonde-haired man with a tanned face, who identified himself as the ship's doctor. He asked, "Is the man still sitting on the balcony?" When Dani confirmed, the doctor placed his key card in the door locking mechanism and entered the room. He instructed Jake and Dani to remain in their room.

They did as they were told, but after two minutes, they heard the doctor on his phone through their open balcony door. The words were muffled so they couldn't understand what he said. However, ten minutes later, they heard the rattle of an ambulance stretcher gurney on squeaky wheels being pushed through the door of 8834.

Dani got up to answer a tapping on the door connecting them to the adjoining room where Emilie was supposed to be sleeping. Her daughter poked her head inside and mumbled, "What's all the racket in the hall? I hope it won't be like this every night."

"No, dear. I'm sure it won't. The man next door is not feeling well, so they brought a stretcher to take him to the Medical Centre. It will be quiet soon. These rooms are soundproof. Get some sleep, and we'll see you for breakfast in the morning."

Emilie closed the door again as Jake got up to find out who was knocking at the open door to their state room. The man had a swarthy complexion and dark hair. Thick eyebrows the size of caterpillars hung over eyes that were never still, as though on the lookout for someone or something. He wore the white shirt and shoulder stripes of an officer. He asked if he could come in, introduced himself as Eduardo, and proffered a badge, identifying him as the Chief Security Officer. Jake and Dani sat side-by-side on the sofa as Eduardo rolled the chair away from the desk and sat.

The security man said, "Unfortunately, the man in the next room did not survive, so I would like to ask you a few questions for the record, if you don't mind." He browsed the iPad in his hand. "I see you're from Ottawa. This will only take a few minutes. I don't want to spoil your vacation."

Jake said, "Of course not. We're sorry to hear he didn't make it. That's incredibly sad."

Dani nodded her agreement.

Eduardo said, "A cruise ship has many passengers of all ages and health conditions, and these things often happen, unfortunately. Let's start with when you first noticed the gentleman."

Dani described how she had been leaning on the ledge of the balcony when she first noticed the man with his head at an odd angle, and she thought he was sleeping. She mentioned he remained in the same position about an hour later, and that's when she became worried. She said she thought it unusual that he was already asleep on the cruise, but he must have been extra tired or had too many drinks before boarding.

The Security Chief squinted back and forth between Jake and Dani. "Well, we have no reason to believe it's anything more than natural causes, and on behalf of the crew, I would like to apologize for any inconvenience. We want to assure you there is no danger, and we want you to have an excellent cruise."

Eduardo got up to leave when Dani asked, "What will happen to the body?"

The Chief Security Officer sat down again with a stony stare and whispered as if someone else might be listening, "We have a morgue downstairs."

"Will the death be reported to a law enforcement agency?"

"I don't think you should trouble yourself with these questions Miss, uh..." Eduardo checked the iPad. "Miss Daniela."

Dani continued. "I had difficulty seeing in the light, but it looked to me like he had staining around his lips. It could suggest some kind of poison was injected or administered through a liquid, like a drink. I suggest you order an autopsy as soon as possible."

Eduardo sat speechless, staring at Dani. After what seemed like minutes, he said, "May I ask your qualifications to suggest such a thing?"

"Yes, of course. I'm the Head of the Homicide Division for Ottawa Police Services." Dani produced her credentials from her wallet, which Eduardo diligently examined. "I've seen cases before where the victim had similar colouring. It turned out to be poisoning. There are other explanations, of course. Have you heard of the term cyanosis?"

Eduardo said, "I am familiar with the term from my days in the military before I retired and started working for the cruise line. Please remind me about the details, though."

Dani continued. "The lips and fingertips turn blue after death because of a lack of oxygenated blood circulating through the body. A heart attack or internal bleeding results in this happening faster than an infection or organ failure. But the distinct colouring would suggest the death could have resulted from poisoning. That, and the fact the bluish tinge rarely shows up for an hour or two after death if it's from a heart attack or internal bleeding—longer if it's organ failure or infection. I just think it's something you should consider."

Droplets of sweat dappled the security man's upper lip, and his face took on the shade of his white shirt. Jake had been taken aback by Dani's suspicions, but Eduardo's reaction made him think that a murder onboard would be terrible for business.

Eduardo said, "We treat all deaths on board seriously. The doctor will do what he can, but he is not equipped to do an autopsy. You understand we must be discreet about this matter. Rumours spread like wildfire on the ship. Before long, someone will make a video with crazy conspiracy theories about a murder on the ship. I will relay your concerns to the doctor, so he can do a preliminary examination. Our standard procedure is to inform the U.S. Centers for Disease Control and Prevention in the event of any death onboard in case the cause of death is contagious. Should the doctor find something suspicious, he will request that the body be turned over to the local authorities at our first port of call, and the FBI will be informed. Under normal circumstances, the body would remain in the morgue until we return home."

"Okay," Dani said. "I just wanted you to know what I observed based on my experience. We're here if you have more questions."

With that, Eduardo got up, wiped his upper lip with a tissue, and left.

Chapter Four

The next morning, while Dani showered, Jake scrolled through the cruise ship app he had downloaded at Dani's urging. He found scrolling through it annoying compared to the paper copy of the daily planner they received, so he shut down his phone. The list of things to do for the various decks turned out to be mind-boggling, and it just seemed more manageable on the paper copy. After a few minutes, as he heard the shower stop, he returned to the app where he perused the breakfast menu. As Emilie suggested, he would have an idea what to order before they arrived at the dining hall. He showered when Dani finished and dressed in beige shorts, a white patterned golf shirt, and sandals with no socks, something else Emilie insisted upon.

Jake, Dani, and Emilie wandered along the corridor toward the elevator. The light brown carpet in the hall featured a diamond-shaped pattern with a darker brown image of a compass inlaid every few feet. The carpet complemented the beige walls, providing a peaceful setting for the travellers.

They stopped to gaze over the rail down to the common area on the fifth deck, where a lineup of passengers waited for coffee, and eager people could book another cruise. Further down on Deck Four, musical equipment lay scattered on a compact stage to be used later, and passengers could book shore excursions or have their questions answered by Guest Services.

The red walls were bright and cheery, and a plush red carpet with a huge circular geometric pattern was visible four decks below in the middle of Deck Four. They had noticed the night before, on the map conveniently in front of the elevator, that the common area led to an art gallery on one side. They had passed through the shopping area on the other side on their way from the dining hall to the theatre the night before. The glass walls of the elevators revealed throngs of passengers as they ascended and descended. Jake gulped at the sight of frothing tips on the ocean waves through the glassed-in wall behind the coffee shop.

A bell dinged, announcing that one of the six elevators, and the one farthest away, had arrived. They rushed to board, and Jake noticed the plaque on the floor had magically changed over to Monday. Someone on the ship had been assigned the duty of changing the plaques every night at midnight.

After the events of the previous evening, Jake and Dani expected a pleasant day at sea, although Jake wasn't sure what that would entail. Emilie had already run around the track a few times on Deck Twelve. She announced as they boarded the elevator that two and a half times around the track represented about a mile. Jake didn't have that on his list of things to do on the cruise, but Dani agreed to go with her daughter the next morning.

After another liberal dose of hand sanitizer, a pair of different waiters from the night before greeted them at the table, asking them about their evening. Jake and Dani both thought about the dead man in the next room, but they replied that it had been great. After they placed their order, they opened the apps on their respective phones to figure out what they were going to do for the day. Jake's thoughts of reading and snoozing on the balcony didn't really require an app.

Emilie settled on a line dancing course in the common area at 11 a.m. Jake set his phone on the table and waited to see what Dani had in mind.

While Dani scrolled through the list of activities, she noted an information technology group had a meeting scheduled in a conference room later in the week on Deck Five. It meant little to her, but her career taught her to observe everything. The location of the conference room surprised her, since they had undoubtedly walked by it several times. Dani spotted nothing that appealed to her for the morning, so hanging out on the balcony won out. "Unless you want to go to a napkin-folding class," she suggested to Jake with a smirk.

When they finished their breakfast, Emilie headed off to continue exploring the ship before her line dancing class, and Jake and Dani returned to their room. A frog cleverly constructed from towels by the cleaning staff sat on the back of the sofa. A light flashing on their phone signalled a message. Dani listened while Jake donned his sunglasses and opened the balcony door to the warm sunshine. When she finished, she joined Jake.

She handed him a bottle of water and said, "The Chief of Security, Eduardo, would like to meet with us. He invited us to his office on Deck One. He might be worried that we'll tell everyone on the ship about the dead man next door."

Jake squinted as he gave Dani the once-over. Her face looked gorgeous framed in brilliant sunshine. He pried the top off the bottle and said, "Hmm ... okay ... Deck One? That sounds like it will be below water. It seems like a strange request, but I understand them being worried about rumours spreading. What time?"

"He said anytime that's convenient, so since we aren't doing anything, now is as good a time as any. Are you ready?"

"Sure, let's get it over with."

They went inside, and Jake sipped his water as Dani called Eduardo to arrange for their meeting. "He's sending someone up to get us," Dani said.

A few minutes later, a short young woman in the cruise line uniform of black pants and a white shirt with black and gold epaulettes on the shoulders arrived at the door to their stateroom. She said little as she led Jake and Dani to an elevator that she summoned with a passkey. They found out on the way down that the elevator they were on was reserved for the crew. They got off on Deck One to an austere floor with no carpets or bright colours. Only door after door after door to rooms, most of which they were told were tiny and served as the living quarters for two people. The young woman referred to the corridor that seemed to run from one end of the ship to the other as I-95, suggesting the main north-south highway through the United States. They passed an enormous, noisy laundry room and arrived at a security office that turned out to be not much larger than their stateroom. Eduardo rose from his desk and beamed at them.

"Thank you so much for agreeing to meet me," he said. "I promise I won't take much of your time so you can go back to enjoying the cruise. Perhaps I can give you a tour of the ship later. As a courtesy from one law enforcement official to another, I wanted to give you an update to set your mind at ease. Please follow me."

They did as he suggested and rode the elevator once again, arriving in front of a locked door on the 10th-floor bridge deck. Eduardo used a phone on the wall to announce their arrival. When the door opened, they entered an immense space with wall-to-wall windows and stations in the middle and on both sides with various buttons, knobs, and switches. The horseshoe-shaped station in the middle had the same buttons, knobs, and switches, but was supplemented by dials, computer terminals, and comfortable office chairs. It reminded Jake of images of the space shuttle's command centre. The motif was blue: walls, ceiling, and the horseshoe. Calming, Jake thought, but also a reminder they were at sea. The front window overlooked a helicopter pad at the front of the ship and, beyond that, nothing but ocean.

Eduardo introduced them to the captain, a tall, poised blonde woman in her forties named Ingrid Svenssen, who spoke with a Scandinavian accent. She wore a spotless white uniform, with gold stripes at the shoulders, a gold name tag, and polished shoes. Her blue eyes were sharp and observant. Jake said, "I don't see any wheel for steering the ship." "No," Ingrid said with a laugh. "It's all done with a joystick now." Her voice was level and clear, accustomed to answering questions from thousands of curious tourists. She spoke with a hint of Norway in her accent. "Everything is electric/hydraulic to turn the pods at the back of the ship. It also has autopilot. We can operate it from the stations in the middle or the sides. All the controls to operate it from the sides are identical, but more condensed." Jake thanked the captain and followed Dani and Eduardo, but he was shocked at the few people on the bridge required to keep the behemoth running smoothly.

Eduardo led them to a separate room with a large opening overlooking the bridge. The room held an array of closed-circuit television monitors. He said, "The man's name was Alan Brindley, from Vancouver, and he was employed as a computer security specialist. He was onboard for a convention at which around seventy-five people are registered."

Dani leaned forward, harkening back to the information technology convention listed in the daily planner.

Eduardo continued, "This ship is older, so it isn't a smart ship, but we have CCTV with some facial recognition we can use to track most people's whereabouts most of the time while they are onboard. There are blind spots, of course. It's not perfect, but it's much better than we used to have.

"We tracked Mr. Brindley from the time he boarded almost to the time he entered his cabin." Eduardo gestured to a middle-aged man sitting in front of a monitor. "Please show our friends here the videos of Mr. Brindley."

They crowded in behind the man operating the computer and watched as a lanky, healthy-looking man arrived onboard to receive his safety briefing at one of the muster stations. Dani recognized him as the man sitting in the chair on the balcony next door to their state room. The video switched to a different camera showing him getting on the elevator and exiting on Deck Eight to walk along the corridor to the stateroom next to Jake and Dani. The video ended there.

Dani asked, "So, this Alan Brindley didn't go for dinner or leave his stateroom to do anything?"

"No, that's the last time our cameras picked him up. The doctor thinks he suffered a heart attack in his room. Very unfortunate."

Jake noticed Dani cross her arms at the mention of a heart attack. The diagnosis wasn't sitting well with her.

She said, "Do you have a different camera angle of Mr. Brindley boarding the ship?"

Eduardo nodded to the man sitting behind the terminal. *Big Brother really is watching,* thought Jake.

The second angle showed Brindley on the gangplank, walking toward the ship surrounded by several other passengers. He wore a flowered shirt, white pants, a Panama-style hat, and sunglasses. Everyone around him stared straight ahead or chatted with the person next to them, but what stuck out was his lengthy stride, upright posture, and tanned complexion. He stood head and shoulders above everyone else in the crowd. It was difficult to believe the man died in his cabin a brief time later.

Dani said, "I know the camera won't recognize Brindley from a distance, but can you back that sequence up a little to show him as he's approaching the gangplank?"

Another nod from Eduardo, and the man at the terminal tapped the keyboard to move the video backward. They could barely make out Brindley as he shuffled along with the other passengers, but his tall frame stood out above the others. He stopped and dumped something into a garbage can before continuing.

The video ended, and Eduardo regarded Jake and Dani with his arms outstretched and his lips pursed. "You see? There's no suggestion of anything untoward. Mr. Brindley, unfortunately, had a health incident, which turned out to be fatal." He turned to leave with his hand on Dani's back, gently nudging her toward the door. "On behalf of the Ocean Wanderer captain and crew, I want to wish the two of you and your daughter a wonderful cruise. You will find three complimentary meal passes for yourselves and your daughter, in the exclusive Swordfish Restaurant, added to your account as a thank you. Please enjoy them on our behalf. Lead the way. I think you know where the elevator is."

Chapter Five

In the elevator, Eduardo told Jake and Dani that the ship was built in Germany in 2002, had a top speed of 25 knots (29 mph), 13 decks, and accommodated 2800 passengers and 850 crew. The stats interested Jake, but Dani stared at a spot above the elevator doors as the numbers rolled by floor by floor. The elevator resembled one found in an office tower rather than the luxurious, glass-enclosed type they had become accustomed to riding on the ship.

They thanked Eduardo for the restaurant passes as they disembarked from the elevator on the eighth deck. Country music floated up from the public area below, so they stopped to peer over the railing. A male and female instructor in cowboy garb, right down to the neckerchiefs and boots, led a group of about twenty people of all ages in line dancing. Each had their left thumb in their belt and waved their right hand over their head. The male instructor encouraged the group of smiling people. "To the right, to the right, to the right, to the right... To the left, to the left, to the left, to the left... Now kick..." Emilie shuffled along in unison in the middle of the front row. The girl had rhythm and had no problem keeping up. Jake thought she could probably teach the course before the cruise ended.

Jake and Dani went to The Mainmast Grill on Deck Eleven for a burger and fries before heading back to their room to change into bathing suits. Dani had warned the outside air would get cooler as they got closer to

Alaska, so they should enjoy the sunshine around the pool while they had the chance. Dani put on a stunning carbon black one-piece bathing suit with a scoop neckline that revealed just the right amount of cleavage. Jake shuddered as he peered in the mirror at the yellow, red, and orange patterned suit he wore. The coloured stripes were intertwined like a woven basket. The image of a clown wearing a bathing suit in springy curly hair, huge shoes, a red bulbous nose wormed its way into his subconscious. He wondered how on earth Dani and Emilie had talked him into buying it. Although it was modest enough, ending at his knees, the modern pattern didn't seem appropriate for a middle-aged guy with grey streaks in his hair and a slight overhang of his paunch. He decided he would never run into anyone from the ship again and shrugged at the mirror as he heard Dani leave a message for Emilie on the ship's phone, letting her know where they would be.

The pool deck was crawling with people of all shapes and sizes, laughing and chatting, holding drinks, some in the pool, but most milling about or lying in the sun. Luckily, an elderly couple vacated lounges as they approached. The mustached man with a fringe of grey hair and an age-spotted dome said, "Too noisy for us. You're welcome to it."

A young man who identified himself as the cruise director yelled that the cannonball competition was about to begin into a P.A. system over the blaring music. Eight hefty men and one woman in a blue bathing suit who could have been north of 300 pounds lined up in front of a diving board that hung about six feet above the pool. Participants from late teens to mid-fifties chatted excitedly with each other now that they had entered the competition and experienced something in common. Dani said, "There's still time to sign up." She pulled her floppy hat down over her face as she said it.

"Are you kidding? I will not make a spectacle of myself in front of this crowd in this bathing suit, although I'm sure you would have to help me hold the women off." They both laughed, and the competition started with the first man launching himself into the air with his hands around his knees, landing with a mighty splash that soaked onlookers standing around the pool. His landing drew wild cheers from the crowd until a group of volunteer judges awarded scores from five to seven. That brought a blend of groans and jeers.

Jake gazed around the pool area. He decided there wouldn't be much more flesh exposed in a Turkish bath. Everywhere he looked, thin pieces of cloth barely concealed private areas, and exposed butt cheeks were plentiful. It wasn't hard to figure out what the men packed either. Emilie's shorts were normally, well, short, but modest by comparison to what ran around the pool deck.

After growing tired of wondering what kept some suits in place, Jake said, "Okay, spill it. What's bothering you? Your mind has been somewhere else since we left Eduardo."

Dani peeked at Jake from beneath the brim of her hat. "Am I that obvious? I didn't want to say anything that might spoil the cruise. Are you sure you want to hear this?"

"Of course I do, but maybe we should get a couple of drinks first. The drink of the day is a margarita. Sound good?" Another roar from the approving crowd accompanied the question as the female competitor tugged her top back into place after she crash landed in the water belly first. Her dive didn't meet Jake's definition of cannonball, but the crowd loved it.

"It sounds very good," Dani said loud enough to make Jake hear above the crowd noise.

Jake signalled to a server who stood chatting with some young women halfway down the pool deck. He ordered two drinks, and he and Dani wordlessly soaked up the sunshine until they arrived.

The noise level dropped except for cheers or jeers when the poolside judges held up numbers to allocate scores to the competitors. The woman won the cannonball competition, and the crowd couldn't have been louder if their favourite team scored the game-winning goal at the World Cup. But as the competition wound down, even the music seemed to drop in decibels. Dani enjoyed her drink and said, "I'm sure Alan Brindley didn't die of natural causes. I've seen colouring like he had around his mouth too many times, and I would bet my next paycheque someone poisoned him. He dropped something in the garbage. Unfortunately, the garbage would have been emptied last night, so it will be in a landfill by now, but if they had retrieved it soon enough, they could have tested it. My guess is that a slow-acting poison was mixed with whatever drink was in the cup, and it took effect after Brindley got to his cabin."

"Are you sure your detective mind just hasn't shut off yet? It's not your problem."

"No, it isn't, but if Brindley was murdered, someone should be looking for the killer. I'm not convinced the ship personnel are equipped or interested in doing that. They have a schedule to keep. You saw the rivers of sweat Eduardo produced when I suggested something other than death by natural causes. I think he was thinking about how to control the situation, so we didn't blab it all over the ship."

"Well, should you try again to convince them that the cup and Brindley's colouring suggest someone poisoned him?"

"I'm not sure it would do any good without more evidence. I think Eduardo fell all over himself demonstrating to us that nothing untoward happened to Brindley for fear we would tell everyone on the ship. He certainly didn't have to show us the video. And then you heard him on the elevator. He wanted to talk about anything besides Brindley's death. He delightedly told you all the statistics about the ship. The restaurant coupons were a reminder to us to keep quiet and forget about it."

"Well, if your theory is correct about the poisoned cup, at least the murderer isn't onboard."

Dani sipped her drink. "How do we know that, Jake? He or she could have come on the ship before we set sail. There could be a murderer among us."

Jake finished his drink and set it on the deck beside his lounge chair. "Okay, what are you going to do? Your instincts are great ... better than anyone I know. You won't let this go, so tell me your plans."

Dani's response was interrupted when Emilie spun through the revolving door to the pool area. She wore a stunning yellow bikini that drew admiring glances from a group of young men playing ping-pong at a nearby table. Although the bikini was small, it covered more than some suits Jake had seen.

Jake and Dani listened as words about the line dancing course cascaded out of Emilie's mouth. When she finished, Dani said, "So, what's next?"

"A guy about my age named Leif danced beside me. He said he wanted to play mini putt. It's on Deck Thirteen. I haven't been up there yet. Then there's a video arcade on Twelve. We'll probably hang out there. Is that okay?"

Jake recalled a slim young man with curly black hair beside Emilie during the line dance as Dani said, "Sure, but don't you think you should put something on?"

Emilie swung the bag she'd been carrying on her shoulder around to show her mom. "I have shorts in here. I'll put them on over my bathing suit. Don't worry, Mom." She dragged the word "Mom" out for emphasis.

Emilie squinted against the sun at Jake. "Nice bathing suit," she said, her face splitting in a huge grin as she turned toward the exit.

Jake smirked at Emilie's comment as Dani said, "Okay, dear. Have fun. Keep me posted. Be back in your room by 5:00 so you can freshen up in time for dinner."

As they watched Emilie leave through the revolving door, Jake reached for Dani's hand. "She's a good kid, Dani. She'll be fine."

Dani nodded. "I know. She has grown up too fast. Yesterday, she was learning how to ride her bike with training wheels, and today, the boys are after her." She took a deep breath to compose herself. "Anyway, you asked what I was going to do about Brindley. I'm going to use the internet package we bought to ask someone in my office to check into his background. If nothing comes of that, I'll leave it alone, and you and I can enjoy the rest of our cruise. What do you think?"

"I think the first margarita tasted like a second. Where's that server?"

Chapter Six

Jake and Dani continued to order drinks and talk about delving into the life of Alan Brindley. They observed people enjoying themselves in the pool and on the deck. A live five-piece band played the syncopated rhythms and heavy percussion of reggae music. Conversation only became difficult when some new game started, designed to embarrass players to the delight of the onlookers. Right now, people just swayed to the music in front of the band. One woman on the dance floor, who appeared to be in her forties, swung her hair and lifted her sunglasses to attract the attention of the twenty-something-year-old singer who ignored her. Jake and Dani relaxed in the brilliant sunshine, enjoyed their drinks, and laughed along with the onlookers.

Jake: "Don't you think people watching is the greatest activity ever?"

"I do, my dear. It's a wonderful way to spend an afternoon."

During lulls in the lively crowd noise, they discussed what the next day would bring. They would arrive at their first port of call at noon and spend the afternoon touring Ketchikan. Visiting a salmon fish hatchery may not seem exciting to some, but it would be the highlight of the day, and Jake anxiously awaited it.

As a young couple wrestled in the pool, soaking everyone nearby, Dani pointed out that the internet onboard would be spotty and unsecure, so she wouldn't be able to discuss much about the case online. She declared she would use some of their time in Ketchikan before their excursion to call Constable Davidson.

"Davidson," Jake said. "His name keeps popping up. Isn't he the one I've run into from time to time?"

"Yes, that's him. I asked to have him transferred to Homicide. He's such a skilled detective, and he was delighted with the transfer."

"What's his first name, anyway?" For all I know, it's 'Constable.'"

Dani lay back in her lounge with her eyes closed. She laughed. "Sorry. It's Lonnie. Lonnie Davidson."

Jake remembered Davidson from the crime scene when a body had been discovered in a marsh close to Ottawa. He drove Dani to the location and didn't think Davidson was investigating the murder, but rather that he was there simply to direct traffic and keep onlookers away. They had met a few times earlier. He remembered once when the young police officer investigated a break and enter at his house. Davidson seemed pleasant enough, and if Dani, with her exacting standards, considered him to be a talented investigator, it made perfect sense to bring him into the Homicide Unit. He was certainly handsome enough.

Wait! What? Jake laughed to himself. *Why did any of this matter?* He knew the reason, but he didn't intend to tell Dani. Shakespeare's green-eyed monster from *Othello* and *The Merchant of Venice* had raised its head. *I must have had too much to drink*, Jake concluded. Dani mentioned she had known Davidson for years, and now they worked together. Jake gazed at Dani in her stunning bathing suit and the floppy blue hat that shaded all but the bottom of her nose, her mouth, and chin. She sensed him admiring her, and she glanced back as she drew on her straw with a slurping sound, suggesting her drink had reached the bottom. She exaggerated the sound a second time, suggesting time for another. Her face lit up in that amazing smile. With a huge wink, she turned back to face forward and closed her eyes. Those dark eyes, so full of uncompromising intelligence that attracted Jake at first glance.

Jake lost count of the drink specials they had consumed. He wondered what would happen when he stood. He concluded the number of drinks he had consumed contributed to the sudden twinge of jealousy.

People drifted away from the pool area around 4:00, and Jake and Dani decided to leave. Nothing dragged tourists from their activities faster than the promise of another delightful meal. Jake and Dani wobbled unsteadily toward the revolving door leading inside and giggled when Jake missed the section of the door that Dani claimed and bounced off the glass wing into the next section.

When they emerged from the revolving door, Dani pressed the elevator button for Deck Seven. "I'm not sure I'm in any shape to email Lonnie," Dani giggled. "I thought those margaritas would be watered down. Nope."

The elevator had barely enough room for two more, but people shuffled to the back. Jake said, "This is cozy," and then remembering Dani's comment about the emails, he added, "Maybe between the two of us, we can construct one."

The comment hung in the air, meaning nothing to the people on the elevator, and someone snickered at the back.

"Construct! Now that's a big word. Too big to be used on a cruise." Dani giggled as the elevator door swung open on Deck Seven, and they disembarked. She waved to the baffled crowd on the elevator. "Have a good day," she said.

"Have fun constructing," someone replied.

They turned left to the computer room and waited several minutes until a machine became available. Dani sat, inhaled a deep breath, and placed her fingers on the keyboard. "Okay, I'm sober now," she said. "It's amazing how some laughs and focusing on something will sober you up." Jake wasn't sure he could say the same as he pulled a vacant chair from beside the wall and sat beside her, blinking his eyes to focus.

The circle on the computer screen wound for several seconds and eventually connected. Dani logged into her email account and glanced at the string of unopened messages. She ignored them for fear of falling down a rabbit hole, clicked on "compose," and typed. As Jake peered over her shoulder, he noted the gist of her message was to tell Davidson to find out what he could about a man named Alan Brindley. She offered no more information because, Jake assumed, of the lack of security. She ended the message by asking Davidson to reply by email with basic information as soon as possible, and that she would speak with him in more detail by phone in the morning.

"Do you want to check your emails? See if you have anything from Avery?"

"Nah, I'll do it in the morning while you're talking to Lonnie."

She exited her account, and she and Jake returned to their room. Dani tapped on Emilie's door to make sure she had returned. Her daughter stuck her towel-wrapped head around the door, assuring them she would be ready for dinner in a few minutes.

Every night featured a theme in the dining room, and tonight was French night. They all enjoyed appetizers. Jake ordered herb-crusted salmon, while Dani and Emilie asked for beef bourguignon. Dessert was Crème Brulé for Jake and Dani and ice cream for Emilie. Throughout the meal, Dani's daughter bubbled about the arcade and the rock-climbing wall she had tried. Jake and Dani told her about the cannonball contest. Emilie's face told them she was sorry she had missed it. Dani also talked about Alan Brindley. It shocked Emilie to hear about the body in the room next to her mom's.

"Why didn't you tell me?"

"I didn't want it to spoil your enjoyment of the trip. We can't tell anyone. I need to follow up to make sure something isn't being missed. I hope you won't worry about this."

"Are you kidding?" Emilie gushed. "This is amazing. Just make sure you tell me everything."

A lull fell over the conversation. The servers wandered back to talk about their homes in the Philippines. Jake glanced toward a porthole as he listened. The horizon, visible in the distance, wasn't the static land mass one sees in an open space on a sunny day. This one rose and fell. Jake's head spun, and his stomach lurched at the unusual sight of the dynamic changes as the land mass apparently drifted up and down. His eyes wandered away for a moment before glancing back. Nothing changed. The horizon still dipped and dived, kind of like the line dancers did as part of their routine. He tuned back in when Maria asked what they planned to do in Ketchikan and reminded himself the motion of the ship caused the optical illusion. When he peeked back, the horizon still moved, but Jake's stomach didn't. At least, not as much.

After finishing their meals and enjoying a comedian and musical performance in the theatre, Jake and Dani headed back to the computer room to check for a response from Davidson. When her account finally opened, it pleased her to see an email from him highlighted at the top of the lengthy list of unopened messages.

But what she read surprised her. She reread the message three times to assure herself that she read it correctly, but it left little doubt. The message was brief, but shocking.

Dani, I couldn't locate the person we talked about in any of our databases. We need to talk. Let me know when you are available... Lonnie.

Chapter Seven

"That was a cryptic message," Jake said as they walked down the corridor to their room. What do you suppose Davidson meant?"

"It can only mean Alan Brindley has no identity in the databases. He must have been travelling incognito. But why would someone be on a cruise ship with an assumed name? He was by himself, so maybe he was hiding from a wife. Stranger things have happened. Even more suspicious is why a man travelling under an assumed name would end up dead on said cruise ship. The plot thickens, as they say. I'll call Lonnie as soon as we arrive onshore. It won't take long. We'll still be able to go on our excursion."

When they entered their room, a towel monkey hung suspended from the ceiling. Emilie tapped on their door around 9:50 to tell them she had returned. Jake already lay in bed, and the gentle motion of the ship lulled him into a deep sleep, but Dani had that fluttering undercurrent in her chest. Questions about Alan Brindley spun through her head. She didn't want to ruin the trip for Jake and Emilie, but she couldn't let it go. She was certain Brindley was poisoned, but she needed to understand more to convince the security detail onboard. She fell asleep around 2 a.m.

They woke to the sound of the phone ringing. It was Emilie calling from the onboard phone by the running track. When Dani mumbled a hello into the phone, Emilie explained she had just finished running a mile and asked her mom if she was coming up to join her. When Dani said she wouldn't be joining today, Emilie said, "I was going to tell you to wear something warmer. I'll grab something to eat at The Mainmast Grill. I'll catch up with you before we go for our excursion."

When they hung up, Dani climbed out of bed and pulled a robe on over her pyjamas. She opened the drapes to an overcast sky. The city of Ketchikan loomed through the mist in the distance.

Jake opened one eye and squinted through the patio door to encounter the dull day. "Is it raining?"

"No, but it's overcast. It looks a little misty. Em says it's cool out."

Dani threw off her robe, slipped out of her pyjamas, and stopped at the foot of the bed to give Jake a view. She climbed into bed and snuggled under the covers, pressing her body against Jake's. He said as he put his arm around her, "Well, if Em says the weather is cool, it must be freezing. I read last night that Ketchikan is the 'Rain Capital of Alaska' with heavy cloud cover and high humidity most of the time. Why did you bring me here again?" He kissed her as he let his hand wander over Dani's naked body. "How much time do we have?"

Dani whispered between nibbles of Jake's ear as she unbuttoned his pyjama top, "To answer your first question, you know how we like to warm things up when it's cold. To answer your second question ... enough."

Later, they showered and held hands as they bypassed the elevator and ascended the stairs to The Mainmast Grill on Deck Ten for scrambled eggs and toast. They found a table near a window to watch thin waterfalls cascading down the mountains and chunks of ice from glaciers float by without so much as a whisper. An indecipherable announcement came over the P.A. system. They caught enough to know they had entered Tracy Arm Fjord.

Thin clouds obscured the peaks but sporadically lifted enough to reveal towering cliffs and blue-tinted glaciers sparkling like diamonds against the rugged landscape. Lush green forests covered the lower half of the mountains. The water resembled frigid greyish glass, disturbed only by the ship's movement. Each waterfall appeared more spectacular than the previous one.

After they satiated their coffee habits, they wandered through the sliding doors to the outer deck to test the weather and admire the scenery. To Jake's delight, the outside temperature actually wasn't that bad. They decided a light sweater and shorts would do the trick. The mist had stopped, but they agreed packing rain jackets in their backpacks would be wise in case the clouds dropped something more substantial.

The ship navigated the channel, which Jake judged to be about a mile wide. He drew some comfort from the proximity to the shore, although the frigid-looking water didn't appear that inviting. The Ocean Wanderer turned in a slow U-turn in the channel before heading back in the direction it came. The scenery was just as spectacular on the other side.

Jake and Dani returned to their cabin and rested until the ship neared Ketchikan's dock. More trucks than cars travelled along the street running parallel to the pier. Commercial buildings of assorted colours stood arm-in-arm across the street, including a white structure with Moose Lodge 224 painted in huge letters across the front and, just in case no one noticed, again under the veranda. Houses dotted the hillside, towering above the commercial buildings, while trees loomed farther back, dwarfing the manmade structures.

They changed into shorts and light sweaters, retrieved Emilie from her room, and headed to Deck One to disembark. "Isn't this the deck the security office is on?" Jake asked. "Yes," said Dani, "but I don't know if we can get to it from here. We'll call Eduardo if there's anything to tell him." Dani impatiently waited to make her phone call onshore. Either that or the coffee consumption made her fidgety. They strode down the gangplank and arrived at a yellow wood-clad shack that also served as a souvenir shop, where they received a number designating which group and bus number they belonged to. Emilie raced off to explore the souvenir shop while Jake and Dani moved to one side away from the crowd to make her call. "Good thing we bought these eSIMS for our phones," said Dani. The card allowed them to access a digital network while travelling, rather than paying exorbitant fees for roaming. She hit a key on the phone to place the call on speaker.

"Hi Lonnie, it's Dani. I don't have a lot of time but tell me what you found."

"Hi Dani. I hope you're enjoying your trip. What I found is nothing. Alan Brindley doesn't exist. There are people with the same name in the system, but none that fits the profile you suggested."

Dani knew Davidson would have checked records of health cards, driver's licences, credit card transactions, and anything else that might reveal something about who Alan Brindley was.

Emilie returned from her brief shopping spree and sat beside Jake to listen to the conversation.

Dani continued. "That's interesting. Okay, I'm going to send you a picture of Alan Brindley. Send it to Vancouver Port Security, and ask them if they can spot his movements through their CCTV from the time he arrived at the terminal until he boarded. The picture isn't very clear."

"Uh, okay, I hate to question your idea, but aren't you a little out of your jurisdiction, boss? Shouldn't the cruise line security people do this?"

"Probably, but they haven't acknowledged that the death was a result of anything more than natural causes. I'm suspicious it was more than that.

Tell Port Security I'm a passenger on the ship, and we're using our resources to help. I'll contact you again before we board the ship."

When Dani hung up, Jake opened his mouth to say something, but Emilie beat him to it. "Mom, where did you get a picture of this guy?"

"I took a picture of him on his balcony."

"You took a picture of a dead guy!?"

Dani and Jake both scanned the surrounding faces, hoping no one heard Emilie's outburst. Everyone seemed to be engrossed in their conversation, excited to get going on their adventure.

"Well, yes. The photo might be useful later. Just call it intuition."

"What if somebody scrolled through your phone and found pictures of dead guys?"

"I'm not too worried about that, honey. Oh, look, there's our bus."

Jake noted Dani's tone of relief that the bus had finally shown up.

They drove away, and the bus passed under a sign that welcomed visitors to Ketchikan and declared the city "The Salmon Capital of the World." The sign featured a carved fisherman decked out in yellow fishing attire from his floppy hat down to his rubber boots. The silent fisherman leaned back in his wooden boat with his fishing pole bent almost in half, struggling to land an equally determined salmon.

On the way, Jake showed Dani the messages he received from two of their breakfast buddies. Pierre Chevrier expressed himself in one sentence. *Hey Jake, I hope you two are behaving yourselves. Don't freeze up.* Ryan Cambridge's message took a little more space. He asked about the weather and said the group missed them and looked forward to their return. Jake replied he wished them well. In keeping with his long-standing tradition of stumping his friends with unusual words, he added, "We're enjoying our fugacious vacation." When Dani raised an eyebrow, he told her it meant that the vacation would last only a brief time. He imagined with a smile his buddies searching for the definition.

He also showed Dani a message he sent to his daughter, Avery, with love to her, Nick, and Ava. He had attached three scenic photos from Tracy Fjord to the email.

The bus driver pointed out highlights and the city's history as they toured, climbing the steep roads, and eventually winding up at the Macaulay Salmon Hatchery, where a controlled environment mimics natural conditions, enabling the growth and survival of the fish. They learned, among other things, that in the wild, only about 10% of salmon survive the trip from the stream to the ocean. Hatcheries have closer to 90% success rate. While Jake assumed Emilie would be bored at the hatchery, it pleased him she appeared enthralled by the process.

They boarded the bus again and toured the city, hearing more highlights and history for another thirty minutes before the driver announced they had two choices. Stay in the downtown core, do whatever tourists like to do, and walk three-quarters of a mile back to the ship, or he would drive them back to the dock and drop them off. The bus divided almost equally, as some chose to shop while others opted for the ride back. For Emilie, it wasn't even a decision. Jake and Dani followed her off the bus.

Chapter Eight

They agreed to meet back at the ship before Emilie hustled off to explore the various shops with a reminder from Dani that the ship would leave at 5 p.m. Two women passing by smiled sympathetically at Dani as she raised her voice to Emilie's departing back. "If you're late, you're on your own to find a way to Juneau."

As they wandered along the crowded streets of Ketchikan, Jake said, "Are you sure you want to do this, Dani?"

"Of course, Jake. Why not? I want to experience as much of Alaska as we can. However, the only ones in shorts appear to be the tourists. Everyone else is wearing long pants and a jacket. I'm putting my coat on." She unzipped the backup Jake carried and pulled out her jacket. "Do you want yours?"

"Yes, I'm ready for a jacket, but I don't mean whether we should wander the streets of Ketchikan. I meant digging into Alan Brindley's death. Or whoever he is. You heard Lonnie. This isn't your jurisdiction. You could get in trouble over this."

Dani stopped walking in front of a restaurant advertising Alaskan delicacies. "Let's go in for something sugary. We can talk more inside."

"Find a seat," a server shouted from behind the counter. The restaurant appeared to be stuck in the seventies with a black-and-white floor in alternating squares that could provide a suitable board for playing checkers. Each table, draped with black-and-white checkered tablecloths, sat a respectable distance from the next and featured chrome legs. Four reddish-brown chairs surrounded each table, and chrome stools with matching fabric lined up like sentries in front of a chrome counter. Stuffed animal heads stared unseeing at the customers and stood guard over the jukebox playing a hit from the nineties in one corner. The servers wore black pants and white tops with aprons the same colour as the upholstery. The delicious aroma of baking hung in the air. A handful of patrons lost in their conversations or staring at their phones occupied the tables, so Jake and Dani slid into a corner booth big enough for four.

The server who told them to find a seat wandered to their table with a carafe of coffee. She appeared to be in her early thirties, and she wore the seventies' theme on her head with what she described as a side bun in response to Dani's compliment about her style. She identified herself as the restaurant owner. Her deep blue eye shadow accented her platinum blonde hair. Tattoos emerged from the bottom of one sleeve and wound around her arm to end at her wrist. If a dangling cigarette bounced on her lips, each time she chewed her gum, the image of a gangster moll would be complete.

The menu displayed a variety of Alaskan delicacies, including reindeer sausage, but Dani ordered rockfish chowder while Jake asked for a piece of the huckleberry pie. Their server assured them they had made good choices and poured coffee for each of them before disappearing in the back to prepare their orders.

Dani: "Okay, you asked about my concern about Brindley. All I'm doing is trying to help the ship security team. They're not equipped for a situation like this. Whatever Lonnie comes up with, I'll share the information with Eduardo, and he can decide what to do. Right now, I would like to know if they turned the body over in Ketchikan to examine the toxicology.

If they did, good. At least that would determine if someone poisoned him. Maybe it was rotten food, but if that's the case, the place where it came from should be shut down. More needs to be done.

"And besides, Eduardo or the captain should have advised the next-of-kin by now, so if they found somebody, they probably know his real name. Like I said, I'll share whatever Lonnie tells us, and that will be the end for me." The server brought their orders as Dani added, "Did you like the fishery?"

Jake cut a piece off his pie with his fork and slid it into his mouth. He closed his eyes and savoured the pie before responding. "The fishery was great. Really interesting. They play a significant role in stocking the lakes and ponds, and the ocean, for that matter. I guess once the fish are in the wild, they're on their own."

They finished their meals, paid their bills, and opened the door to find the clouds dropping heavy mist again. Their server checked her phone. "The radar says the mist is just passing through. Are you folks from the cruise ship?"

"Yes," Dani said. "We're from Ottawa, Canada, and enjoying a cruise of your beautiful state."

"Ottawa? I've been there. The nation's capital, right? Beautiful city. So many parks and bike paths. Why don't you enjoy a coffee on me and wait out the mist?" The woman checked her watch. "You have an hour and a half before the ship leaves. The mist should lift well before then."

Jake and Dani gladly accepted her offer with thanks and chatted more until Dani's phone rang.

"It's Lonnie," she said as she peered at the screen. "I can't put it on speaker," she added as she raised an eyebrow toward the woman standing within earshot behind the counter.

Jake nodded in understanding.

Dani sat listening in silence, then said "okay" in acknowledgement every few minutes. Finally, she said, "You're sure about the shoes, right?" More listening. Then, "Fine, can you send it to me?"

She hung up and turned to Jake, keeping her voice low. "Lonnie said Port Security officials tracked Brindley on their CCTV from the time he entered the terminal until he passed through Security. He's sending me the video. Apparently, he met a man who gave him a folder. The man never showed his face, but Lonnie said he wore distinctive designer running shoes. He says he knows the brand because he considered buying some, but they were way out of his price range. He called them IceCloud10s, all one word. Have you heard of them?"

Jake placed his palm on his chest. "You're asking me if I've heard of designer running shoes when I buy cheap ones when they're on sale? Not likely, my dear."

Dani's phone pinged, announcing a message. She downloaded the video, flipped the phone sideways to its horizontal orientation, and leaned forward so she and Jake could both watch.

The video was grainy and black-and-white, but they saw Brindley coming through the terminal doors and striding purposefully toward the escalator, which he boarded to ride up to the next floor. A second camera picked him up as he walked off the escalator toward a coffee shop. He purchased a coffee and turned to greet a tall, blond man in what appeared to be tan pants and an open-neck white shirt. Dani and Jake both focused on the trendy running shoes the man wore. Dani paused the video and spread her fingers on the screen to enlarge it. She and Dani squinted as they peered at the screen. The shoes looked to be grey and white or two shades of grey with some kind of logo imprinted on the side. It could have been lettering under the laces down the tongue as well.

The blond man never showed his face on camera, but he gawked around furtively as if concerned someone might observe him. He handed a folder to Brindley, which the latter stuffed in a briefcase, and said something while shaking his head as if admonishing Brindley not to do something. The blond man turned and walked in one direction while Brindley took his coffee and headed toward the security area, where the ship's cameras later picked him up dumping the coffee cup in the trash.

Dani sat back in her chair without saying a word.

"Do you still think he might have been poisoned, Dani? It seems unlikely since Brindley bought his coffee from the coffee shop."

"I'm sure he was poisoned, but there had to have been another form of transference. It's interesting the way the mystery man avoided being caught on camera. Like he knew every camera location in the terminal. Almost like he had inside knowledge."

While Jake pondered that, Dani searched on her phone for IceCloud10 shoes and turned the image to Jake when she found a match to the ones worn by the man who met Brindley. The shoes were grey and white with an icy cloud logo. Red lettering under the tongue further identified the brand.

"Yes, but it's all circumstantial, Dani. All you have to go by is body language that's impossible to read, a guy you think somebody poisoned, and a theory that you're trying to put together. Almost like you're trying to force a narrative to fit your agenda."

Dani's narrowed eyes made Jake think he had gone one step too far. He added before she could erupt, "Look, like I said before, your intuition is as good as anyone I know, but there aren't any facts yet. I believe you when you say somebody poisoned Brindley, but you don't have jurisdiction here, and it's unlikely you would get any cooperation from the ship Security Chief even if you wanted to investigate further. Of course, I'll go with whatever you decide, but maybe you should just let it go. We're on vacation, remember?"

"Maybe you're right," Dani said as she shrugged into her jacket. "We'd better go. I'm going to ask our server if she'll take anything for the coffee." She turned on her heel and strode to the counter.

Jake had made his point, but even though the sky cleared, Dani's demeanour on the walk back to the dock became as icy as the logo on the running shoes.

Chapter Nine

Dani's mood hadn't softened when they arrived at the dock, and it was about to worsen. She and Jake walked up the gangplank without saying a word and pressed their cruise cards against the reader to gain access to the ship. In Jake's mind, silence, at least until they arrived at the state room, might be the best course of action. Forty-five minutes remained until the ship's scheduled departure.

Jake took off his jacket, and Dani handed hers to him so he could hang them in the closet. He sidled up to Dani and put his arms around her. He asked, "Are you mad at me?"

Dani returned the hug half-heartedly and then moved away. "Just leave it, Jake. I'm aware I shouldn't be pursuing this, but I'm convinced somebody poisoned Brindley, and if I'm right, a murderer could still be on the ship. I have to investigate it, but I promise it won't ruin our vacation."

Jake sat on the sofa with his mind racing. *How could someone poison Brindley? How could someone administer the poison? Brindley bought his coffee at the shop. Unless the server poisoned his coffee, but three servers worked behind the counter. How would a server poison Brindley when the coffee shop was hopping with activity? And how would they put poison in the cup without someone noticing? It makes no sense. The other guy handed Brindley a folder. Could the papers inside have been poisoned? Wouldn't the guy need to wear gloves to protect himself if that was the case? Brindley was never out of the view of the cameras, so there wasn't another opportunity to poison him. But Dani's seldom wrong about anything. It was maddening and endearing at the same time.*

Dani tapped on Emilie's door to announce they had returned. No answer. She knocked louder. Still nothing.

She crammed her hands in her pockets. "I wonder where she is."

"Probably upstairs in the video arcade. Do you want me to check?"

"No, it's okay. I'll call her, and then I'm going to take a shower. The rain chilled me to the bone. I'm sure she's all right."

But when Dani called, Emilie didn't pick up.

Worry creases appeared on Dani's forehead. "Okay, that's bizarre. She always has her phone with her. Well, there's nothing I can do, so I guess I'll take that shower. Knock on the bathroom door when she comes back."

When Dani emerged in her bathrobe ten minutes later, Jake sat on the sofa with his arms crossed and one leg folded over the other. "There's no sound from next door, Dani. I just knocked about two minutes ago."

"I hope she remembered she had to be back before 5:00. This is concerning. It's unlike her not to call or text. What if she forgot the time to be back or didn't check her watch?"

"She won't forget, Dani. She would remember we go for dinner at 5:00 if nothing else. I'm sure she's on the ship. The video arcade would be the best place to start. The weather is too cool for mini putt or the rock-climbing wall, but teenagers have a higher threshold to cold and rain than we do. I'll take a quick look."

Dani glanced at her phone, her dark eyes a combination of fury and worry. "The last thing I told her was not to be late," she fumed. "She is going to be in a lot of trouble. I'll check the schedule to see if there might have been an activity at 4:00 she would be interested in. Maybe another line dancing class or something. Check the running track, too. She might be smart, but she's run in cold, rainy weather before. I wouldn't put it past her to run on the ship in the cold just for the experience."

Dani dialled her phone again, but still no response.

Fifteen minutes to departure.

Jake bounded up the stairs two at a time until he reached the 13th deck, gasping for breath. A yellow hinged triangle sign warned passersby that the deck was slippery, and indeed, his running shoes slipped in the moisture from the mist. He poked his head around the corner of the mini putt course, expecting to see Emilie. Only a pair of preteen boys with wet hair and glistening rain jackets laughed as they each putted two balls that left a rooster tail of water in their wake. Next, he checked the rock-climbing wall, even though he expected it to be closed in this weather. The rocks would be too slippery and dangerous. Still, he had to check. A fence surrounded the wall closing it off. No sign of Emilie on Deck Thirteen. No sign of anybody other than the two preteens, in fact, as the mist became thicker. He entered the dark video arcade crammed with kids. He pushed his way through the crowd and the cacophony of blips and bongs, but no Emilie. Down a flight of steps to the track revealed it glistened with water, unused.

Now, *his* anxiety level ratcheted up. He inspected his watch.

Five minutes to departure.

Jake shivered as he descended the stairs to the eighth floor. He had forgotten his jacket in his haste, and the chill in the air wormed into his bones. That, plus he now wondered like Dani if Emilie had lost track of time. He prayed that this would all turn out to be a misunderstanding, that she would be in her room when he got back.

Dani was close to tears when he entered the room. He had never seen her like this. She was always the stoic one.

He put his hands on her arms. "Dani, what is it? Did you hear something?"

"Nothing. Where is she?" Her voice cracked, close to breaking. "Where could she go? And why won't she answer her phone? What the hell is going on? She's smarter than this. What if she's stuck in Ketchikan? We need to talk to Security and find out what to do."

A shudder and movement under their feet caused them both to lean to the left. Dani's eyes widened in fear, and her hands clenched.

The ship moved away from the dock, and still no Emilie.

Chapter Ten

As Jake held Dani in his arms, he realized in their panic, they had forgotten to do something. He breathed into her ear, "Yes, we have to call Security, Dani, but to ask if she boarded the ship. They'll have a record of who is on the ship because every passenger is required to show their cruise pass coming and going. That's how they ensure everyone has returned. They'll already know if she isn't on the ship. The good news is that they didn't call us, so that's a sign she boarded. I'll call to confirm."

Jake pulled himself away, and his heart sank at the sight of Dani's misty eyes. Understandable, but he had never seen her so vulnerable. She sniffed and sought a tissue from the bathroom while Jake sat on the sofa and dialled. A woman picked up the phone and answered with a terse, "Security."

"Hello, this is Jake Scott from Room 8835. Our daughter, Emilie, is in the next room, 8836, and we haven't seen her for an hour. We expected to pick her up in her room and go for dinner, but now we're worried she may not have boarded the ship on time. Could you please confirm that she's onboard?"

Jake's stomach flipped when the woman said, "Some passengers didn't make the boarding. Just a minute, please." He tried to avoid giving anything away to Dani, who now sat beside him, by maintaining eye contact straight ahead with the logo identifying the brand on the mini fridge.

"Hello, sir, no one named Scott missed boarding."

"I'm sorry, her name is Perez. She's my girlfriend's daughter."

"That name sounds familiar. One moment, please."

That name sounds familiar. Is this woman trying to give me a heart attack? She hadn't been standing in line when they handed out the empathy ability. Jake continued staring at the mini fridge logo, hoping Dani couldn't hear his thundering heart trying to climb out of his chest like a prisoner attempting to hoist himself over the prison wall.

The clock in Jake's head ticked off the seconds and rolled into a minute. He looked at Dani as she held her hands palm up to question what was going on. He turned back to the logo on the fridge as the woman came back on.

"Emilie Perez from Room 8836 has been on the ship since 3:20, sir."

Jake's shoulders sagged, and his hand drifted to his chest before he turned to Dani and flipped a thumb-up. He exhaled an explosion of pent-up breath.

"Whew, that's a relief. Thank you so much, ma'am. It seems like this has been a misunderstanding. I appreciate your help. I hope the other people who didn't make the ship will be okay."

"Our onshore staff will take care of them, sir. Have a good night."

Jake turned to Dani whose face softened. He said, "We can relax now. She's on the ship. Would she go straight to the dining hall?"

Dani's mouth turned up in a tentative smile, but her eyes revealed annoyance bubbling beneath the surface. "I think I'm going to kill her" was the first thing she said. Then, "We might as well get ready for dinner. She'll turn up. I'll be setting some ground rules."

The phone rang again as they rose from the sofa. This time, Dani snatched up the receiver and answered with little more than a grunt.

"Hello."

It always amazed Jake how invisible frost could dangle from a single word out of Dani's mouth when she was in that kind of mood. It reminded him of icicles left hanging from tree branches after a harsh Canadian winter storm.

It was Emilie on the other end of the line. "Where are you guys? I've been sitting in the dining hall since 5:00. I thought you must have missed the ship."

Dani's eyes brightened, but she said, "We've been looking for you. We thought *you* missed the ship. Why didn't you call?"

"My phone died. I forgot to charge it last night, so I plugged it in when I got back from Ketchikan. We arranged to meet in the dining room."

"No, we didn't. You should have called. Anyway, we'll be down in a few minutes."

The side table shook, and a pen rolled off when Dani thumped the phone's receiver down on the cradle, still fuming. It would take her a few hours to get over the combination of worrying about Emilie and her belief that Jake's support of her suspicions about Brindley's death remained less than convincing. Hopefully, a satisfying meal and a glass of wine would settle her down.

They dressed in casual clothing, and Jake chose not to say a word on the way to the dining room. When they arrived at their table, they sat opposite Emilie, and Dani stared stonily at her daughter. Jake ordered a glass of wine for himself and Dani. Dani said, "Do you know how worried Jake and I have been?" The question was rhetorical, and Emilie knew it. Dani continued, "We've been worried sick. We thought you would have to find your own way to Juneau, or something worse happened to you. I distinctly told you to tell us when you arrived back on the ship. I have a good mind to make you stay by our side the rest of the trip."

Emilie's eyes sparked. Once again, Jake saw her mom in the young lady sitting across the table, "Actually, you didn't say that, Mom. You said that we would meet back on the ship and to make sure I returned in time for dinner. I came back to the ship, changed, and hung out with my new friends until the time came to come here. I was surprised you weren't at the table when I arrived. José and Maria told jokes while we waited."

Dani looked briefly at Jake for corroboration of her understanding regarding the last thing she said to her daughter, but he remembered the conversation the way Emilie explained it. He took a healthy swallow of wine and concentrated on the menu.

Emilie pushed her knife around on the table with her index finger and said in a voice barely above a whisper, "I'm seventeen years old, Mom. It's time you trusted me."

José arrived to take their orders, but sensing tension in the air, he asked, "Do you need a few minutes?"

The headline on the menu trumpeted Mediterranean Night in the dining hall, which Jake considered being kind of odd when they sailed in Alaskan waters, but they agreed they were ready and ordered. Jake could tell the way Dani slumped in her chair that Emilie's comment stung. Emilie had grown to be a responsible, trustworthy teen, soon to be a woman. Dani's reaction was only a response to her fear when she didn't know where her daughter was. He knew the feeling, having gone through similar situations as Avery grew older.

He tried to lighten the mood by asking Emilie what she did in Ketchikan. She described a toque she bought at one store and entering every other shop along the street. When the meals arrived, they all focused on eating until a child of about twelve at the next table spilled ice water on his mom's tan coloured pants. The embarrassed mom tried to wipe off the water before leaving to change. The dad suggested to their server that he shouldn't refill the kid's glass. *That kid will be in more trouble than Em,* thought Jake. When the commotion settled down, Dani talked a little about the seventies-style restaurant she and Jake visited. Jake filled in the blanks.

After dinner, they sat through the production together in the theatre, and Emilie said she was going back to her room to watch a movie she had downloaded. She and Dani hugged before she disappeared into her room.

"Do you want to go for a drink?" Dani asked Jake.

"Sure, I'm always up for that."

They found a bar with a reasonable decibel level and ordered margaritas. None of the bars would meet the definition of the word "quiet," but this one, with a marine motif of fishing nets, ship steering wheel, and models of schooners under glass, was as close as they would come.

When their drinks arrived, and they settled into their soft faux leather armchairs, Dani said, "Do you think I don't trust Em enough?"

"Well, Dani, I'm not an expert certainly, but Mia had a theory about raising teenagers I think made sense, and we tried to treat Avery that way. Admittedly, we were guilty of worrying too much on many occasions. We had our share of discussions like the one with Emilie tonight. I can share Mia's theory with you if you like."

"Of course. I want Em to enjoy this cruise. This could be our last vacation together since she's going to university. She would be hanging with her friends right now instead of sitting in her room in front of her iPad if I hadn't overreacted. I'm not sure now what I said to her before we left Ketchikan. I feel like I told her to tell us when she arrived, but I could be wrong. Tell me Mia's theory."

Jake inhaled deeply. "Mia always said our responsibility as parents is to give our kids wings to fly. That's all we can do. We can prepare them to make responsible decisions, and then it's up to them to put the concepts into practice. That doesn't mean we will ever stop worrying. That's natural. But we can take some comfort knowing that our kids have all the tools in their toolbox to make the right decisions. And if they occasionally make the wrong decision, they'll learn from those mistakes. You've done an incredible job of giving Emilie her wings, Dani. Emilie is a great kid. It was understandable to be nervous when she didn't show up. I felt the anxiety, too. If we made a mistake, it was that we didn't check the first place she would go at 5:00, which was the dining room. Lesson learned by both of us. We can learn from our mistakes, as well."

Dani reached across the table to take Jake's hand. She said nothing. She didn't have to. Everything that had to be said glowed in the chestnut brown eyes that stared into Jake's.

Before realizing it, they both reached the bottom of their drinks, and Jake ordered refills. They each sipped the second one slowly. Dani thanked Jake and reminded him how much she appreciated his support with Emilie, and they spent the rest of the time talking about everything but Alan Brindley or teenagers.

After they finished their second drinks, they returned hand-in-hand to their room. When they arrived, Dani raised her fist to tap on Emilie's door but hesitated. "Should I say goodnight, or would that look like I'm checking up on her?"

"Go for it, Dani. If she doesn't answer, she's asleep. I'm sure she could use a hug as much as you."

Dani tapped, and Emilie answered. As they hugged and said their good nights, Jake noticed the message light flashing on the phone. He dialled to retrieve the message and listened. When he hung up, he said goodnight to Emilie just before she closed the door.

Dani hurried to use the bathroom and returned in her pyjamas. Jake said, "I picked up a message on the phone."

"Now what?" Dani asked before her mouth formed an "O" as she applied face cream in the mirror between the two shelving units in front of the sofa.

"Eduardo. He wants to see you in his office at 9:00 tomorrow morning. It didn't sound like a request."

Chapter Eleven

T he next morning, Dani left early to spend time with her daughter running around the track a few times, so Jake took his time showering. They agreed to meet for breakfast in the dining room at 8:15. When he finished showering, he lathered on ample shaving cream and examined himself in the mirror as he dragged the safety razor through the two-day-old stubble. He liked to tell Dani that the boyish charm of his face had been replaced by the rugged handsomeness of an older gentleman. To be honest, from the little overhang above his belt, he concluded he should be running too. Maybe tomorrow.

He pulled on a white T-shirt and blue shorts and wandered out to the lobby, greeting fellow passengers along the way. The plaque on the floor of the elevator informed the riders it was Wednesday. Jake grinned at the people on the elevator. He said, "A woman on the first night told us we wouldn't know what day it is without this plaque. She was right. The person who does this every day deserves a medal."

A woman standing next to him shrugged. "I don't know. I think I'd rather not know."

Jake sauntered around the ship, stopping at the casino on Deck Six to watch early birds playing the slot machines. The sound of music and dings and dongs from the machines filled the air. The sound had been almost deafening on previous nights when they walked through the casino to the theatre. He discovered the players used their cruise card to place their bets. *That could be dangerous,* he thought, as he imagined the debt piling and delivering a shocking surprise at the end.

A woman got up to leave the slot machine she had been playing. She had won nothing, so he sat on the stool in front of the machine, hoping it might pay off for him. He plugged in his cruise card, pressed a large red button. The numbers spun. Seconds later, three unmatched numbers settled in a row. Nothing. He tried again. Same result. Within minutes, he spent more than he expected to when he walked in. One more spin, he decided. The numbers spun until they stopped with three sevens across, giving him a payout of $20. *Must be my lucky day,* he thought, even though overall, his cruise card would reflect more expense than revenue from this visit to the casino. It all took about fifteen minutes, and it was now 7:45.

He took the stairs back to Deck Five and lined up for coffee at the shop. People of all shapes, sizes, and nationalities wandered past, and Jake received his coffee and sat in an armchair to people-watch. He wondered what Eduardo wanted, but one thing was for sure: This would reopen the disagreement with Dani about her involvement.

At 8:15, he dumped his empty cup in the trash and wandered to the dining room. José, their dinner server, confirmed he also worked the morning shift. He greeted Jake at the door and led him to Dani and Emilie, who sat with three people at a table on the opposite side of the room to where they normally sat. Dani introduced him to a couple and their daughter who seemed to be about the same age as Emilie. They lived in Mozambique and spoke little English, but they communicated with a few laughs and hand gestures. They introduced their daughter, Katia, who spoke better English than her parents, so she and Emilie giggled about different topics.

At 8:55, Emilie told her mom she was going to the arcade with Katia, and Jake and Dani excused themselves for their meeting with Eduardo. On the way down the stairs, Dani said, "I'm not looking forward to this. You and I disagreed about what I wanted to do, and I don't enjoy arguing with you, especially when we're on holidays. Let's hear what he has to say and then move on."

"Okay, Dani. Just remember I'm on your side no matter what happens."

They arrived at the open door to the security office, and Eduardo invited them in.

"Welcome," he said. "I hope you're enjoying your cruise. Have you enjoyed the restaurant coupon I gave you?"

"Not yet," Dani said, "but we will."

Jake took it as a reminder that Eduardo was in control, and they should not think otherwise.

Eduardo started. "The reason I wanted to see you is that I understand you conducted some investigations on your own, Ms. Dani. And outside your jurisdiction, I might add. I'm told by our onshore security in Vancouver that one of your staff asked for and received Security footage from the port. Might I remind you that anything that happens on the ship is ship business, and we can handle investigations. We appreciate your efforts, but please just enjoy your cruise, and leave managing the ship to us."

Dani's face coloured.

"I understand your concern, and I won't make excuses. You can handle any investigation that comes your way. I'm sure Brindley was poisoned, and I'm sure you notified next-of-kin and requested a toxicology report. I'm comfortable everything is well in hand."

This time Eduardo's swarthy face reddened from the neck up. He spluttered, "We took every measure to do so. Inform the next-of-kin, that is."

Dani caught Eduardo's eyes with hers. "You might have tried, but I doubt you notified the next-of-kin because, Eduardo, Alan Brindley doesn't exist. He travelled under a fake name, so it would be impossible to notify the next-of-kin."

Eduardo squirmed in his seat, and that same line of sweat they observed last time they met appeared again. A lengthy breath of air escaped his lips.

"You're correct, Ms. Dani. We were unsuccessful at notifying the next-of-kin. That job has been turned over to the FBI office in Anchorage. I'm sure they're investigating Mr. Brindley's real identity. It's out of our hands."

"Can I ask you another question? Did you find a file folder in Mr. Brindley's room?"

Eduardo hesitated. "There was a briefcase. We didn't look inside. We turned it over to Shore Security in Ketchikan. I don't know if there was a folder or not. Why did you think there might be?"

"We saw a folder on the video. Someone handed Brindley a folder, which he slid inside his briefcase. I suggest you tell your security staff in Ketchikan to examine those papers. It might shed some light on Brindley's identity."

"They will do their job, Ms. Dani. Is it possible for me to look at the video?"

Dani reached into her purse. The fact Eduardo wanted to view the video encouraged her. Maybe there would be some cooperation after all. She retrieved her phone, found the video, and hit play.

It was the video she and Jake had looked at earlier, but Jake leaned forward to watch it again.

Dani anticipated what Eduardo would say. When the video ended, the Security Chief leaned back in his chair with his hands clasped over his stomach. "I did not detect any opportunity for someone to poison Mr. Brindley, did you, Ms. Dani? If the poison was in the folder, the man handing it to him would have been poisoned as well. I just saw someone meeting a friend or business associate before boarding the ship. You are worrying for nothing."

"Perhaps. I hope you're right. But just in case I'm right, will an autopsy be done on Mr. Brindley? That would be the proper course of action since the cause of death is unknown, and he seemed to be a healthy man."

"Once again, Ms. Dani, that is out of our hands. Our job on the ship is to make sure the passengers have an enjoyable time and are safe. The captain must ensure we get from port to port in a timely manner. These inconveniences while at sea are handed off to Shore Security so we can be on our way and ensure that one unfortunate incident does not affect the thousands of passengers travelling with us. I'm sure you understand. The FBI will investigate if there is any reason to. My staff and I will continue to ensure the safe passage of everyone onboard. This is a business decision by Head Office. Do you have an excursion planned for today in Juneau?"

It wasn't lost on Jake and Dani that the subject had abruptly changed. They were about to be dismissed.

Jake answered while Dani narrowed her eyes. "Yes, we're going to see the Mendenhall Glacier. The forecast doesn't sound good, but we're hoping it will be sunny for the trip."

"Excellent, I wish you a pleasant stay in Juneau." He directed his gaze to Dani. "Ms. Dani, please put all of this behind you, and enjoy the rest of your cruise. I'm former military, so I know it's difficult to forget the job. Once a cop, always a cop, right?" Eduardo got up from his chair, patted Jake on the back, and moved toward the door of the office.

Dani's mood was grim when they left, and Jake understood why. She must be feeling like everyone was ignoring her suspicions, including him. He waited for her to say something as they climbed the stairs to the coffee shop on Deck Five.

Music wafted up from Deck Four when they found seats with coffee in hand. They peered over the railing where a young curly-haired musician took requests and played an acoustic guitar.

Finally, he interrupted her thoughts. "What do you think of the meeting, Dani?"

She sipped her coffee and regarded Jake with a wry smile. "I get it, Jake. I understand Eduardo's position. If he and his team discover something that has to be dealt with on the ship, like a fight breaks out, they handle it until they reach port, and then the situation becomes someone else's problem. The offenders are handed over to the port authorities. I should leave the investigation alone, but my instincts tell me there is more going on."

"Okay, so what are you proposing? I'm all in with whatever it is. I shouldn't have questioned your instincts, and I apologize."

Dani used her free hand to grab Jake's. "No apology necessary, dear, but remember Eduardo told us Brindley was on board to attend some sort of information technology conference? I checked today's schedule before I left to run with Emilie, and there's a meeting of the group this morning at 11:00. Since the meeting is on the schedule, it must be a public event. We should go."

Chapter Twelve

As Dani sat on the balcony in a puffy rust-coloured fall vest over a light sweater and jogging pants, Jake slouched on the sofa reading about the upcoming excursion to Mendenhall Glacier. The overcast sky through the window told him all he needed to know about the weather. Even though the sun peeked through heavy clouds hanging over the mountains, their snow-capped peaks remained obscured. Like a giant hand draped a shroud over the area.

He tossed the brochure aside and felt himself circling the drain at the idea of going to the information technology meeting. Figuratively, at least. If they found out something at the meeting that raised Dani's suspicions further, he would be racing down the drain into an investigation to support her. Despite the tremors of trepidation, he admitted to a sense of excitement coursing through his veins. He had always been up for an investigation during his time as a reporter. That was his job, and he relished in the anticipation, the sense of the unknown, and yes, the potential for danger. Life had been good.

Then, everything came crashing down. First, the newspaper became more digital and opinion-based, which turned out to be fancy words for downsizing. The official words they used to push him out the door were that his position had become redundant. That started a downward spiral as he lost the sense of adventure that energized him. The sense of everything else soon followed when his wife, Mia, suddenly became stricken with an aneurysm and passed away. More than a few months of misery followed. His daughter, Avery, had still been at home offering whatever she could, but she needed support as well. Losing her mom got the best of Avery, and she eventually moved to Toronto. That left another void for Jake. A love-hate relationship with Mia's temperamental cat, Oliver, was all that remained. The cat wandered around the house just as lost as Jake, so it turned out they needed each other, and the relationship grew into one of mutual tolerance. Now, he admitted he would miss the cat if something happened to him.

The other thing that kept Jake going was three supportive friends who understood he needed them, and the four of them would gather each week for breakfast at Brew and Buns, a restaurant on Wellington Street within walking distance of Jake's house. During breakfast one Saturday morning, Jake's life took a turn for the better under the strangest of circumstance.

A thump outside the front door of the restaurant caught the attention of everyone seated in the place. Police officers had chased down a man with matted hair, a torn jacket, and ragged, filthy pants and subdued him on the sidewalk at the door in full view of everyone inside. The drug-addled man took a few swings at the officers, but they quickly subdued him with the help of a taser and led him away. While her colleagues took the cuffed offender to the police station, a female officer entered the restaurant. She used the washroom, and all eyes followed the lithe woman in a close-fitting police uniform as she ordered coffee. While she waited for her order, she wiped her sleeve across her forehead to remove beads of sweat remaining from the struggle with the man. She brushed at a stubborn dirt mark on her pants to no avail. Her chest still heaved from the exertion. As the restaurant's owner handed her the coffee, he said, "No charge," and everyone in the restaurant applauded.

Her utility belt rattled as she found a table next to where the four friends sat. Jake couldn't help but notice her captivating face framed by shimmering black hair. Her eyes shone like deep brown marbles, but wrinkles at the corners told a tale of years of happiness mixed with sorrow. To Jake, her lips were soft and enticing. She sensed the four men, and when she greeted them with a modest toast of her coffee cup, they couldn't help but smile back.

Jake and his friends invited her to join them at their table, and after considerable cajoling, she agreed. Pierre practically tipped a chair over in his haste to drag it to their table. They found out her name was Daniela Perez, and she was of Venezuelan descent. While the other three stumbled over themselves to ask about the incident in front of the restaurant, Jake remained quiet. He was immediately attracted to her, and his quiet demeanour interested her. Over time, the attraction grew stronger. She became a regular of the breakfast group, and it always disappointed Jake when he walked into the restaurant if her chair sat vacant because of some case she worked on. She seemed to need the get-togethers to bring some normalcy to her life. Jake found out Dani had her own issues, raising a teenage daughter alone after her husband left, so it took a while for the relationship to develop. They agreed to take their time, and it had been for the best. Their relationship poked along at a snail's pace as they overcame the respective issues that held them back, and Jake got to know Emilie. Now, here they were. Jake would do anything for Dani Perez and her daughter.

At 10:45, Dani returned inside to change.

"What do you suppose we should wear to this meeting?" Jake asked.

"Casual clothes, I would think. While I sat out there, the thought occurred to me to try something. What would you think of introducing yourself as Alan Brindley?"

Jake had been walking to the dresser to retrieve a casual outfit. He stopped in mid-stride. "You can't be serious. What if someone knows Brindley? Don't you think that would be asking for trouble? We might end up in the brig downstairs. I would be impersonating someone who was impersonating someone else."

"Yes, I suppose you're right. We don't know Brindley's role at the conference. Maybe he was supposed to deliver the keynote address." She broke into a wide-eyed chortle, full of excitement. "I don't think you could do that."

Jake laughed as he realized Dani was just giving him a hard time. At least he hoped she was. "You're just jerking my chain, aren't you? I can barely turn on my computer, let alone give a keynote address on technology."

He changed into tan slacks and a yellow golf shirt. Dani wore a blue skirt accentuating her muscular legs, along with a white top. They met in front of the mirror and embraced.

"Are you ready?" Jake asked.

"Let's do this," said Dani.

Chapter Thirteen

The conference room was on Deck Four opposite the Art and Photo Galleries. Jake and Dani didn't want to rush to the meeting, preferring to enter at the back after it started. They arrived at 11:05. One entrance led into the room, about equidistant from the front and back.

About seventy people sat chatting in the steel-framed chairs with comfortable red padded seats and backs. A large screen occupied most of the wall at the front. A tall, distinguished, silver-haired man wearing a light brown sport jacket over a khaki T-shirt, faded blue jeans, and sandals on his bare feet fiddled with notes on the table. When he stood to face the crowd, his features became more apparent. His slicked-back hair had streaks of dark that matched his sideburns and beard. He smiled thinly as he surveyed the crowd, his lips barely moving when he spoke to someone in the front row.

A coffee urn and cups sat on a table at the back, and Jake and Dani helped themselves before finding two empty seats in the second-to-last row. A machine projected a circular image filled with coloured swirls and dots of orange, red, and blue on the screen. To Jake, it looked like someone's worst nightmare. A round silver cylinder with a lens supported by a columnar tube occupied the middle of the maelstrom of colour. The company name, CamGuard Solutions, appeared underneath in a shape parallelling the curvature of the bottom of the logo.

"Closed-circuit TV," Jake whispered to Dani who nodded in agreement. She said, "That camera in the logo is old school. The newer versions are much sleeker and less obtrusive. The modern ones have a lens inside a half-moon-shaped glass. But I think we're about to hear about something like that."

A hush fell over the room as the man at the front attached a lapel mic to his jacket and softly blew into it. "Good afternoon, ladies and gentlemen. My name is Zachary Felton, and I'm the founder, President, and CEO of CamGuard Solutions..." The room burst into applause like they were cheering for the supreme leader. Jake and Dani clapped along. Felton held his hands up to quiet the crowd and continued. "Thank you, I hope you all had a pleasant journey here and that your cruise is everything you hoped for so far. Thanks to Angela Lee for helping pull this together." More cheering. "What did everyone do in Ketchikan? Isn't that a beautiful city, by the way?"

Shouts of whale watching, crab fishing, and kayaking rose from the crowd. Someone said they went to the salmon hatchery, and Jake and Dani peered over the top of the crowd to see if they had seen the person at the hatchery but saw nothing but the backs of heads.

The CEO continued. "Well, it looks like everyone had a wonderful time. I'm happy to hear it. Today, I want to walk through the latest plans we have for CamGuard Solutions. You've all been working hard on our products, and you should know it's appreciated. We value our employees. Each one of you. We're entering an exciting new phase of our operation, leaving behind the old technology and embarking into a new world to stop the bad guys dead in their tracks." He flashed a photo of a swarthy-complexioned man being led away in handcuffs by police. It reminded Jake of the day Dani and her colleagues apprehended the man in front of Brew and Buns. The day that changed his life.

Felton talked about the business which turned out, as Jake and Dani suspected from the name and logo, to focus on security technology and, particularly, closed-circuit cameras. Throughout the next half hour, Felton described how CamGuard Solutions planned to become the leaders in closed-circuit camera technology. He explained a multi-faceted approach to develop cameras that use artificial intelligence to assess individuals from facial recognition against databases to identify potential terrorists. The innovative technology would also zero in on objects that could be problems based on shape, location, or if left unattended. The cameras could identify people loitering where they shouldn't be or other unusual behaviour and alert authorities in real time. They could even identify people under stress or other human emotions, which would be telltale signs of someone up to no good. The next phase of development would involve cameras capable of sniffing distinctive odours like explosive material or even sweat. Everything would happen instantaneously, so authorities could take immediate action.

Only the odd murmur drifted from the crowd as they grasped the magnitude of the presentation. Jake sensed their pride in being part of the enormous advancements. Dani leaned forward, resting her elbow on her knee and her chin on her hand. She seemed mesmerized as well. Jake suspected she imagined the law enforcement potential of the technology. His thoughts circled around how people would react if they knew their every move, their emotions, and even their scent were under surveillance. *What about the ethics of all this? How close are we getting to George Orwell's "1984" when the government controls people's thoughts? The book, written in 1949, took a depressing look into the future. Is that where we're headed?*

The CEO talked about integrating the cameras with drones to control traffic flow in cities and provide more immediate disaster response. *Not so bad*, thought Jake.

Throughout the presentation, Felton flashed AI generated images on the screen to amplify his points. He spoke enthusiastically, and even Jake concluded there were definite benefits to the technology.

At the end of Felton's talk, people asked technical questions that neither Jake nor Dani understood. They followed Felton's responses even less.

At the conclusion of the presentation, the attendees engaged in conversation among themselves. Several approached Felton to introduce themselves personally or to remind him of their attendance. At the back, a young woman poured coffee from an urn. Observing that she appeared to be alone, Dani discreetly directed Jake's attention to the coffee area with a nod.

On the way, Dani whispered, "Let's ask her about Brindley. See if she knows him."

Neither of them noticed a man walking behind them, but if they had, they would have seen his eyes shoot open and his eyebrows arch. The surprised expression was fleeting, precipitated by the mention of Brindley's name.

The young woman appeared to be in her late twenties. She wore round, oversized glasses that emphasized her expressive, almond-shaped eyes. She wore her black hair pulled back in a messy bun with a few rebellious strands framing her round face. Her bright and flowery top and knee-length shorts were patterned with pansies and daisies. Jake thought the woman, or at least her ensemble, would remain in his memory banks for a long time. The hint of jasmine perfume supplemented her seasonal attire. The woman spilled coffee into her saucer as she lifted the cup to her lips. As Jake and Dani approached, she exclaimed, "Oh, that's hot," as if to cover for her clumsiness.

Dani and Jake each poured a coffee and introduced themselves. The woman said her name was Angela Lee.

"Ah, so you helped organize this cruise," Dani said, remembering what Felton said.

"I had the pleasure of helping a bit, yes. Mr. Felton is too busy to do everything, and his secretary is, uh, kind of brainless. Dresses great and looks gorgeous all the time." She scanned the room. "I'm surprised she isn't on the cruise. Anyway, I'm in the design department. The new technology is so awesome. It's been a challenge to work on, but it's so satisfying because it's going to revolutionize the industry. No one else is even close. I haven't seen you two before. Are you in Administration? I don't get up to that floor much. We're kind of like moles, buried in the basement. But it's okay. I love the work."

"Oh no," Dani said. "We don't work for the company. We're just here on vacation, but we read about this meeting concerning information technology, and since we're both interested in the subject, we thought we would sit in. There isn't one technical skill between us, but we like to remain current on recent developments. It's so intriguing." Jake hid a smirk. Before Angela asked what they did for a living, which would be the next logical question, and a difficult one to answer, Dani said, "Where is the head office for CamGuard?"

Angela said, "If I were you, I'd be sitting in a lounge right now, not attending some meeting. Anyway, each to their own." She laughed heartily, pushing back her glasses that had slid down her nose. "The head office is in Ottawa. In Kanata, to be precise."

"Is it in the Kanata North technology park? Jake asked.

"Yes, are you familiar with the area?"

Jake said, "We're from Ottawa, so we're familiar with the area. Not well. At least not me, but I'm aware of it."

They continued to talk about CamGuard Solutions and found out that Angela had worked for the company for four years. While they talked, Jake became aware of a man standing nearby. In fact, the man stood uncomfortably close. *Maybe he wants to join the conversation*, Jake thought.

The man stood about six feet tall and wore a white shirt with blue stripes and navy pants. His dark hair was greying at the sides and tousled like he had just woken up. He wore a light stubble. Worry lines wove across his forehead, and his eyes shifted around the room.

When the man saw Jake staring at him, he started for the doorway. That's when Jake noticed. The man wore running shoes similar to the ones in the picture. White and grey with a logo on the side and the brand name on the tongue under the laces. The man moved too fast to identify the branding, but Jake instinctively knew. The shoes, IceCloud10s, belonged to the person who handed the folder to Brindley or whomever the guy turned out to be.

Chapter Fourteen

D ani appeared to be about to say something more to Angela when Jake grabbed her arm, nearly knocking the cup out of her hand. "Wha ...!?"

Jake placed his cup and saucer on the table and said to Angela, "I'm sorry, I just saw someone we hoped to run into on the cruise. We heard he would be on this trip, right, darling? What a coincidence he's at this meeting! I'd like to catch up to him before he disappears among the thousands of passengers on the ship. Genuinely nice meeting you, Angela." He took Dani's cup from her hand and placed it on the table. "Maybe we'll run into you again during the next four days." He addressed the last to the startled Angela again as he steered Dani toward the door with a firm hand on her back.

Dani said, "What are you doing? Who do we know on the ship? I was about to ask Angela if she knew Alan Brindley."

"Here's one better. Someone resembling the man who gave Brindley the folder just left. I'm almost certain it's him. He must have attended the meeting, and he stood right beside us at the coffee table as if he wanted to overhear what we said. Didn't you see him?"

"No, I was concentrating on my conversation with Angela. How do you know it was him?"

"Same running shoes. He left a minute ago."

Jake and Dani lost valuable seconds maneuvering through the people chatting near the doorway. By the time they exited, the man had disappeared into wall-to-wall people taking part in a scavenger hunt at the art gallery.

"Dammit!" Jake muttered as he realized he couldn't see the man.

"You go that way. I don't know what he looks like, but I'll look for the shoes," Dani said as she turned toward the shops. Jake pushed his way apologetically through the crowded art gallery toward the theatre. He finally got through and turned the corner to the theatre but saw no sign of the man. A quick check inside the darkened theatre confirmed it was empty, although he heard murmuring behind the stage area. Deciding there was no point to this, he turned back to find Dani. Only a few minutes remained to have a snack before the ship docked in Juneau. They had to disembark for their excursion at 1:00.

The hairs stood on the back of his neck as he pushed his way back through the crowd. The sense someone tracked him crept up the length of his spine, but when he turned, nobody was there. Oh, there were people. They surrounded him. But no one he recognized. He decided the claustrophobic uncomfortableness of being surrounded must account for the weird sensation of being followed. The farther he walked, the more it clung to him. He quickened his pace, but the feeling refused to leave him.

It relieved him to see Dani walking toward him just before he reached the shopping area. The area had shops on both sides with kiosks running down the middle displaying jewellery and assorted trinkets under glass countertops. Signs boasting huge discounts stood atop the counters. Dani shrugged her shoulders with both hands turned up, suggesting she hadn't seen the man either. They met in front of a kiosk with signs promoting expensive watches at reduced prices.

"Obviously, you didn't see him," Dani said as soon as she arrived within a few feet of Jake.

"Nope, our mystery man disappeared into thin air."

"Well, now we have two mystery men. We don't know who Brindley is, and we don't know who this guy is, but we know he's on the ship. We're bound to run into him again."

Just then, Jake sensed someone sidling up to him close enough that their arms touched. Jake's eyes flashed down to the man's shoes. IceCloud10s.

The man pointed at a Cartier timepiece under the glass, suggesting his interest and pretending to ask Jake about it.

He said in a low whisper, his lips barely moving. "Don't say a word." He gestured toward a clothing store. "In two minutes, go into the store, and check out the sweaters on the shelf near the back. I'll meet you there."

With that, the man disappeared into the store.

Jake and Dani examined jewellery while monitoring the time. When an enthusiastic salesclerk approached, they advised her they were just looking. "Ask if you need anything," the clerk said cheerily. In precisely two minutes, they wandered into the shop toward the back and started thumbing through the sweaters. The man appeared beside them and did the same.

"How do you know Alan Brindley?" He mumbled his question barely loud enough that Jake and Dani could hear as he pulled a purple sweatshirt emblazoned with a graphic of a polar bear and the word "Alaska" on the front off the shelf and held it to his chest. To a casual observer, it would appear he asked the opinion about the sweatshirt of the two people standing beside him.

Dani held the arm of the shirt up as if to size it better. "We don't. He died on the balcony next to ours."

The man's face turned ashen. "Shit! Dead!? Are you sure?"

"He's definitely dead," Dani said. "Who are you?"

"It doesn't matter who I am. You didn't know Brindley?"

Dani bristled. "No, I told you."

The man seemed to forget he held the sweater in his hands. "You seemed to search for me after I left the conference room. Why?"

Dani said, "Because we know you handed a folder to Brindley before he boarded the ship. We saw you on closed-circuit television. I think someone poisoned him, and you might know something about what happened. Your shoes are pretty distinctive."

The man frowned as he looked down at his shoes. "I know nothing about any poisoning. Look, we can't talk here. Are you going ashore at Juneau?"

"Yes, we're going to see the glacier." Dani let the arm of the sweater drop and checked her watch. "We'll be going ashore in about forty-five minutes to do the Mendenhall Glacier excursion."

"Okay, I've visited Juneau before. There's a restaurant and a bar called the Gold Rush Grille on Seward Street. Restaurant at the front. Bar at the back with pool tables. It's dark inside. The bar is kind of seedy, and only the locals use it. I'll be at a table at the back. Meet me after your excursion."

The man turned and, within seconds, melded into the crowd, leaving Jake and Dani standing with their mouths agape. Dani put back the sweater she had been holding. When Jake found his voice, he said. "Well, that seemed very spy-like. What do you suppose that was about?"

"I guess he has information he wants to share with us. It's nice of him to let us go on the excursion first." Dani's sentence dripped with sarcasm.

"Are we going to meet him?"

"Of course. He could have valuable information. Then again, he might be a killer. At least we're meeting in a public place. Although it sounds like some interesting characters frequent the bar."

"Are you going to tell Eduardo?"

"Not yet. Let's find out what our mysterious friend has to say first. He could be feeling us out to find out what we know. We'll tell Eduardo after we talk to him. Besides, the meeting is taking place on shore. Eduardo has no jurisdiction."

And you do? thought Jake.

Chapter Fifteen

The morning passed quickly. They didn't check the weather, but water drops mottling the ship's windows revealed enough. As the ship moved along, the clouds seemed to drop even lower.

"Did we pick the wrong month?" Jake asked as he stared at a drip slithering in a zigzag pattern at snail speed toward the bottom of the window.

"No, Alaska receives a lot of rain in the summer. I seem to recall it rains something like nineteen days in Juneau in July. That's over 60% of the time by my calculation. We're here for one of those days. Buck up, buddy. The scenery is still gorgeous."

Time ran out to go to the dining room, so they climbed the stairs to The Mainmast Grill. Passengers occupied all the seats along the windows, so they filled two coffee cups and staked a claim at a table for two in the inside area. Dani said, "We'll be right back" to a slight, young, pretty Caribbean server who seemed poised to scoop up the coffee cups in her haste to make way for other diners. She smiled warmly as they went to get their food.

On their way, they stopped at a window to admire the view. The channel had narrowed with soaring mountains on both sides. A causeway in the distance connected the city centre with houses on the other side of the water. The clouds hid the mountaintops, but the dense green trees stretching upwards suggested the peaks rose high into the sky. The bright coloured buildings of Juneau grew larger in the mist as their ship glided forward. A ship from a different company cruised past in the opposite direction while another mammoth vessel sat hulking at the dock.

Once the other ship passed, a white chartered fishing boat chugged through its wake. Twelve-foot-long fishing poles attached to the side of the boat vibrated from the movement. Anglers wearing glistening yellow rain gear hunkered unmoving in the rain along the sides at the back of the boat, peering at the boundless waves, greyed by the overcast sky. A few fishermen raised their hands in a lacklustre wave. Jake wondered who they saw on the ship to wave to since most passengers remained inside out of the rain. The anglers looked miserable.

The boat appeared tiny compared to the ships that passed, but it had to measure 50 feet. Its rumbling, powerful engines echoed across the swells. Closer to Juneau, a float plane bounced across the waves before lifting off and disappearing into the thick, dark clouds. The plane reminded Jake of a seagull as it climbed from the water, its sound muted by the distance.

They returned to the grill counter, where Jake ordered a hamburger and fries while Dani chose scrambled eggs and fruit. Jake poured relish and mustard on his burger at the garnishment station and salt on the chips at the table. They sat, and Jake tasted his coffee. *Not bad,* he thought. Dani picked at her fruit with her fork.

"You know what's frustrating, Jake? Our standard practice at Ottawa Police Services is that we treat every sudden or unexpected death as suspicious until there's proof it's not. In Ontario, the Office of the Chief Coroner and the Ontario Forensic Pathology Service work together to ensure no death is overlooked, concealed, or ignored. They'll gather information from the family, co-workers, neighbours, doctors, hospitals, and police services."

Dani speared a piece of pineapple with her fork and spun it around in the juice in her dish. "The coroner and the pathologist will decide if an autopsy is necessary. If the family expresses concerns or if the death is suspicious, an autopsy will be done. A report is quick, but toxicology results take longer. Of course, if the person is older or has suffered from an underlying medical condition, they would conclude natural causes based on the medical history and comments from the family and leave it at that."

Jake finished his burger and dipped each chip in ketchup before savouring it. He said, "And what makes you believe that is not being done? I'm sure the FBI is working on Brindley's identification and notifying the next-of-kin. They're rather good at their job from what I understand."

"Yes, I suppose you're right. Eduardo seemed a little cavalier about the death, but I understand that, too. They're on a tight schedule, and the last thing they want to do is spook the passengers by suggesting a murder might have been committed on board. They're better off keeping it quiet." She scanned their immediate area to make sure no one heard. "A ship is not the best place to get murdered; that's for sure. Not if you want your death solved quickly."

Jake drained his coffee. Obviously, someone murdered Brindley in Dani's mind. One thing for sure. Dani would do her best to understand it. "Finished your coffee?" he asked. When Dani's head bobbed once in agreement, he said, "Are you going to change before our excursion? We don't have a lot of time."

"No, but I need a bathroom, and we should get our rain jackets and find Emilie. She's going on the whale watching excursion, remember? She's so excited about that. It looks like it's still coming down rather good. She'll be treated to the same drowned rat experience as those poor souls on the fishing boat."

They rode the elevator back downstairs to their stateroom. Jake packed the backpack while Dani rapped on Emilie's door. Her daughter came into their room wearing her red waterproof jacket and jeans and carrying her grey backpack. Jake and Dani decided not to change, and the three of them stood at the patio door as the ship drew closer to Juneau.

Emilie said, "I read Juneau has about 32,000 people, but another 21,000 come and go from cruise ships. No roads connect the city to the rest of the state. When you're here, you're here, unless you want to fly out."

Jake said, "I would feel isolated. Maybe even claustrophobic. Everybody probably knows everybody else's business in town. Not for me."

The city lay at the foot of steep mountains that Emilie informed them were around 4,000 feet high and appeared from their vantage point to be long and narrow. She gleefully told them that officials renamed the city to UNO after the card game for one day on April Fool's Day in 2016. "They've also experienced natural disasters like earthquakes and avalanches," she announced with wide eyes. "Two avalanches last January. One covered some road just outside town."

Jake would have appreciated not hearing that. He stared at the mountains towering over the city. Although the tops were not visible, he still imagined an avalanche roaring down the mountainside and burying the town. And as for an earthquake? A ship would not be the place to be. He resolved to do more research on that.

The ship docked, and they made their way to the first deck to disembark. After a long walk on the creaky wooden pier, they arrived at a souvenir hut to get their tokens and the bus numbers for their respective excursions. The streetlights above the parking lot reflected off the raindrops on their waterproof jackets. Jake and Dani hugged Emilie before she headed for her bus. "See you at supper in the dining room?" Dani said.

"Yes, Mom, see you at supper in the dining room."

"Be safe," Dani whispered to her departing back.

Chapter Sixteen

Jake and Dani checked their emails right after retrieving their tokens for the bus. Dani's were work-related while Jake's were from Avery and his buddies at Brew and Buns. Avery told Jake that Ava missed him. Although the message made him feel special, he doubted his granddaughter missed him since Ava didn't see him that much, plus she was only a year old. Nice of Avery to say, though.

"I wonder if I should call Lonnie," Dani mused as they walked toward their bus.

"Wouldn't he contact you if he had something to report?

"Yes, I suppose you're right. I may contact him later, depending on what our mystery man has to say."

A standard coach waited for them, like you would see on the highway, with plush seating for about fifty people and 18-inch television sets hanging at the front and about halfway toward the back. There was a rack for backpacks and the like, handy for a day like today. A short, rotund female tour guide welcomed the tourists aboard with a laugh and the promise the weather would clear someday.

When everyone sat, the driver/guide introduced herself as Mable. She welcomed them again and said a twenty-minute ride, give or take, would get them to the Mendenhall Glacier. She pointed out a sundial commemorating fishermen lost at sea as she drove the bus away from the port.

Jake noticed they turned onto South Franklin Street, and Mable pointed out artwork and the Red Dog Saloon. She gleefully explained to the tourists that the saloon owners displayed Wyatt Earp's gun from Nome inside, along with a bunch of stuffed animals. Mable elaborated that Earp moved from Arizona to Nome after being indicted for the murders at the O.K. Corral. Jake unfolded his paper map. Seward Street, where they would meet the mystery man, lay a couple of blocks from their current location.

The streets seemed narrow and the sidewalks wide, suggesting a tip of the hat to the tourists. Mable made a slight left onto Marine Way at one of the many gift shops in town. The bus's windshield wipers thrashed back and forth to clear the vast window. Rain combined with fog on the window made driving difficult, but Jake imagined Mable faced much worse conditions driving in Juneau, Alaska.

They rode for about 10 miles while Mable regaled them with stories about Alaska generally and Juneau in particular. She related tales of Juneau being founded in 1845 with the name "Victory." Local lawmakers changed the name to "Dodge Center" in 1846, but the official name became "Juneau" in 1852, although Joe Juneau didn't discover gold until 1880.

Their route took them onto the Mendenhall Loop Road, a nice smooth highway except for the waves launched into the ditch as the coach splashed through the puddles. They finally arrived at the glacier parking lot, but their arrival didn't generate any cooperation from the weather or much enthusiasm from the tourists. The rain still fell in torrents. Mable announced they could view the glacier from the second floor at the Visitor Center or walk about a third of a mile on the Photo Point Trail to get a better view. The bus would leave, so staying onboard to wait out the rain was not an option.

Since the weather didn't make for great viewing from the Visitor Center, Jake and Dani walked through the pelting downpour to the photo point. They zipped their waterproof jackets to the neck, pulled up their hoods, and hunched down as they hurried along the paved trail. Rivulets of water wide enough they couldn't leap across left them with soaking wet running shoes. They slowed periodically to marvel at the wide glacier that gravity pulled into the valley from the Juneau Icefield above. The sheer width and craggy features would have sparkled on a bright day as if diamonds had been seeded from the heavens. Today, the glacier, sandwiched between two mountains, featured a still picture-worthy dull greyish sheen. To the right of the glacier, water roared down from the mountaintop in two radiant streams to combine into one thunderous waterfall called Nugget Falls before it splashed into Mendenhall Lake.

A trail to Nugget Falls veered from the Photo Point Trail, but Jake and Dani took their photos of the glacier and the falls through rain-spotted lenses and turned back. "I wonder how Em's doing on her whale watching excursion," Dani said through gritted teeth.

"She's probably having the time of her life," Jake replied, his voice vibrating from shivering. "We are. Right? Tell me we're having the time of our lives." He grinned at Dani as he shoved his hands as deep as they would go into his jacket pockets. His neck ached from the strain of his hunched shoulders.

They reached the Visitor Center and hurried inside to find a crackling fire in the fireplace upstairs. Dani nudged her way between other rain-soaked tourists to dry her clothes while Jake went to retrieve coffees. She took off her soaking running shoes, and her wet socks left imprints on the wooden floor. Jake returned carrying steaming mugs of hot chocolate. "Best I could do," he said as he handed one mug to Dani. "This fire feels so good."

Others returning from their hikes needed a piece of the fireplace, too, so Jake and Dani found a seat on a ledge by the window. Dani pulled her running shoes back on and poked Jake as she pointed to the crowd by the fireplace. Angela, the young woman from the meeting, stood rubbing her hands together in front of the fire. "Let's ask her about Brindley," Dani said. The minute she said it, Angela looked over her shoulder and started walking with a crowd moving toward the door.

Jake said. "She must be leaving on the bus just ahead of ours," as Angela reached the door and quickly descended the stairs. The woman vanished long before Jake and Dani had the opportunity to talk to her.

"I'm sure she saw us," Dani said. "She made a beeline for the door like she didn't want to talk to us."

"Maybe she didn't like the way we blew her off after we saw the mystery man. Like you said, it was kind of rude."

"I don't know. It seemed to be more than that, but you might be right. I'm going to the souvenir shop to buy some postcards for my staff. It could be Christmas before they get them, but the thought will be there."

Their clothes dried a little by the time they walked up the slight incline to catch their bus a few minutes later. The bus returned on the same route, with Mable telling the passengers a few more tidbits about Juneau. As the driver did in Ketchikan, Mable gave the passengers the option of staying on the bus to go back to the ship or get off downtown and walk about half a mile back to the port. Because of the rain, most stayed onboard, but Jake and Dani had no choice. They had a meeting to go to, wet clothes and all.

To their surprise, when they descended the stairs from the bus, the clouds lifted, the rain stopped, and the sun peeked through, revealing the stunning mountaintops. The dense, tall conical trees gave way to brown earth about three-quarters of the way up.

Dani pulled out her phone and entered the name of the restaurant, the Gold Rush Grill, in her GPS. They headed in a northeasterly direction along Franklin Street to Marine Way and eventually arrived at Seward Street. An uphill climb from there left them digging deep for breath. They hurried as they didn't know what time the mystery man would arrive or how long he would wait.

They passed buildings that looked like they were built a century or more ago. Just past 4th Street, they found a flat-roofed two-story grey building with a glass door bearing a stencilled welcome sign and frosted windows on either side. The top floor might have been apartments. A neon sign in script above the door announced the Gold Rush Grill except the "G" was burned out and the rest flickered and hummed. Jake said, "I wonder how long the sign has been like that. Maybe years, and they left it hanging as a joke."

The mystery man's description of the place as "seedy" was close to hitting the mark, although the description might have been unfair. It was old as the sign suggested. Chrome tables sat on patterned blue and white linoleum that lifted in the corners and buckled enough to crack in front of the bar. Four wooden chairs sat spaced around each table. A man occupied a chair at one table. He was the size of a small house with a scruffy salt and pepper beard that brushed the tabletop, a grease-stained plaid jacket, and a matching hat that occupied the chair beside him. His dirty hair lay plastered against his head. He ignored Jake and Dani as he read a folded paper he held in one hand while spooning soup into a mouth well concealed by whiskers. Drops of orange soup clung to his moustache.

Wood panels punctured by nail holes where pictures had been removed covered the walls. A handful of photos of Juneau from decades past still hung askew in several places. A bartender in a blue T-shirt that strained against his muscular frame regarded Jake and Dani from behind the wooden bar as he polished a beer mug with a towel. A mirror threw back an image of the pair as they passed. Damp beer mugs fresh from the dishwasher sat upside down in a tray, and a row of five beer taps extended above the bar. Chrome stools with ribbed fabric sat in front of the bar, and cardboard coasters lay scattered across the counter. Jake expected a gold miner with a cowboy hat and six guns at his hips would walk through the door from the 1800s any minute.

Loud voices and laughter greeted Jake and Dani as they approached the back half of the building. They stopped in the doorway as a man leaned over a pool table, about to take a shot, while another in fishing attire and a woman in blue jeans and a yellow sweatshirt chirped him. Two other men threw darts at the last of a row of five dart boards lined up along the wall. Jake wondered how they accommodated dart players and pool players at the same time as the line for the dart players occupied the same space as someone taking a shot from that side of the pool table. A jug of beer and three half-full mugs sat on one table while two other full mugs sat on another. A country song played in the background. The place smelled of stale beer and sweat. Not unlike a gym ... except for the beer.

Jake and Dani waited for the man to take his shot. The white ball fell into a side pocket, much to the delight of the onlookers. The pool and dart players stopped talking and stood to stare at Jake and Dani as they passed. At a table in the back corner sat a man with a baseball hat pulled down over his eyes. He picked at a large plate of bacon and eggs with a fork. A half-finished glass of orange juice sat on the left side of his plate, a cellphone on the right. Above his head hung the enormous head of a stuffed grizzly.

Jake and Dani stopped in front of his table. The man peered at them from under the peak of his baseball hat and sipped his orange juice. "Have a seat," he said.

The meeting with the mystery man was about to begin.

Chapter Seventeen

The man shoved his half-finished plate forward and thumped his glass down on the table. He brushed his lips with the back of his hand as he squinted past the brim of his cap, regarding first Dani, then Jake, through semi-slit eyes. He surveyed the room, taking in the pool and dart players and, through the doorway, the back of the enormous man in the front room.

The server from behind the bar sidled up to the table. "Get you something?"

Jake still shivered from the walk in the rain to the glacier, so he ordered an Old Fashioned, a mixture of whiskey and bitters. The mystery man across the table visibly shook. Even his lips trembled. Dani took Jake's lead and ordered a Bloody Caesar. The server said, "Ah, you must be Canadian. You need to ask for a Bloody Mary in the U.S."

Jake observed Dani had detected the mystery man's nervousness. When she requested the server to elaborate on the differences between the two drinks, he understood she intended to increase the pressure on the man across the table by making him wait. Dani and Jake had discussed the differences between the two drinks with Amanda, the owner of Brew and Buns, only days earlier before they left home.

The server's chest puffed out, happy to expound on his knowledge to the newcomers. He replied, "We make a Bloody Mary with tomato juice. I understand Canadians make a Bloody Caesar with some combination of tomato and clam juice. I think you call the combination Clamato.”

Dani replied, “Okay, thanks. Let me check the menu. Jake, do you want anything to eat?”

The server said he would be back in a few minutes and left Jake and Dani to mull over the food choices.

As soon as they left, the mystery man hissed, “There’s no time for this. Someone might see us.”

Dani glanced up from the menu. “Why would it be a problem if someone saw us? Do you have something to hide? Maybe start by telling us your name. I’m Dani, and he’s Jake.”

“Okay, my name is Gavin Holt. I’m the Vice President of Human Resources at CamGuard Solutions. I need to know if you told the truth about not knowing Alan Brindley and how you knew about the folder.”

“How can we trust you, Gavin?” This from Jake.

Holt hesitated for a few seconds before answering. The server returned to take their orders, so it gave him even longer to ponder. Jake and Dani decided not to order food, and when Jake asked Holt if he wanted another beer, he declined.

When Holt hesitated to answer their questions, Dani thought about how nervous he appeared to be. Something was going on here. Holt was holding his own personal tug of war. One side didn’t trust them while the other wanted to. She put all the cards on the table.

“Alan Brindley wasn’t the deceased’s real name. I think someone murdered him. As I said earlier, we have video of you handing the folder to Brindley. As of now, if it’s confirmed someone murdered Brindley, you’re suspect number one. You’re obviously scared to death of something. We can’t help you if you don’t tell us everything.”

“How do you know all this?”

Dani reached into her purse and produced her credentials for Holt to see. "I'm a detective from Ottawa. Jake is a former investigative reporter. We have no official capacity in this. Brindley died on the balcony next to ours, and since we reported the situation, the Chief of Ship Security naturally wanted to question us."

Holt seemed to react more to Jake being an investigative reporter than to Dani being a detective.

Finally, he said, "You're right, Alan Brindley wasn't his real name. His name was Mark Reynolds. He worked as an investigative reporter from Vancouver and was undercover on a story about CamGuard. I gave him the credentials so he could attend scheduled CamGuard meetings, but if he was murdered, someone must have discovered he was investigating the company. Since I work in Human Resources, I can access credentials. The real Alan Brindley worked for the organization for about a week in Vancouver two years ago. Nobody would remember him."

Jake asked, "What kind of story did Reynolds work on that had to be done on the sly?"

"CamGuard is working on advanced closed-circuit television technology as you know. It will revolutionize security at airports, shopping malls, and any other public space. Once the technology is up and running, it will be much easier to spot someone doing something they shouldn't and alert the authorities immediately. The software uses artificial intelligence, so the technology will develop patterns and eventually will predict with a high accuracy rate what that person is planning. Law enforcement will be able to address situations before they happen.

"The technology will eventually be able to go even further. It will sniff explosives. The software has enormous potential to be a boon for law enforcement."

Dani leaned forward in her seat. "That's what we heard at the meeting. The capabilities of the software are astonishing. We would love to use that kind of equipment at the city level. The technology sounds so remarkable. I must be missing something. I don't understand the problem."

Holt glanced around again before he continued. "What if the authorities thought the software worked, but someone with the source code manipulated it so that the images displayed something totally different? The people watching the monitors would see something entirely different from reality."

"Are you saying this will happen? You mean the software can be hacked?"

Holt shook his head. "The software has so many built-in hidden redundancies, it's almost hack-proof. You can never say never in this business, but right now, it is 99% impossible."

The drink Jake ordered warmed his body as it slid down his throat. "Okay, so the software is hard to hack. What is it about the source code, then?"

Holt said, "The source code is fundamental to any software. It's used to design, edit, customize, or upgrade it. Someone with the source code has the power to do what they want with the software. Countries with ill will for the West, like some in the Middle East, China, Russia … take your pick … would pay a lot of money for that source code."

The picture became clearer for Jake like he had driven from a tunnel into the light. "You're saying that someone in the company who is working on the software and with access to the source code wants to sell it to the highest bidder? CamGuard can't make enough money from the software itself?"

"The money from the software will be substantial, but not in the same league as what someone would pay for the source code. We're talking hundreds of millions. I'm pretty certain that's what's happening, and now that Reynolds is dead, I'm convinced I'm right."

Dani asked, "How did you discover this?"

Holt sighed deeply. "Mark Reynolds was a friend of mine. We lived on the same street, and our kids played together. He was researching computer hacking, and he stumbled across some encrypted messages about CamGuard. He couldn't decipher them completely, but he was a pretty bright guy, and he discovered enough to make him think someone in the organization would give up the source code for a truckload of money. I've been feeling forgotten in the organization lately because I've been left out of senior management meetings. Like I don't exist. Something must be going on, and when Mark brought this up, I became more suspicious. He asked me to help him dig up anything on four people with access to the source code."

Dani said, "Why didn't you or Reynolds go to the police?"

"We had nothing solid enough to take to the police. It was all based on assumption. Mark promised he would go to the police if he uncovered anything provable." He sniffed. "Now he's dead. I feel sick for his family."

Dani said, "Last we heard, the authorities couldn't reach his family. They don't know who he is, and it's unlikely anyone has reported him missing since he is on a short cruise. I'll alert the authorities so they can tell his wife at least. If someone found out he was snooping around, that might put you in danger. According to the Chief of Security, they didn't find a folder in Reynold's room. They found a briefcase, so the folder could have been inside."

"Oh my God! This has gone way beyond anything I expected." Holt's eyes tightened, and he stared at the opposite wall, his lips pressed together. He wrung his hands as if trying to remove a sticky substance.

Jake asked, "Why didn't you just give Reynolds the folder on the ship? Why all the subterfuge by handing it to him before boarding?"

"Mark didn't want to risk anyone seeing us together on the ship."

Dani said, "I suggest you tell your boss you're sick and stay in your room. Order something in for food, and only answer the door when the steward brings it."

Holt nodded grimly. He raised his head slightly when Jake asked, "So, there were dossiers on the four people in the folder?"

"Yes, two of them were new employees, and the other two have worked for the company for a long time. We have been hiring lately because of the new push toward advanced technology. We think we have some of the best and brightest on the planet now."

"Can you share the dossiers with us?" Dani asked.

Holt's pallor suggested Reynold's death had spooked him. That, and the suggestion his life could be in danger. "How can I be certain I can trust you?"

Dani said, "We've been completely open with you. You've seen my credentials. Jake is a former investigative reporter, so he has tremendous skills for ferreting out information. We want to help. If there's a murderer onboard, we want to stop them before anyone else gets hurt. Help us, Gavin. Show us the dossiers. It will be a good place to start."

"Okay, I need to recreate them because I didn't want to keep a copy of what I gave Reynolds. I can give you the names. I can't send the dossier to you by email, obviously, because the ship is crawling with computer experts, many of whom could hack into the ship's system. Come to my door at ten o'clock. I'm in 7575. Knock on the door three times, and then after a few seconds, another three times. That way I'll be certain it's you."

Dani took out her phone. "We'll figure out who's behind this and who killed your friend, Gavin, I promise. Give me the names, and I'll put them in my phone."

Holt drew in a deep breath, scanned the room, and leaned forward. In a whisper barely audible to Jake and Dani, he said, "I don't have any particular suspicions about any of these people. The first one you saw already. He's the company president, or CEO as he likes to call himself, Zachary Felton. He also founded the company. The second is a new guy working in the Design Division, Raj Patel. The Design Division works on technical design and engineering of CCTV systems. They ensure the hardware and software components are compatible and meet the required specifications. Felton recently hired Patel as a manager. The third one is also new. His name is Brendon Thompson, and he's a senior researcher in the Research and Development Division. They come up with wild possibilities for future development, some of which see the light of day. They work on developing new features, enhancing image quality, and integrating advanced technologies like AI and machine learning for better surveillance capabilities. The final one is Angela Lee. She's the lead developer in the Design Division, so she has access to the source code and deep technical knowledge. She works for Patel."

Dani stopped typing. "Angela Lee? Short? Large glasses?"

"Yes, that sounds like her. Do you know her?"

Dani said as she typed, "No, but we met her at the meeting, and she showed up on the same excursion as us. You don't have any idea why these four interested Brindl ... uh ... Reynolds?"

"No, like I said, I have no idea. My only thought is that they would be the ones in the organization entrusted with the source code. I pointed out that Angela and Patel have direct access to the source code, but they aren't the only ones in the organization." Holt glanced at a large clock on the wall. "You better go. I'll wait a few minutes before I leave."

Jake and Dani got up and put on their coats. "Don't answer your door unless it's us or the steward bringing food," Dani said.

All Gavin Holt could do was watch them go with his elbow on the table while his fingers tugged at his bottom lip.

Chapter Eighteen

They left the Gold Rush Grille or "Old Rush Grille" as the sign suggested, walked for a few minutes, and turned left on 4th Street. The next left took them onto Main Street and back to Marine Way, where the brilliant sun gleamed off their waiting ship. They removed their jackets as they walked to combat the sun now beating down with intensity. They remained quiet, each lost in their thoughts.

Finally, Jake said, "Do you think the dossier will provide anything that you couldn't get from Davidson?"

"I doubt it, but I wanted Holt to think we need it. It will keep him in the game, so to speak. I'm still not sure Holt is as innocent as he pretends to be, although he puts on a pretty good act. He seemed scared to death about something. We're at sea all day tomorrow, so it's going to be difficult to reach anyone unless we can get access to the ship's communication system. We're persona non grata as far as Eduardo is concerned. I'm going to call Lonnie."

She dialled as they walked. Lonnie answered on the first ring and asked about the cruise. "It's great," said Dani. She put the phone on speaker so Jake could listen. "We found out Alan Brindley's real name is Mark Reynolds. The FBI may not have his name yet, so would you call the Anchorage office and tell whoever is trying to notify the next-of-kin? They'll owe us one if we help them with this information."

"Okay, but what else should I say? How do I tell them you got this information?"

"Be honest with them. Tell them who Jake and I are and that we met someone on the ship who lived on the same street as Reynolds. Reynolds was an investigative reporter working on a story about a company called CamGuard Solutions. The company executives and some of the other major players planned to meet on the ship, so he was incognito, trying to get inside information. I would be happy to talk to the FBI at the next port if necessary. Please also ask them when the preliminary report from the autopsy will be completed. We still don't know for sure if Brindley, uh, I mean Reynolds, was murdered."

"Okay, will do. Are you going back to the ship now?"

"Yes, we set sail at 5:00. Email if you need to reach me. One other thing. Please run background checks on these five people. She gave him the names of Gavin Holt, Zachary Felton, Brendon Thompson, Raj Patel, and Angela Lee. Don't tell the FBI we're looking into these people for now. We'll alert them if you find anything."

Dani disconnected at the same time they arrived at the entrance to the ship. They showed their passes and boarded, heading straight for their room. Dani tapped softly on Emilie's connecting door. The teenager opened it immediately, stunning in a peach-coloured, form-fitting dress. Stunning, but frazzled. Emilie gaped from Dani to Jake and back again with her hands raised, palm up.

"Have you guys forgotten it's formal evening? Get dressed up, remember? We're already late. Sheesh!"

"I completely forgot," Dani said. "You look gorgeous! So … well … grown up. Give us twenty minutes."

Jake flashed a thumbs-up as Emilie said grumpily, "I'll meet you in the dining room."

When Emilie returned to her room, Jake bounced across the floor on one leg as he peeled his still damp pants off the other. He flung them onto the bed and headed toward the shower.

"Wait," Dani said. "Let me go first, so I can work on my makeup while you shower. I'll be five minutes."

Twenty minutes later, he and Dani looked far different from earlier. She wore a form-fitting blue dress while Jake wore a grey suit with a white shirt and red tie that Dani and Emilie had picked out for him. They stood side-by-side in front of the mirror.

Jake said, "You look breathtaking." Unaccustomed to wearing a shirt and tie, he tugged at the neck of his shirt, trying to loosen it as he gazed at his stunning girlfriend.

Dani replied, "Yeah, except for my hair, but no one will see me again after this cruise, so I guess it doesn't matter. And you're very dapper yourself, Mr. Scott."

They hustled out of their room and headed for the dining room. A cameraman stopped them in the hallway on the way to take their picture.

"What about Emilie?" Jake asked.

A maître d' standing at the door overheard and asked if they were waiting for someone. When Dani said her daughter was inside the dining hall at Table 144, the man hurried off to retrieve her. He came back with Emilie right behind, her face aglow with excitement.

"Mom, exciting news. We've been invited to sit at the captain's table. I was talking to the server, Maria, when a man came along telling me about the invitation. Isn't that cool? They said to wait until you and Jake showed up. Now that you're here, we can sit with the captain."

Jake frowned. Based on what he read before coming on the cruise, an invitation to the captain's table was usually random and delivered to the room on an embossed sheet of paper in an envelope. It was considered a privilege to dine with the ship's highest-ranking officer. The invitation seemed suspect, but he lined up with a smile for the photo with Dani and Emilie. The photographer took several shots and assured them the pictures would be available for viewing at the photo gallery on the 4th deck. Jake assumed a hefty price tag would accompany them.

A maître d' hovered until the photo session finished and gestured for Jake, Dani, and Emilie to follow him. As they wound their way around the corner toward a large round table in the middle of the dining room, Dani asked, "Em, did you enjoy your excursion?"

"It was awesome, Mom. We got soaked, but so much fun! Most of the people looked old, but they talked to me."

"I hope you won't catch a cold."

"I'm fine, Mom."

Full wine glasses sat in front of each occupant at the table, and three chairs remained vacant. Captain Ingrid Svenssen sat facing the passengers occupying other tables around the massive room. Two couples sat around the captain's table, and one man sat beside her with his back to Jake, Danie, and Emilie as they approached. He sat bolt upright, and Dani thought she recognized his silver hair as they drew near.

The maître d' led them around the table and pulled out the chairs for them to sit. He removed the napkins from the table and spread them out on the laps of the newcomers. A server appeared out of nowhere, as if he had been conjured up, carrying a bottle of red wine in one hand and white in the other. Jake and Dani both chose white, while Emilie asked for a Coke.

Captain Svenssen reintroduced herself without acknowledging Jake and Dani's earlier visit to the bridge. The Swansons from Calgary and the Barretts from Manitoba introduced themselves. Finally, the man sitting next to Captain Svenssen took his turn to introduce himself. He didn't really need an introduction to Jake and Dani. He announced his title,

Founder and Chief Operating Officer of CamGuard Solutions, and his name, Zachary Felton.

Chapter Nineteen

"**I**'m very pleased to meet you. Haven't we met somewhere? You seem so familiar." Felton directed his words at Dani as he held her eyes with his. The man's expression appeared predatory to Jake as Felton leaned across the table to take Dani's hand. His wine glass rocked on the verge of tipping when his tuxedo jacket swung open, and his sleeve lifted above his wrist to reveal a watch that cost the price of a small car.

Before Dani answered, Jake said, "We haven't met, but we sat in on your lecture the other day. We know nothing about technology, but we had time to kill, and your session sounded interesting. Advancements in technology fascinate us."

Felton ignored Jake as his eye's swept Dani from her chest to her face and back again. Captain Svenssen said, "Dani and Jake and their lovely daughter were chosen at random, like all of you, to sit at our table tonight, and I'm delighted to meet you all."

Jake assumed the captain didn't want to acknowledge that Dani worked as a detective, their role in discovering the murder victim, or that they had been on the bridge. Felton exclaimed, "Daughter? You two aren't sisters?"

It may have been an attempt to compliment Dani, but Emilie's expression shouted that she considered it an insult. The evening was not off to a great start. Dani said, "Yes, this is my *seventeen-year-old* daughter Emilie. Jake and I are delighted she joined us on the cruise since she'll be heading to university in the fall. Captain Svenssen, we consider ourselves fortunate to have been invited to join you this evening. I understand the invitations are random but thank you." The Swansons and Barretts, who said nothing to this point, nodded in agreement.

The menu turned out to be the same as everyone else's in the dining room. While the service at their usual table was exemplary every night so far, the captain ranked as the most important person on the ship, so their servers were more senior and fussed to ensure everyone received everything they needed or wanted.

The Barretts, who were farmers from north of Brandon, Manitoba, and the Swansons, who sold farm equipment in Calgary, shared common interests, leading to plenty of conversation between them. Dani said she worked in retail, and Jake said he was a retired reporter looking for a job. Felton bragged about his 1986 29-foot sloop and his love for and experience on the water. "The boat is too big to handle by myself, so if any of you are interested in coming to Ottawa for a ride sometime, I would be happy to take you. I've been sailing for years, so it's perfectly safe." He looked directly at Dani.

Then, Felton talked about his CCTV camera system nonstop, which Captain Svenssen seemed to find fascinating. She said, "I would love to have that kind of technology on the ship. Some of our ships are being equipped with smart technology as we speak, such as facial recognition, so if something happens, we could track anyone just by identifying them from their picture on their sea pass. This is an older ship, so it doesn't have that capability yet."

"You must have CCTV, though," Felton suggested as he cut into his steak.

Svenssen tilted her head. "Yes, of course, but there are blind spots. It's improving."

Emilie, who sat quietly until now asked, "Who's driving the ship when you're here?"

Captain Svenssen laughed and wiped her mouth with her napkin. "That question comes up a lot. Some people are nervous when I'm not on the bridge."

"I know I am," said Jake. That drew a laugh from everyone around the table.

The captain continued, "I can't be available 24/7, but my quarters are close enough to the bridge that I can be there in 12 seconds if they need me. There are typically at least two people on the bridge besides the Quartermaster. The Quartermaster handles lookouts, so he or she scans the water for approaching vessels or, since we're on an Alaska cruise, ice. Anything that can cause a problem. I control the engines and thrusters, but I will give the responsibility to my 2nd or 3rd in command to give them experience. So, to answer your question, my 2nd is in charge now. The Communications Officer monitors the VHF radio. If you're wondering about safety features on the ship, everything on the bridge has three backups, so if one fails, another will take over. They're called redundancies. There is a fire detection system, so fires can be identified and dealt with. And remember, the crew on the bridge can see everything, so be careful what you do on your balcony."

Felton said, "I imagine you've seen quite a bit." He almost leered.

The captain smirked at Felton. "More than you can imagine."

Jake directed a question to Felton. "I've always been curious about security when companies develop high-tech software. There must be many people involved. How do you secure the engine of the system? What's it called? Something code?"

Dani hid a thin smile behind her napkin at Jake playing dumb as she pretended to wipe something from her mouth.

Felton's chest puffed out, thrilled to have someone at the table interested enough to pose a question. "It's always a concern, but everyone is vetted before they join the company and must sign an NDA, a Non-Disclosure Agreement. The code you're referring to is the source code. Only a few most trusted employees are given access. There are safeguards that alert people monitoring the system if someone is messing with it. You said you're an investigative reporter. Are you interested in doing an article on the software? We can use all the publicity we can get."

Jake assumed anyone with advanced knowledge of the source code could find a way around the safeguards, but he let it go for now. Dani's foot nudged his under the table. He picked up on her gesture and said, "I *was* an investigative reporter, so I don't have a direct link to a mainstream newspaper anymore, but magazines and online sites are always looking for freelance submissions. I would be delighted to work on an article. I would need access to some of your staff. Maybe the Design Team or Research and Development can help fill in the background. How does that sound?

Felton stroked his chin. "It sounds great. I'll get back to you on setting that up."

Dani picked up on something the captain said earlier. "You said the Communications Officer monitors the VHF. What's that?"

"Oh, VHF gives us the capability to communicate with other vessels and the pier. UHF allows us to communicate with departments onboard. We have an emergency position indicator and a search and rescue transponder, and an orange box, which is like the black box on airplanes."

"And what about internet?" This was from Emilie.

The captain laughed. "That's always been a problem and one of the biggest complaints from passengers. Our internet is spotty at best, as I'm sure you've experienced. We're testing an improved satellite system on the bridge now, and if it works out, I'm sure all passengers will have access to it on all ships soon enough."

Emilie said, "I wear out my phone battery every time we're onshore. We bought electronic SIM cards for our phones, so we don't pay roaming charges."

Felton changed the subject back to something that interested him more than a teenager's concerns about the internet. "It sounds as if ships like this need to be equipped with our state-of-the-art CCTV cameras to make it even more secure. I'll contact the corporate CEO about that."

Captain Svenssen sipped her wine and set the glass on the table. "Can you speak Norwegian? These ships are built in Norway and fly under the Norwegian flag."

Felton carried most of the conversation while they finished their desserts. Emilie raved to Jake, who had tuned Felton out minutes earlier, about her chocolate brownie. Suddenly, the servers gathered on the stairs leading to the dining room on the upper deck. After a few minutes, Svenssen excused herself and took a mic set up in front of the servers. She welcomed the passengers and mentioned that the servers represented twenty-four different countries. The servers then marched through the dining room, waving, smiling, and clapping as they sang their version of a popular song.

When the captain came back to the table, Felton announced he had a meeting to attend, and the Barretts, Swansons, and Emilie said they wanted to change before the theatre production. That left Jake and Dani alone with the captain. As the servers cleared the remaining dishes from the table, Svenssen said quietly, "You're probably aware our Security Chief, Eduardo, isn't thrilled with you." She stopped speaking to have her picture taken with an elderly Asian couple before continuing. "Eduardo is worried you could spread the news around the ship that someone was murdered on-board and start widespread panic. We can't have that, of course. I promised

I would speak to you. That's why I arranged for you to sit at the table this evening. I'm sure based on your careers that you will be discreet. Oh, and thank you for not mentioning you're in law enforcement. The less said about that, the better."

Dani said, "Captain, we will be discreet, of course, but you should know we spoke with the VP of Human Resources for CamGuard Solutions, and he promised to give us some information he passed on to the deceased just prior to his death. It was in a file folder, and according to Eduardo, the folder might be in a briefcase, which is with the FBI now. We're meeting with the whistleblower later this evening to get our copy of the information. We're just trying to help where we can."

"Okay, well, please keep Eduardo informed if there is something to be concerned about. Although he may seem uncooperative, he received a warning when he first started, so he has a reason. He was too exuberant with an incident on board. He threw some people in the brig who he thought were fighting, but they were friends just fooling around. Of course, the friends recorded everything and posted it online. He's extra careful now.

"In the meantime, please enjoy your cruise. I hope you savour your time on the ship when we're at sea tomorrow. We will head into the Gulf of Alaska during the day. The forecast predicts a sunny day, so it should be beautiful sailing." The minute she rose, a server arrived to pull her chair back.

Dani said, "There is one thing we found out. The deceased travelled under an assumed name, Alan Brindley. His real name is Mark Reynolds. The FBI probably knows already, but we'll mention it to Eduardo. Reynolds was an investigative reporter doing an article on CamGuard Solutions and travelling incognito."

The captain sat again. "Why would he do that?"

"According to the whistleblower, named Gavin Holt, someone might be trying to steal valuable data from CamGuard, and they've chosen this cruise to work out the details. I suspect the deceased knew too much and somebody killed him, but that could be my detective brain working overtime. Hopefully, that's all it is. I've asked my staff to investigate the backgrounds of the people working at CamGuard and will pass anything I find out to Eduardo."

Creases formed around the captain's eyes as she contemplated the information. Finally, she said, "You're taking an extraordinary interest in all of this. Are you sure you're enjoying your cruise?"

"Yes, of course. The scenery is breathtaking. It was a little soggy today, but we expected as much when we chose Alaska. There is something else I wondered about, though. You mentioned testing satellite internet on the bridge. Is there any way we could have access to it? I don't want to trouble you, but it would help us investigate further."

"I would need to request permission from the shore to do that, and I'm not sure it's possible. Sorry, but I must say 'no' for now."

Jake and Dani shook hands with the captain and thanked her again for inviting them. After she left, Jake checked his phone and glanced at Dani. "Just enough time to catch the show before we visit Cabin 7575 to see Mr. Gavin Holt. Shall we?"

Chapter Twenty

Jake and Dani hurried straight to the theatre. They found two empty seats near the back and ordered the drink of the day—a Cosmopolitan. Jake undid his shirt collar and pulled his tie from around his neck. He breathed a sigh of relief as he folded the tie and stuffed it in the pocket of his jacket. Dani leaned forward and scanned the room. After a few minutes, she pointed. "There she is." Emilie sat about six rows back from the stage beside the curly-haired boy they had seen her dancing with. They appeared to be sharing a joke as they laughed.

"She's having a good time," Jake said.

"Yes, I'm glad she found a friend. Her standards are high, and she sometimes has difficulty making friends, but this time it looks like she found one. I wanted her to tell us about her excursion before she forgets and starts looking forward to the next one. You know how teenagers are. Sometimes they have the memory of a gnat."

Their drinks arrived, and they handed the server their passes to pay for them just as the lights dimmed. Jake said, "What do you think of doing an article on CamGuard Solutions? That kind of fell in our lap. I'm not sure I'm prepared to write an article again, but it's a great opportunity to interview some people working there."

Dani's face displayed a map of skepticism. "If he ever follows through with the interviews. That guy is so full of it; his eyes are brown. Is there a hole in my chest from him staring at my boobs all night? If you ever do an article, he will make sure you write about the amazing Mr. Zachary Felton and little about the company. But I agree, this presents a great opportunity to do some digging."

This time on stage, the cruise house band presented covers of hits from the fifties and every decade after. Hearing the songs played back-to-back reminded Jake how music had changed over the years. The show lasted about an hour, after which they watched Emilie and her friend leave. Jake and Dani sauntered through the door to the outer deck. Stars twinkled overhead as they snuggled close together in the chilliness of the Alaska evening. The ship's lights illuminated the waves gently slapping against its side.

Dani continued to survey the heavens as she leaned her head on Jake's shoulder. "Were you aware that stars are a symbol of mystery and wonder?" Jake had no chance to answer before Dani exclaimed, "Look!" He scanned the indigo blue sky in the direction her finger pointed, just in time as the tail end of a comet flashed across. At least, it could have been a comet. Or the international space station, for all he knew. He was more focused on the breathing beauty in front of him, but he said, "Isn't a comet supposed to be good luck?"

"That's one interpretation. Another is that it signifies a journey we are not sure of taking."

Jake thought of Dani's insistence to get involved with the death of Mark Reynolds. "Well, that's kind of creepy," he said.

Dani viewed her phone. "It's time."

They returned inside hand-in-hand to the warmth of the ship and ascended one flight of carpeted stairs to Deck Seven. A short walk brought them to Room 7575. Jake tapped on the door with three knocks followed by three more as agreed, and they waited. And waited. He tapped again with the same combination, more sharply this time. They still waited. Dani checked her phone again. 10:10. "I hope he followed instructions not to answer the door without the knocking pattern we agreed on."

Jake tried one more time, but still nothing. "What do you want to do?"

"Let's wait in the chairs at the end of the corridor. We'll spot him if he shows up."

They did as Dani suggested. They listened to the piano styling floating up from a lower deck and monitored the people coming and going. An hour went by, and still no sign of Gavin Holt. Jake spied the cabin steward in the hallway. "Excuse me," he said as he hustled down the corridor to talk to her.

The woman stood about five feet two inches and wore black pants and a white shirt. Her name tag identified her as Ana, and she appeared to be in her early twenties.

"Hi Ana, I'm sorry to bother you, but my friend and I expected to meet a colleague in Cabin 7575, and he's over an hour late. It's not like him, and we're concerned. Do you think you could check on him?"

Ana smiled at Jake. "Sir, I can't tell you how many times this happens on a cruise ship. People get distracted in a bar or meet someone and they're late to meet a friend or for a business meeting or something." She smiled politely while pushing her cart of cleaning supplies. She added, "There are many distractions on the ship." Jake detected a Spanish accent.

Dani joined them and chipped in. "Our colleague's name is Gavin Holt, and he wouldn't miss this meeting. It's just so out-of-character. He was ill earlier, and we would be so grateful if you would just open the door to make sure he's okay." She touched Ana's hand with a folded $20 bill.

Ana crouched down away from the prying lens of the cameras as if re-trieving something from her cart and tucked the money inside her blouse. She stood and whispered, "Please don't tell anyone I did this. I could get removed from the ship." She knocked on the door and said loudly, "Housekeeping."

Jake snuck a look at Dani. Neither planned on telling Ana that Dani told Holt not to answer the door for anyone. Just like before, Holt didn't answer. Ana placed her card into the reader and opened the door just wide enough to repeat who she was. Nothing. She opened the door wider to see Holt sprawled on the bed. Ana put her hand to her mouth in a silent scream and stepped backward, bumping into Dani. Holt's eyes stared at the door, but nothing registered.

Chapter Twenty-One

Dani sensed nothing could be done for Gavin Holt, but she pushed past Ana toward the bed. Jake gently nudged Ana inside and let the door to the room slam shut. Dani said to Ana, "Call the doctor." As Dani climbed on the bed to administer chest compressions, she shouted, "Touch nothing. Even the door handle could be infected." She surveyed the room as she pressed on the middle of Holt's chest with one hand on top of the other, fingers interlocked. A bluish tinge around the dead man's mouth caught her attention, but what interested Dani the most was a gift bag on the dresser. She looked beyond that to an open laptop on the desk. An image of the room reflected on the black screen, but a tiny light on the side shone brightly, indicating the machine was powered. A USB thumb drive stuck out of a slot on the other side of the computer. Dani wondered if the dossiers waited for her on the drive. If Holt had ordered food, it wasn't apparent. No empty dishes in the hallway.

While Holt faced the door, his half-turned body lay with his left arm across the far side of the bed beside the wall. His open hand dangled off the edge. Below that lay a half-eaten chocolate bar on the floor. Death could have come quickly if someone had poisoned the bar.

Ana seemed frozen in time. Dani said sharply, "Ana, call the doctor, and you should contact Security as well."

Ana's face contorted, a picture of anguish. She exclaimed, "How am I going to explain this? I shouldn't be in here."

Jake peeked in the bathroom. Holt's used towels hung on the rack. "Ana, think. You have every right to be in here. You can say Mr. Holt asked for a fresh towel, and when you brought it, he didn't answer the door, so you planned to lay it on the bed. We stood here knocking on the door when you arrived, so we asked you to check on him. That's when you found him. Can you do that?"

Ana was still afraid to move. Tension crackled in the air at the idea that a toxin could be on any surface in the room. Dani wondered how anyone could get into the room without a passkey. She made a mental note to check into the control over the master keys that would access any room. For now, she decided, until they determined otherwise, they must assume any of the surfaces could be contaminated. She glared at Ana, who finally uncrossed her folded arms, her eyes wide in fear. Ana dialled her phone with trembling hands. After she hung up from speaking with someone in the Medical Centre, she said, "Are you sure we need to call Security?"

Dani gave up on the chest compressions. She moved from the bed to the sofa, shoved a crab made of towels aside, and sat down. She said, "Yes, I'm sure. Mr. Holt is dead, and there's a suggestion of foul play." She gestured to the gift bag on the table. "Do you know where that bag came from?"

Ana shuddered with her hands clasped beneath her chin. Her voice barely rose above a whisper. "It sat outside Mr. Holt's door when I came to clean the room. His name is on the bag, so I brought it in and set it on the desk where it is now. Are we in danger because we touched the doorknob? I'm so scared."

Dani said, "Symptoms can take minutes or hours. You would feel chest pain, dizziness, or weakness, but I'm sure you're fine."

Ana put her hand on her chest. "I feel ... we ... weak."

Jake put his arm around the young woman. "It's just because you're scared, Ana. Take a deep breath. We can assume the outside doorknob would be safe. We should stay away from the inside knob and other solid surfaces. Besides, the clinic onboard would have an antidote." He peeked at Dani, whose eyebrows raised. Jake read her mind. They would have no antidote.

A sharp knock at the door startled Ana as she dialled the security office.

Jake took a handkerchief from his pocket and used it to turn the knob to open the door. The doctor entered the room.

Dani said, "Please be careful where you walk. And don't touch any surfaces. This could be a crime scene, and it should be preserved until further investigation takes place. There's a half-eaten chocolate bar on the floor that should be tested, along with the gift bag on the dresser. All the solid surfaces should be tested for toxins."

The doctor appraised Dani and then Jake. He said, "I remember you two. You were next door to the deceased person on Deck Eight. Why shouldn't I touch any surfaces?"

Ana stared wide-eyed at Dani and Jake. Her pinched lips showed she would rather be any place but in that room. The doctor already wore rubber gloves as he hurried to the bed, avoiding the chocolate bar and any solid surfaces. He checked Holt's pulse with his fingers and his heart with a stethoscope. Finding nothing, he made a note on a sheet of paper attached to a clipboard.

Dani said, "Notice the bluish tinge on the lips. The man who died in the room next to ours had the same colouring. It could be poison. If it is, whoever administered it could have put it on the chocolate bar, but they could have also dabbed it on any solid surface as a backup."

The doctor regarded Dani. "Yes, I noticed the tinge. I asked for a toxicology report on the other victim, but it will take a while. The tissue would be sent to Anchorage, and the tests done there." After covering Holt with a blanket that he carefully removed from a top shelf, the doctor called the Medical Centre for a gurney.

A few minutes later, another solid rap on the door startled everyone. When Jake opened the door, Eduardo stood outside. "You again," was all he said. He pushed the door open and surveyed the room. By now, the standard cabin of about 180 square feet or 15 square metres was getting crowded. Eduardo stared at the body covered in a blanket on the bed. He said nothing more before another knock followed the squeaking wheels of a gurney rattling outside.

Everyone looked at the Security Chief for guidance, who finally said, "Doc, you take the body to the morgue. I want to talk to these two." He gestured to Jake and Dani. "Meet me in my office in twenty minutes." It wasn't a request. To Ana, he said, "You come with me."

Dani said, "You need to secure this room. Nobody should come in here until it's been thoroughly cleared by a hazmat team. There could be a toxin anywhere in the room."

Eduardo was not happy about getting orders from Dani, but he placed a call to have his security team tape off the room.

They all traipsed out the door that Jake pulled open with the handkerchief. The doctor held the door so the man pushing the gurney could enter. Jake and Dani headed for the stairs and took them to their room while Ana and Eduardo walked in the opposite direction. Dani said, "I wish we could check Holt's computer. There might be something useful on it. I think the USB could have the dossiers."

"Couldn't we use gloves?"

"Depends on what the toxin is. Some toxins can penetrate gloves." Jake shuddered as they arrived at their cabin, thinking about the thin handkerchief he used. Dani tapped softly on Emilie's door while Jake went into the bathroom to scrub his hands. Emilie wasn't in her room, so Dani left a note. She explained that the Security Chief wanted to see them, that it was nothing to worry about, and that they would catch up with her in the morning. Twenty minutes later, they descended in the elevator to the first deck and Eduardo's office. It surprised Jake to see the word "Wednesday" still on the plaque. It had been a long day.

When they arrived, Eduardo rose from his chair and stood with his arms crossed and his feet spread apart. His chest puffed out, and his head tilted upward. This was not a man to be trifled with. He uncrossed his arms and gestured toward the same two chairs Jake and Dani had sat in the last time they visited the office. He didn't waste any time. He said icily, "The captain called me."

Jake glanced at Dani from the corner of his eye. She remained rigid in her seat, leaning forward, her hands clasped on her lap.

Eduardo said, "You found out the name of the deceased in the cabin next to yours, and you didn't bother to tell me. Don't you think that's vital information I should know?"

Jake said, "We got back late to the ship. We planned to reach you after we talked to Gavin Holt. We thought he might have more information that you would be interested in, so we planned to tell you everything then." Jake realized the excuse sounded hollow. He and Dani took the time to go to the theatre. They had time to call the Security Chief but simply chose not to. Dani obviously thought little of Eduardo's investigative skills.

Eduardo rose from his chair and started pacing. "Start at the beginning. Why were you meeting this Gavin Holt?"

Dani explained Holt had seen them at the CamGuard Solutions meeting and overheard them talking about Alan Brindley.

"Okay, stop!" Eduardo exclaimed with a red face. "Why did you go to the meeting?"

"I told you from the beginning I thought there was reasonable evidence to suggest someone murdered Alan Brindley. You said yourself that Brindley planned to attend a high-tech conference, so we sat in. It was a public meeting, so anyone could attend. Holt overheard us talking about Alan Brindley. He found us after and asked for a meeting. We met him in Juneau, and he said he would give us a file at ten o'clock. We knocked several times but didn't get a response. We were about to leave when Ana came with a fresh towel, so we asked before she went in if she would tell us whether Holt was asleep inside."

Dani's eyes darted to Jake and back as she inhaled deeply. She hoped Ana told the story Jake suggested about the reason she was in the room.

Eduardo didn't react. He stopped pacing and sat in his chair opposite Jake and Dani. He ran his fingers through his hair, his eyes narrowed.

Dani regarded him and resolved to herself to ask Lonnie to check into Eduardo's background. Eduardo told them he was former military, but the man reacted strangely to this situation. The captain mentioned a problem Eduardo had with a previous incident, and there was the whole business thing to keep the ship on schedule without upsetting the passengers, but this didn't seem right, and it became worse.

The Security Chief said, "I recall asking you to stop investigating and enjoy your cruise. I even gave you passes to The Swordfish Restaurant, yet you continue to stick your nose where it doesn't belong. You embarrassed me by sharing information about Mr. Reynolds' real name with the captain before me. I have a good mind to lock you up in the brig until the next stop and put you off the ship." He glared back and forth between Jake and Dani.

Jake bristled. "You're right, we should have informed you about Reynolds' real name, and we apologize for that, but as for the rest of it, Dani is a well-respected detective in Ottawa. You would be wise to listen to her when she says there could be a murderer on board. In fact, now that Holt has been found dead, it's even more probable. Since both men worked for CamGuard Solutions, there's a common denominator. Everyone working for that company could be in danger." Jake's voice rose, punctuating every syllable. He leaned toward Eduardo until their faces remained inches apart, his right hand slicing the air with every word. "In fact, if I were you, I would beg Dani to help, because you're not able to do it yourself. You're former military, so you should know well enough to stop threatening us and use Dani's skill to your advantage before someone else gets hurt."

Eduardo seemed to shrink at the onslaught as Jake sat back in his chair, looking defiant. The silence was fraught with tension. Eduardo sucked his bottom lip. Suddenly, the shrill of a satellite phone on the desk broke the silence. The Security Chief seemed thankful for the distraction as he rose from his seat, grabbed the phone from the desk, and fumbled with it to connect. He listened with his eyebrows scrunched together, responding in monosyllables for a good two minutes.

Dani reached to cover Jake's trembling hand with hers. Her wry half smile and wink expressed her appreciation for his diatribe. Their moment of quiet sharing received a dramatic interruption when Eduardo said into the receiver, "They're right here." He handed the phone to Dani. "Someone from the FBI wants to talk to you."

Chapter Twenty-Two

Neither Jake nor Dani reacted when Eduardo announced the call from the FBI. After all, Dani asked Lonnie to call them. They were curious about the call and amazed by the sudden change in temperature of the room. Eduardo's face expressed awe compounded by anger that the agent wanted to talk to them. Dani wondered as she answered the phone if she should expect another lecture on butting out of looking into the deaths.

She answered with a professional, "Detective Daniela Perez." The woman on the other end sounded equally professional. "Detective Perez, this is FBI agent Sloane Parker from the Anchorage Branch. Your officer contacted me, Officer Lonnie Davidson. I understand you suspect there is a situation onboard the Ocean Wanderer."

"We have a situation with the potential for getting worse, yes," Dani replied. "Based on the skin colouring around the lips of the two deceased men, they could have been murdered. Eduardo tells me that Mr. Reynolds' body tissue was sent to Anchorage for toxicology testing."

Parker said, "That's correct. May I call you Dani? Please call me Sloane. Yes, as I'm sure you're aware, toxicology tests take a long time because the overworked lab technicians are focusing on testing the living since the dead are … well … dead. We can't blame the technology for taking so long. It's the human factor. Staff shortages."

Dani nodded at the phone, as if Sloane Parker stood right in front of her. The Anchorage agent just exposed a universal problem.

Sloane continued, "I inquired with the lab about conducting a preliminary test, and they agreed. They grumbled, of course. They prefer to avoid speculation until they complete thorough research. According to the initial results, Mr. Reynolds was poisoned, likely by ingesting cyanide. This situation presents several potential concerns, as cyanide on the ship poses a risk to all passengers. I agree with you that two possible poisoning victims have worsened the situation. I'm going to send a helicopter out to collect the second body. We can't wait until the ship arrives in Seward. This is too serious. Can you provide information about this second individual?"

Dani related the story about meeting Gavin Holt and the list of people who could try to steal the source code from CamGuard Solutions. She described the same colouring on Gavin Holt as Mark Reynolds.

"But why would someone use a cruise to murder people?" Parker asked. "They won't steal the source code on the ship. That would need to be done in an office somewhere. Or could they? I suppose they could do it remotely."

Dani said, "I asked myself the same question, but judging by the speed of the internet we've been dealing with onboard, we can rule out stealing the source code while on the ship. They must have carried the cyanide onboard to get rid of Reynolds. Then they discovered Holt was the informant after they boarded. Perhaps there's no better place than a ship. There are 2800 people onboard, and they would be just another passenger. The perpetrator might try to get off the ship at the next port." She wanted to add that the security department was great for dealing with rowdy passengers, but not equipped to investigate murders, but Eduardo's scowling face stopped her. Instead, she said, "This ship isn't a smart ship, so the security is not as sophisticated as it could be.

"The bigger reason revolves around the way cyanide works. When cyanide is administered, death is from cardiac arrest. It's difficult to detect unless you're looking for it. I recognized the unusual colouring, having seen it before. Otherwise, the death could've been deemed the result of natural causes. A cyanide solution of as little as 200 mg, or exposure to airborne cyanide of 270 parts per million, suffices to cause death within minutes. It's hypertoxic. If the perpetrator has enough, they could expose this entire ship through the ventilation system."

Dani sensed Eduardo taking a deep breath at the mention of mass distribution of the deadly toxin.

Dani continued. "Bringing the cyanide onboard wouldn't be a problem since there are no real liquid rules on a cruise ship. From my experience, a shampoo bottle or sunscreen is acceptable to bring on a ship, unlike an airplane. They can be brought onboard in a traveller's carry-on. We need to investigate further so nothing worse happens."

Parker said, "You're right." Dead air hung between them until Parker said, "You're under no obligation to do what I'm about to ask you to do. I understand you're out of your jurisdiction. I could get in trouble for this, but would you be willing to continue investigating? You're in the best position to do so. You have the skills. I looked up your record. I'll speak to the captain to make sure you gain access to whatever you need onboard and ensure Security cooperates to give you whatever help they can. Would you be willing to do that? I could send you a letter of authorization. I would just ask that you keep me informed."

"Yes, of course I'll do what I can," Dani said. "The limitations I mentioned for the perpetrator apply to an investigation, too, though. I would ask that we get access to the faster internet system that's being tested on the bridge and to the communications systems used by the security staff here. That would be helpful."

"Who is 'we'?"

"Oh, I'm sorry. My partner is a retired investigative reporter by the name of Jake Scott. He has a tremendous record of tracking down criminals, sometimes whether I like it or not." Dani winked at Jake and chuckled.

"Okay, I appreciate this very much. I'm sorry for ruining your cruise, Dani, but anything you can do on your end will be helpful. I feel helpless sitting here in my office. We don't want this to turn into a major disaster. I'll call the captain right away. Oh, and one more thing. Please do everything you can to make sure no more innocent people get murdered on that ship."

"I'll do my best, Sloane," Dani said as she hung up, knowing that calling the captain would be the second thing Sloane Parker would do. The first would be to run a background check on Jake.

Chapter Twenty-Three

Dani handed the phone back to Eduardo and stared at the carpet as she gathered her thoughts. Eduardo broke the silence. "Several people on staff can help with the investigation. A Deputy Security Official, a Security Officer, and several guards report to me. I'm still not convinced we need to do much investigating before we dock in Seward. We'll arrive the day after tomorrow."

Dani patiently reminded him that cyanide had the potential to wipe out the entire ship in minutes. She said, "But I don't think that's the aim. This doesn't seem like a terrorist act. Someone is attempting to eliminate anyone with the knowledge to expose the scheme to steal the source code. The only death would have been Reynolds if the murderer hadn't found out somehow that Holt was the informant. Sloane Parker said she would send out a helicopter to gather Holt's body. We need to eliminate any further risk by narrowing down the potential culprits. We might have to put one or two of them in the brig until we get to Seward. By the way, do you recall seeing a gift bag in Reynolds' room?"

"No, there was no gift bag. You think that's how the person delivered the poison to Holt's room, right? On something in a gift bag?"

"The half-eaten chocolate bar on Holt's floor and the gift bag on the desk are suspicious, but we won't be sure until it's analyzed. As I mentioned, possibly his laptop or something else in the room was contaminated, but to do that, someone would have to access the room. How likely is that?"

"Not likely. The cleaning staff is trained to maintain close control over the passkeys. I'll double-check with Ana to make sure she didn't lose her passkey or lend it to someone else or something. She seemed distracted."

Jake thought it wasn't much wonder since she just discovered a body.

Dani looked at the clock on the wall. "Do you think the captain would still be available? I would like to talk to her tonight, if possible."

Eduardo said he would check and picked up a different phone to connect to the bridge. He reached Captain Svenssen and explained the phone call with the FBI and that Jake and Dani would be coming up to speak with her. He nodded as he hung up the phone and said, "She is waiting for you. She wants me to give you a passkey to the bridge." He rose from his chair and went down the hall. When he returned, he said, "Your passkey will be ready in a few minutes."

"Don't you need a picture?" Jake asked.

"They'll use the one on file."

"Do you want to join us on the bridge?" Jake asked.

Eduardo shook his head. "No, this is your investigation now. Call me if you need me."

As promised, they received their passkeys to the bridge within minutes. As they left the office and entered the elevator to the bridge, Jake said, "I don't think he likes us much."

Dani's face tightened in a thin smile. "I can't blame him. He's in charge of ship security, and we've waltzed in here and taken over. We'll try to involve him as much as we can in the investigation ... make him feel part of it. This is a jurisdictional issue. Like the provincial police taking over a case that I expected to be mine. I would be right pissed off. We run into jurisdictional issues all the time in law enforcement, but it usually isn't like on TV. Negotiation between the parties works things out. The goal for everyone is to catch the perp.

"Eduardo is out of his league with this investigation. I'm sure deaths on cruise ships are common. We read about people going overboard or deaths from natural causes. It's a floating city with an aging crowd, so deaths are bound to occur, but I get the impression that any situation is turned over to shore police at the first opportunity, and the ship carries on. I wonder how long they would search for someone who went overboard. I don't think Security personnel are trained to investigate a murder on the ship."

Jake said, "I agree," as the elevator opened onto the bridge deck.

They walked down the hall to the door leading to the bridge, and Dani placed her key on the reader. The captain stood inside waiting.

Chapter Twenty-Four

Captain Svenssen led Jake and Dani to an office connected to the navigation bridge. Jake thought she looked a little more tired than the perky host at the dinner table. He imagined the stress of the job taking a toll on a person. She wore the same white outfit with black epaulettes on each shoulder featuring four gold stripes and an anchor. Jake understood the thicker bottom stripe denoted the most senior person on the ship.

The office could have belonged to any executive on land with two leather-covered chairs facing an L-shaped desk and another high-back chair. Personal pictures adorned the wood-panelled walls, and framed photos sat on a wood shelving unit. A laptop sat on the desk, and various monitors around the room displayed navigational maps and other images that meant nothing to Jake. An open door led to what Jake assumed to be the captain's living quarters. Veranda-style windows surrounded the office, rather than a balcony. They seemed to offer little privacy from staterooms overlooking the room.

The bright and open office suggested it would be difficult to get any work done. The captain observed Jake staring at the windows. She said, "You must be wondering if everyone can look in. The windows are covered in one-way film, so I can see out, but no one can see in. The other wonderful thing about the office is that the walls are magnetic. They're called bulkheads." She tugged on a magnet holding a picture of an enormous

German Shepherd until it came free. "I share duties with another captain. We rotate in and out every three months, so the bulkheads and shared storage space allow us to remove and store our personal things easily. We don't carry everything on and off the ship every three months. They make us as comfortable as possible."

She gestured for Jake and Dani to sit while she took the chair opposite. "So," she said. "How serious is the situation?"

Dani replied, "An FBI agent from Anchorage, Sloane Parker, confirmed the first victim, Mark Reynolds, was poisoned with cyanide. Cyanide is a deadly toxin, and we haven't confirmed yet how it was administered. According to Gavin Holt, whom we met yesterday, someone is trying to steal the source code for the program Zachary Felton talked about that improves closed-circuit TV cameras. If a foreign country accessed the source code, for example, they could manipulate the cameras. Say they wanted to terrorize a shopping mall. The security team monitoring the cameras would rely on the new sophisticated technology to alert them if someone looked suspicious. Using AI technology, the cameras would identify anyone loitering, check them against a watch list using facial recognition, and raise a flag if something appeared to be out of line. The security team would rely on the cameras to identify potential problems ... almost lulled into a false sense of security, so to speak.

"If someone were to manipulate the software so that the security team viewed outdated or fabricated footage, this could lead to significant security risks. As I suggested earlier, an incident could occur in a mall that differs from what the team observed, allowing individuals to enter and leave without detection. Similarly, thefts from an art gallery or other organizations might go unnoticed. This issue could also arise on a ship if pirates boarded at night and the security team saw nothing unusual on the cameras. The individual responsible for the source code has control over this scenario. There are many potential situations, none of which are good.

"The stakes have just been raised with the death of Gavin Holt. It appears the murderer used the same method of poisoning, but this time I believe the delivery mechanism was a chocolate bar in a gift bag delivered to his door."

Tiny crevasses formed on Svenssen's furrowed brow as she absorbed the information. She leaned forward, her elbows resting on the arms of her chair, and her hands clasped in her lap. "I already received a call from Shore Security in Anchorage advising that a helicopter will pick up Mr. Holt's body. They received the request from the FBI agent. What's the connection between Holt and Reynolds?"

Dani told the captain that Holt worked as the VP of Human Resources at CamGuard Solutions, and Reynolds was a reporter investigating the possible theft of the source code. She mentioned Holt planned to give them the folder with background on the four people and how Ana let them into his room to find him dead.

Svenssen clasped her hands together as if in prayer, but her chin leaned on her index fingers. She said, "My immediate idea is to let the authorities deal with this in Seward. We could put the four people you mentioned off the ship and ask the local authorities to question them. There is enough suspicion to allow us to do that. I see it as being less disruptive than a full-blown investigation. We will be in Seward the day after tomorrow. Why wouldn't we do that?"

Dani replied, "I agree it has merit, but there are two reasons we need to investigate further now. The first is that the murderer may not be finished. Is there someone else working for CamGuard Solutions who might know too much? We want to avoid another murder. The second thing is the murder weapon. Because of its toxicity, if the killer got desperate, half, if not all, of the population on the ship could be wiped out. We *really* want to prevent that situation. Jake and I will be as discreet as possible. The only people who will be in on what's going on will be those we talk to. If we find nothing by the time we reach Seward, I suggest we follow your approach."

The captain hesitated before answering. "Okay, what do you need from me? I spoke to the people on the shore and, without divulging the details, I convinced them to allow you access to the faster internet. Our information technology people will change your access. You'll have it before morning."

Dani said, "Could we view the security footage for Deck Seven and specifically room 7575 starting from just before Gavin Holt boarded the ship?"

"Of course. Right this way."

Svenssen led them to the room behind the bridge, where they first viewed the video of Mark Reynolds. The captain instructed one of her officers to retrieve the video and excused herself. Jake felt like a voyeur as people walked up and down the corridor on the screen, oblivious to being on camera. Gavin Holt arrived on the video. He appeared to carry the weight of the world on his slumped shoulders as he entered the room. A pang of pity coursed through Jake's veins. The man was frightened for his life and had mere hours to live.

The door closed behind Holt, and people continued to come and go in the hallway. Some laughed, one couple appeared to be arguing, kids in bathing suits ran and dodged other passengers, Ana disappeared in and out of rooms as she cleaned them ... A never-ending parade of passengers went about their lives unaware of being under observation.

Dani asked the officer to fast forward through much of the footage until they came to what they were looking for. A young man dressed in the grey jacket and black pants that Ana wore arrived in front of 7575 carrying the gift bag. Jake asked the officer to freeze the video on the young man. No one questioned the man's identity. He was Jake and Dani's steward from Deck Eight.

Chapter Twenty-Five

"Okay, that's interesting," said Dani. "Can we trace his footsteps backwards to when he picked up the gift bag? If I recall correctly, his name is Rafael."

The officer nodded his head. "The capability of our closed-circuit TV is limited, but I'll try. A different camera picked up Rafael's image on the 8th deck, still carrying the bag. The officer sped up the video until he arrived at a spot where Rafael no longer carried the bag and then slowed it down to normal speed. The steward moved quietly and efficiently, his actions developed from years of navigating the endless corridors of the cruise ship. Jake had noticed his powerful hands, hardened by tidying, lifting, and scrubbing. A couple of strands of black hair hung down over his forehead. The other thing Jake observed from the brief interaction they had was a quiet energy beneath the surface, suggesting Rafael aspired to work beyond the corridors of the ship.

They continued watching as Rafael scurried in and out of rooms, including theirs and Emilie's, but couldn't identify where the bag came from. The rooms had no cameras, but he never came out of any carrying a bag. As the video footage advanced, he disappeared around a corner.

"That's a blind spot," the officer said. "The hallway does a little zigzag where there is a passageway from one side to the other, so he must have left the cart in that spot between where the two corridors join." The footage started again when Rafael entered another part of the hallway without the cart. He walked down the hallway and knocked on a door. When someone answered, he returned to the "zigzag" again out of camera range, only to re-emerge in the original hallway he had been in, pushing the cart in front of him.

Jake asked, "Can you back up the video just before he goes into the blind spot and stop it, please?"

The officer complied, and everyone squinted at the image. Anyone seeing them concentrating wide-eyed in the bluish glow from the monitor would have guessed they were staring at a scene from a horror movie.

"Look," Jake said, "No bag." He pointed at a towel dangling off the top of the cart. "Watch that spot. Move the video forward, please, frame by frame."

The video inched forward, and when Rafael and his cart emerged from the blind spot between hallways, a corner of the bright blue bag protruded from behind the towel. Dani said, "Either we're dealing with someone who knows where the blind spots are on the ship or who's incredibly lucky. Rafael left the cart unattended for what? Forty-five seconds? We need to ask him who put the bag on the cart."

Dani straightened and arched her back. She checked her watch. It was getting late, and her back ached. She was about to suggest to Jake that they start fresh in the morning when something else occurred to her. "I'm sorry to keep bothering you, but if I send you a file from my phone, do you have time to run it on your computer, so we can look at it?"

"Sure, I can do that," the officer said.

Dani tapped keys on her phone until she found the video of Mark Reynolds in the ship terminal. She forwarded the extensive file to the email address the officer gave her using an electronic file transfer software. Even with the advanced internet system used on the bridge, it took a few minutes for the file to show up and longer still for the officer to download it. After a few minutes, he clicked on the link to start the video.

It was the same video Jake and Dani had watched over and over, but on a much larger screen. They peered at the screen as the man they now knew to be Reynolds met the other man they now knew to be Gavin Holt in the coffee shop. Holt handed the folder to Reynolds. They viewed as Holt turned away, and Reynolds hurried toward the area where he would be cleared through Security. While still not the best, the larger images on the computer monitor afforded Jake and Dani the opportunity to focus on things they might have missed. Soon, something showed up. Or at least the suggestions of something.

"Stop!"

The sharpness of Dani's command startled Jake and the officer. "Sorry," she said. "I think I detected something. Please back up the video."

The officer backed up the video and played it forward.

"Do you see it?" Dani asked Jake.

Reynolds made his way through Security and climbed onto an escalator that took him to a crowded boarding area. It was on the way to the boarding area that Dani asked to view the video again. Reynolds was at the far reaches of the camera's field of vision.

Jake said, "What is it? I don't see anything. What are you seeing?"

Dani pointed. "Look there. Just at the edge of the video."

Then Jake caught it. Fleeting, but there. Someone wearing what appeared to be an expensive, thin driving glove reached into the frame and touched Reynold's wrist.

"We might have just witnessed the delivery mechanism for the poison. Reynolds would have become nauseous soon after, but he would have had time to board and get his safety briefing at his muster station. He would have died soon after that."

Jake said, "Everything all happened so fast, we can't even tell if the hand is male or female. It's just a hand."

"It might tell us a couple of things, though, Jake. Assuming we're right about the poison being on the glove, they're already through Security, so the person who murdered Reynolds could be on the ship and potentially the same person who killed Holt. I suppose there are other explanations for someone wearing a glove, but it's just too coincidental. The second thing is that whoever is doing this knows their way around security cameras. Where did the gloved person come from? How did he or she stay just out of camera range? The same thing happened with the gift bag. The person stayed out of camera range. I guess it's no surprise when we're dealing with a company that specializes in security cameras, but any footage the cameras capture will not be that useful. Anyway, this gives us another working hypothesis." She stretched again, this time pushing her arms back and chest out. "I don't know about you, but I'm tired. We need to get some rest and start fresh in the morning."

They gathered up their things and left the room. Captain Svenssen met them on their way out the door, away from the bridge. "Get everything you need? A storm is approaching from the west, so I might be kind of busy tomorrow. The storm doesn't appear serious right now, but weather changes quickly on the seas. We'll monitor the forecast. It could hit the Gulf of Alaska late tomorrow night, so if there's anything more you need from me, now is a good time."

Dani said, "There is one more thing you could help with. Could you provide us with the room numbers for Zachary Felton, Brendon Thompson, Angela Lee, and Raj Patel from your manifest? We might as well get started interviewing them first thing in the morning."

The captain consulted the manifest and provided Dani with the numbers. As soon as they passed through the door from the bridge into the hallway, Jake said, "Did I hear that right? She said a storm is coming, didn't she?"

"Oh, relax, dear. I'm sure they navigate storms all the time. They'll take us inland if the winds get too strong. We can't be that far from land."

"I don't know. It's bad enough when the boat rocks a little. What would it be like in 30-foot waves? Last time I checked, land was way off in the distance."

Dani took Jake's hand. "The ship is made to withstand all kinds of things. I'm sure we'll be fine. We'll make sure the seasick pills are handy." She quietly chuckled to herself as they arrived at their door. Inside, the light flashed on the phone, indicating a waiting message. Jake picked up the messages while Dani went to the bathroom. Emilie wished them a good night in the first message. The second came from, of all people, Zachary Felton, the CEO of CamGuard Solutions. Jake handed the phone to Dani when she returned. "You're going to want to listen to this."

She listened to Emilie's message first with a smile on her lips. The next message widened her eyes. When she hung up, she said, "Why do you suppose he's inviting us to the organization's luncheon?"

Jake sat leaning with his left arm on the top of the sofa, fiddling with the towel elephant left by their room steward, Rafael. "Well," he said, "He seemed enamoured with you. Or maybe he's following through on doing an article on the company. A third possibility is that he's figured out we're looking into the potential theft of the source code, and he's keeping his friends close and his enemies closer."

Chapter Twenty-Six

They woke the next morning around 7 a.m. Jake got up and opened the drapes to the balcony. Ridges of land loomed through the haze in the distance across the water. A twinge of panic set in as he remembered the storm Captain Svenssen had mentioned the night before. They changed into jeans and plain T-shirts. Dani tapped on the door to Emilie's room.

The teenager wore blue sweatpants with her high school logo running vertically in white lettering up the leg and a T-shirt with a picture on the front of a young man holding a guitar with a name emblazoned underneath that was, not surprisingly, unfamiliar to Jake. She entered the room, hugged them, and sat on the sofa. She shrugged out of her backpack and dropped it on the sofa beside her before she spied the towel elephant. "These animals are so cute. I took pictures of all of mine."

Dani said, "So, tell us about the whale excursion. Did any whales surface?"

"Lots. Sperm whales and humpbacks. An Orca showed up that had to be eight metres long. So cool. We got soaked, though."

"You weren't the only ones," Jake said with a laugh. "The captain said there could be a storm coming our way today, too."

Emilie's eyes widened. "That would be *awesome*! The captain? She didn't say that at dinner."

Dani replied, "We saw her later in the evening. We're looking into the man who died in the room next to us, and the captain is cooperating, so she invited us onto the bridge. She even gave us a pass to get in." Dani held up her pass for Emilie to see.

The teenager's mouth turned down in a pout. "Why didn't you wake me up? That would have been fun."

Dani said, "Maybe we can take you on the bridge before the cruise is over. Try the internet. It should be faster this morning."

Emilie pulled her phone from her back pocket and tapped on the keys. "What the …? It is faster. Still not like home, but better. What happened?"

Dani told her about getting access to the test system used on the bridge. Her daughter's expression showed she was impressed. They spoke for a while longer until Emilie announced she was starving. Dani said, "We just want to speak to Rafael, our cabin steward, before we go down to breakfast. Can we meet you there?"

"Sure," Emilie said. "What are you guys doing today? I'm going to spend the day goofing around with Leif if that's okay."

Dani looked at Jake, who said, "Does Leif have curly hair? Good at line dancing? Kind of cute in a rugged sort of way?"

Emilie's face turned a bright crimson colour.

Dani said, "Ignore him. Jake and I are going to a luncheon, so that's okay. Just be careful."

Emilie got up, grabbed her backpack, and shrugged it onto her shoulders as she headed for the door.

"Wait," Dani said. "Aren't you forgetting something?"

Emilie turned and hugged her mom. Then she hugged Jake. "I'll see you at supper then?"

Dani stood with her elbow cradled in her hand and her other hand under her chin, watching her daughter go. When the door shut, her eyes misted over. "She's growing up so fast, Jake."

"They do, Dani. That's a fact of life, but it doesn't make it any easier."

They heard quiet mutterings of Rafael speaking to someone in the corridor. Jake hurried to the door and waited until the cabin steward finished exchanging pleasantries with another passenger before inviting him in. Rafael looked down at his shoes as he entered the room, wondering if he had done something wrong.

Dani said, "Thank you for coming in, Rafael. I'm a detective with the Ottawa, Canada, police force, and Jake is a former investigative reporter." The hollowness of the statement flashed through Dani's mind. Anyone with knowledge of the law would realize she had no jurisdiction outside her home turf. She hoped she could pull this off. "We've been asked by Captain Svenssen to investigate the death of Mr. Reynolds next door, as well as that of Mr. Holt in Cabin 7575. We have a couple of questions for you. It won't take long. Please take a seat."

"Uh, okay, am I in trouble?" was all Rafael mustered. Then he said, "Who's Mr. Reynolds?"

"Of course you're not in trouble. Just answer our questions as honestly as you can. I'm sorry, you might know Mr. Reynolds as Mr. Brindley. Do you recall seeing a folder with some papers in it on Mr. Reynolds' desk at any time?"

Rafael pursed his lips. His hands trembled from apparent nervousness. "I recall seeing a folder along with a gift bag in the garbage. Mr. Brindley had checked in and was sitting on the balcony. I knocked on the door to tell him his suitcase had arrived and it was sitting outside his door. He came to the door to retrieve his suitcase and asked me to empty the garbage. He surprised me because the folder looked new, like it hadn't been touched. There were empty candy wrappers in the gift bag. I did as he asked."

Jake said, "Did he say anything about the folder?"

"No, nothing."

"What happens to waste paper products on the ship?" Jake asked.

"They are compacted and stored for offloading at the next port."

Dani said, "We won't take much more of your time. I know you're busy."

"Yes, ma'am. I will clean twenty-four cabins today. I work ten hours a day, seven days a week. Very busy, ma'am."

"You were seen delivering a gift bag to Room 7575 yesterday afternoon. Can you tell us where that came from?"

Rafael's eyes widened. "Ms. Dani, I found the bag on my cart while cleaning this floor. A note was attached instructing to deliver the bag to Room 7575 and leave it outside the door. I'd normally give it to Ana, who cleans that room, but I did her a favour and left it outside the door as directed. She was working down the hall, and she saw me, so she would have put it in his room right away."

"So, you have no idea who left it on your cart? You didn't see anyone?"

"Uh ... no, ma'am." The hesitation left Jake and Dani curious.

Chapter Twenty-Seven

"Did he tell the truth?" Jake asked Dani as they sat on the sofa.

"The brief hesitation at the end surprised me. Maybe he saw something he didn't want to tell us. Could be he is afraid someone might come after him if he talks. Then again, maybe nerves got the better of him."

Jake flipped the towel elephant around in his hands, examining it. "These things are pretty great. So, what do we have so far?"

"As far as the case goes?" Dani said. "Two murders. Someone poisoned Reynolds with a glove or something in a gift bag, and that person might still be on the ship. Holt could have been murdered with a poisoned chocolate bar delivered in a gift bag. The folder with whatever Holt dredged up and the gift bag from Reynolds' room are now compacted in the garbage to the size of a fingernail and offloaded at Juneau. Holt thought three people might be involved. Four, if we count the CEO of the company. Everything revolves around theft of the source code from CamGuard Solutions. Oh, and the Head of Security isn't cooperative. So, basically, we have conjecture and speculation."

"Yeah, that's pretty much how I see it," Jake said as he put his head back on the sofa and closed his eyes. He dozed for a few minutes before catching up on the news on his phone while Dani showered. Jake opened his email, and a rush of joy washed over him at one from Avery. She had attached a photo of blonde, curly-haired Ava clutching a brown fuzzy teddy bear Jake gave her. The shower continued to run, so he searched online for the Gulf of Alaska. The Gulf stretched from Ketchikan on the east to the Alaska Peninsula on the west side. Their next port, Seward, sat at the top of the Gulf. He tried to combat the urge, but he was drawn to search for the worst storm to hit the Gulf. It happened in 2022 when historic wind and rain battered the west coast of Alaska. The storm started with a low-pressure front in the Bering Sea, which spun itself into typhoon-strength winds that created tremendous surges. He was no weatherman, but the most recent reports referred to a similar low-pressure front. The only difference was that the prognosticators expected this one to go north. The door to the bathroom opened, and he returned to the picture of Ava, which he showed to the towel-draped Dani.

After Jake showered, and they both dressed, they rode the elevator to The Mainmast Grill. Neither starving, they grabbed croissants and coffee and wandered toward a window facing the outer deck, where they spied Emilie at a table. She sat beside the curly-haired boy they assumed to be Leif and a couple in their forties, presumably Leif's parents. When they approached with their food trays, Emilie introduced everyone. Jake and Dani enjoyed a conversation with Leif's parents. The family lived in Ireland, so they discussed the similarities and differences between the two countries, including weather, traditions, and politics. Emilie listened sometimes, and she and Leif had their own conversation at others. The adults agreed to get together again before the cruise ended.

As they pushed their chairs back to leave, Jake spotted a man wearing something that startled him. He poked Dani and gestured. The man was Caucasian, about six feet tall, with a tanned complexion and hair down to his collar. His designer glasses gave him a studious appearance. He was with a woman of about the same age and a youngster of about twelve. The man laughed at something the server said. What captured Jake's attention was the black leather driving glove he wore on his left hand.

Dani saw where Jake gestured. "Oh, that's interesting. It could be the glove we saw in the picture. His hand looks misshapen, though. Like maybe a burn or something."

"Should we talk to him?" Jake asked.

Dani shook her head. "I'm not sure what we would say. Let's talk to the server at the table."

They approached an Asian man in his forties who had served the table. Dani pointed to the man with the glove and asked if he sat at the server's regular table for evening dining. "Yes, ma'am. That's Mr. Duncan, ma'am. A delightful family. It is my pleasure to serve them every night."

"I don't suppose you would know his first name?"

"I think it's Tony, ma'am, but I can't be sure."

Jake and Dani left the dining room and ambled to the outer deck, where they stood leaning over the railing. The overcast grey sky brought with it warm and humid air. Small whitecaps rose off the grey water. Miles in the distance in front of the bow of the ship hung a massive formation with layers of cloud, some rolling and ragged while others hung soft and puffy. They ranged in colour from azure to indigo. Jagged lightning bolts lit the bottom edges of the clouds. It looked spectacular, and the Ocean Wanderer appeared to be heading right for it.

"That doesn't fill me with confidence," Jake said.

"The clouds look wild. It will probably go north or south, and we'll skirt the edge. We might rock and roll a bit, though."

Jake changed the subject. "What makes you think a person on Holt's list is the murderer? Something like seventy-five people attended the meeting. It could be any of them."

Dani stared down the side of the ship toward the bow as a jagged lightning bolt split the sky. "That's true, but what else do we have to go on? Holt seemed plugged into everything going on at the company, so we need to start somewhere. It might be a wild goose chase, but it's a start. We'll see where it takes us."

They held hands as they wandered back inside to peruse the shops on Deck Five. They strolled in and out of the clothing stores and examined the watches and jewellery under glass. It seemed like a long time ago that they met Gavin Holt in this area. Dani felt compelled to solve his murder. It was the least she could do.

They returned to the Conference Centre on Deck Five, which had been expanded since the last meeting they attended. The collapsible partition walls had been widened to accommodate the diners. Several round tables had been set up for the luncheon with white tablecloths and silverware. No name tags sat on the tables, so the seating appeared to be random.

People stood in groups chatting. While everyone pretended to be engaged in their conversations, some gawked at Jake and Dani when they entered. Jake spied the woman from the first meeting, Angela Lee, so he tugged Dani's arm to follow him to her group. She wore a different patterned blouse and a short set this time. Her eyebrows shot up at their approach. She stepped aside from her group, held out her hand, and said, "I don't know if you remember me. Angela Lee. I'm the lead designer in the Design Division. I'm surprised to see you. You said you knew nothing about technology."

Jake shook her hand and replied, "We don't, but I don't know if I mentioned I'm a reporter, and Mr. Felton graciously agreed to give me the opportunity to write a story about the new technology being developed by CamGuard Solutions. It's such a game-changing technology in the security field, and I'm sure people will want to learn about it." He couldn't remember if they had introduced themselves, so he said, "My name is Jake Scott, and this is Daniela Perez." He leaned in and whispered, "There's a rumour going around that someone from CamGuard Solutions died on the ship. Is that true?"

"Yes, sadly, our VP of Human Resources, Gavin Holt, passed away. He was a young man, too. I guess the stressful environment at the office got to him. It was kind of Mr. Felton to bring us on this cruise. It's too bad Gavin didn't get to enjoy much of it."

Angela's expression didn't match her words. While she expressed regret at Holt's passing, she didn't seem that saddened. Dani wondered if she had already visited the bar a few times based on her red eyes and flushed face. She recalled Holt saying he had not been invited to meetings lately. She said, "I presume you and Mr. Holt spent a lot of time together at work, being at the same level. You must have attended the same meetings."

"Oh no, we weren't at the same level at all. Gavin was a VP, and I'm just the lowly Head of Design. I report to a manager. He's new. His name is Raj Patel. That's him." She pointed to a slight young man with a dark complexion, blue shirt, and grey slacks. She leaned in. "He may know something about technology, but not much about managing. Too young. One of Holt's 'great hirings.'" Her air quotes implied a distaste for Felton's hiring practices. "As for Gavin, I attended an occasional meeting with him." She lowered her voice, "Nobody liked him in the organization because he handled hirings, firings, and salaries. Sometimes the firings weren't handled nicely. I shouldn't be telling you this." She leaned forward again and giggled, touching Jake's arm. "Please, don't include this in your article." She punctuated her last statement with a conspiratorial wink.

Dani said, "That's unfortunate. People sometimes blame HR when they should examine themselves for their problems. Do you mean Mr. Felton paid for all of you to come on the cruise? That must have cost a fortune."

"I'm sure it was expensive, but the company is generous with perks like that. We're paid okay, and we get a few perks. The new software is a winner that would pay for a cruise for the entire staff a thousand times over." She laughed and held up her drink for a toast. "Oh, you don't have a drink yet. Can I get you something from the bar?"

Jake and Dani both declined, but Angela said, "Well, I'm ready for another. They're free, you know. I'll be right back." Her skin glistened, and she laughed as she pushed her glasses up her nose.

Jake looked at Dani with his eyebrows raised as they waited for the woman. She returned carrying a martini with an olive. "I love these," she slurred.

Jake asked, "What's your role with the new software? As the lead designer, you must be involved with everything to do with its development."

Angela's lips curled in a smile. "I'm proud to say that after the Research and Design team came up with the concept, my team and I breathed life into the software." Just as suddenly, her face scrunched in distaste. "The R&D team wants to take all the credit, of course. They'll tell you if they hadn't come up with the concept, the system wouldn't exist."

Jake pushed a little. "If you don't mind me asking, how does your compensation work? You said you get perks. Does that include profit sharing or just the occasional trip? The information would be great background for the article I'm writing."

"Pffft … profit sharing! Are you kidding? Felton is so tight that moths would fly out of his wallet if he ever opened it. Sure, he pays for cruises sometimes, but I'm sure he gets a volume discount for the number of people. It's only for the executives and a select few. We're still working here, and we have to show we are by participating in every activity. It isn't a vacation. If we want to bring a spouse or friend, the extra ticket is on our dime, and there's no time to spend together. So hardly anyone does. They save their money for a *pleasure* cruise. Meanwhile, everyone else is back at the office, all pissed off because they're *working*." She leaned forward again, spilling her drink. "When I'm finished with the development, I'm leaving this place. There are companies that would welcome me with open arms and pay a hell of a lot more."

Jake was about to ask about Angela's boss, Raj Patel, when Zachary Felton interrupted. "Everyone, your attention, please." When the room quieted, he said, "I have sad news to share. Gavin Holt passed away from a heart attack last night. He will be missed, and we'll send condolences and flowers to his family. Let's take a moment of silence." After about thirty seconds, Felton continued, "Okay, is anyone hungry? Let's eat."

Chapter Twenty-Eight

Jake and Dani, sharing a mutual understanding, excused themselves from Angela's company and navigated past two tables to join the man Angela pointed to, Raj Patel. The man's eyes held a quiet, brooding intensity, clouded by disappointment or fatigue. He had thick, unruly hair streaked with premature grey. With skilful precision, Jake positioned himself beside Patel at the table and introduced both himself and Dani to the newly appointed Manager of the Design Division.

Patel turned out to be the opposite of Angela Lee. He answered questions with monosyllables, so Jake realized it would be a challenge to get anything out of him. His Indian or Pakistani accent lingered with the rhythms of his homeland. Others at the table were more gregarious, and the conversation flowed around the excursions everyone had taken and what they planned to do in Seward. They focused on everything but the work at CamGuard Solutions.

As their salads arrived, Dani engaged the table with a discussion about how much food they must go through on the ship. The analytical people around the table examined the subject, except for Patel, who seemed disinterested. He quietly picked at his salad with his fork. Jake took the opportunity.

"Raj, Zachary Felton allowed me to do an article on CamGuard. I'm a freelance reporter, so I'll be looking to have it published in a technology journal. Do you mind if I ask a few questions?" When Patel shrugged, Jake asked, "How long have you been with the company?"

Patel turned his head slowly toward Jake with a drop of salad dressing on his upper lip. He cleared his throat before speaking.

"About two months."

"Oh, so you're new at the company. How do you like the work so far?"

More throat clearing. "It's good. It's work."

"Where were you before?"

"Ahem, I worked at another security software design company called Code Fortress."

Jake sensed Patel's annoyance building at being grilled over lunch, but he persisted. The man was instantly unlikeable, distant, and withdrawn. He seemed to expect little from others and offered even less in return. Jake wondered what he was like as a boss. Angela didn't seem to like him much either. The throat clearing that precipitated every sentence was becoming annoying as well. Jake realized it could be nervousness or a habitual behaviour to allow for a reset to give him more time to think before speaking.

"That's interesting. Do CamGuard and Code Fortress do similar work?"

Patel hesitated before answering. Then, after clearing his throat, he said, "They're not as advanced as CamGuard. That's why I joined this company. They seemed to offer more of a challenge." Patel pushed his half-finished salad bowl aside as the main course of fish enchiladas arrived. Apparently, he wasn't that hungry.

Jake hadn't finished his salad for a different reason. He'd been doing most of the talking. He let his unfinished salad go with regret to begin the main dish. "Dani and I met one of your employees, Angela Lee. She's enjoying the cruise."

"Yes, Angela is very outgoing."

Jake pressed on. "I've come across animosity between the Design Division and Research and Development in other organizations. Do you find that? Has there ever been anything like that at CamGuard? It's just natural for both sides to want credit for a fresh development, but really, you can't be successful without each playing their part. Wouldn't you agree?"

This time, Patel didn't look at Jake. He pretended to be more interested in his enchilada, but his face tightened. "Ahem, I suppose. Never given it any thought. I just do my job. I don't care who gets credit for it. They're two independent roles. My job is to deliver the software. We're on the verge of finalizing the development. When that's done, we'll move on to developing the next thing R&D comes up with. If they don't come up with anything, we have nothing to work on."

One of the others at the table chimed in. "R&D always comes up with something. They work night and day over there. I mean we do too sometimes, but it isn't constant. The turnover rate in R&D is something else. They're always under pressure to create new products or improve on the old ones. They're always testing hypotheses and developing prototypes." He peered over his shoulder to find out where the CEO sat. "Felton is demanding, man. He expects them to come up with new stuff all the time."

Patel sent the man a withering look. Jake wondered if the man forgot his quiet new boss sat at the same table.

Dani said, "Yes, but aren't you under pressure to design the blueprints and user-friendly interfaces to make sure everything works? It seems to me that could be pressure packed."

Patel glared at his colleague before answering. "I think he's suggesting R&D has a tougher job dreaming up a concept where technology is moving so fast. But they've been educated to do that just as we've been educated to develop the product."

Jake said, "I've always wondered about the source code, though. I guess R&D wouldn't have to worry about securing the source code, right? That must fall under you guys. It must put pressure on you to ensure the source code doesn't fall into the wrong hands. I mean, it's the foundation of the software. If someone stole that, it would be catastrophic."

Patel sighed deeply as he cut into an enchilada. He put a small bite in his mouth and answered while he chewed. "Many mechanisms exist to safeguard the source code. We use automated code scanning to identify vulnerabilities and security flaws in the development process. The number of users is extremely limited, we use two-factor authentication for the repository of the code, clear policies are in place, and we use encryption tools to secure the most sensitive information. I'm confident the code is secure. No breaches or weaknesses have been found since I've been with the company."

As Jake took another bite of his meal, he said, "This lunch tastes so good, and this conversation has been very enlightening, too. Thank you for the valuable information." *Even though it was like pulling teeth, and I had to listen to you clear your throat countless times.* He leaned forward to look at Dani, who said, "Could you please point out Brendon Thompson? We'd like to talk to him before we leave."

Patel scanned the room and pointed at a man in a red shirt and black jacket sitting at a mostly empty table. "That's him." He seemed to like the fact Jake and Dani were preparing to move on.

Dani said, "Jake, there's room at his table. Why don't we move over to eat our dessert?"

Jake reluctantly left his half-eaten enchilada and prepared to follow Dani to their next rendezvous.

Chapter Twenty-Nine

Jake and Dani excused themselves from the table and wandered over to the one where Brenden Thompson sat. They lurched as the ship swayed. Jake rattled the silverware on a nearby table as he nudged it. He imagined the ship's powerful thrusters pushing back against the waves to reposition it on its path. Through the window, angry grey swells rose and fell. Frothing whitecaps topped the waves. At least this time, Jake's stomach didn't dip as much with the ship's sudden lurch, but the worst of the storm couldn't be far away.

Thompson was a tall man with wavy black hair, thinning at the temples. He wore dark-framed glasses, which imparted his face with a serious, focused appearance. Jake estimated him to be in his fifties. His rounded shoulders told of long hours spent hunched over, analyzing prototypes, sketches, and formulas.

As Jake and Dani approached, they noticed how quiet the table was. Although three people occupied the chairs, there was a lack of conversation. Jake sat beside Thompson with Dani by his side. Jake and Dani introduced themselves to Thompson and the other man and woman at the table. The introductions were polite. It appeared this luncheon was mandatory for everyone except Jake and Dani, and attendance was important to ensure the boss noticed their presence.

Once again, Dani struck up a conversation at the table, this time with the other couple. She quickly realized the couple would rather be alone. An office romance, she suspected, even though he looked to be close to twice the woman's age and wore a wedding band. As she tried to engage them in conversation, Jake explained to Thompson about writing an article and attempted to pry information out of the man.

Thompson turned out to be friendlier than Patel, which didn't say much. He seemed to be a man who said little, but when he spoke, people listened. His sharp eyes sparked with curiosity. Like Patel, he didn't see any conflict between R&D and Design. Jake sensed Thompson would repeat the party line, no matter what. At the very least, he was guarded with his responses.

Jake said, "I understand you're new to CamGuard Solutions, like Raj Patel. How long have you worked there?"

"I started before Raj. Probably two months before."

Jake mused, "It's odd there would be so much turnover at such a crucial time for the company. Do you know what happened?"

"I believe Patel arrived at the company when his predecessor was killed in a car accident. A hit and run. I don't believe they ever caught the driver."

"Wow, CamGuard has had its share of tragedy. First, the senior researcher and now the VP of Human Resources. What was his name? Something Holt?"

Thompson took a sip of his beer. "Yes, Gavin Holt."

"What kind of person was Mr. Holt? Was he well-liked in the company from your perspective?"

"I didn't know him that well. I think people liked him okay."

"One thing I'm curious about and want to include in the article is the security on new software like you are developing at CamGuard. My understanding is that theft of intellectual property is rampant. Especially by foreign countries. How does the company safeguard the software?"

Thompson stared at Jake as if coming to some conclusion. Then, "That's above my pay grade. My division comes up with the ideas. The design team develops them. They're the ones who ensure the software is protected from theft."

Jake said, "For argument's sake, what if someone in the company wanted to steal the source code? Someone outside the Design Division. What would they have to do?"

Once again, Thompson regarded Jake as if he saw him in that moment for the first time. He said, "I haven't given that any thought. Since I don't worry about development, it isn't my concern."

"Doesn't everyone at the company play a role in safeguarding the work you do? What if someone stole your concept? Couldn't they develop the software based on the concept you created?"

Thompson replied, "Oh, sorry, I misunderstood. I thought you meant safeguarding the software. There are all kinds of ways we safeguard the concept. There are physical safeguards, of course, so offices are locked, and security cameras are everywhere. All employees must sign a Non-Disclosure Agreement. Patents and Trademarks are filed. Audits are done periodically. There are firewalls, and data is encrypted. Systems are monitored in real time to detect any internal threat. You're not taking notes. Do you have a photographic memory?"

Jake shook his head. "No, right now I'm just sort of getting the lay of the land. I'll be back with more detailed questions, I'm sure. Let me ask again, if someone who wasn't working in Design wanted to steal the source code, is it possible to do that?"

Thompson closed down, clearly uncomfortable with this line of questioning, but he answered. "Anything is possible, I guess. They would have to hack into the system."

Jake sat quietly for a moment until he realized the rest of the table had become quiet, too. Dani, the man, and the woman all focused on him. He didn't know how long they had been listening to the conversation. People chatted as they drifted away. They had all done their duty by showing up. It was all about being seen by Zachary Felton. Now that goal had been accomplished, they wanted to go back to enjoying the cruise. The older man and young woman at the table excused themselves, soon to be followed by Brendon Thompson. That left Jake and Dani alone at the table.

"What do you think, Jake?" Dani asked.

"You and I need to talk, and then we should speak to Felton. There are people with motive, for sure."

Chapter Thirty

Servers bustled about picking up plates and silverware and scraping crumbs off tables. Felton stood at the back of the room, greeting CamGuard employees as they left. Only a handful of people still sat at the tables. Jake and Dani agreed to go for a drink to discuss Jake's observations.

They got up from the table and wandered toward Felton as the CEO shook hands with Raj Patel. They waited until the Design Division Manager left before approaching the CEO. He wore a big smile aimed at Dani as they approached.

Felton took Dani's hand and held it for an uncomfortably long time. "I hope you enjoyed your luncheon and got to meet some of the staff."

Dani extracted her hand. "We did. We'd like a private discussion with you soon. I think Jake has questions for his article that he would like to pursue." No sooner did she say that than the ship yawed sideways. Jake and Dani lost their balance, and Dani ended up brushing against Felton, who somehow didn't move. She caught her footing and pushed herself back. "I'm sorry," she said. "It must be getting windy out there."

Felton said there was no apology necessary with a leer and added that he would be happy to meet anytime. They agreed to get together in an hour in the Salty Seagull Pub on Deck Twelve.

Jake and Dani proceeded to the tavern following their departure from the conference room. They swayed as the ship pounded through the rising swells. A multicoloured stylized sign depicted a seagull wearing a captain's hat above the entrance to the Salty Seagull Tavern. Two weathered barrels, wrapped in thick rope, flanked the door on either side. The vibrant establishment resonated with mingling voices and laughter. Because of the inclement weather, patrons sought refuge indoors, making the tavern a popular choice. Jake and Dani navigated through several groups—one engaged in exuberant German toasts and another in solemn discussions. This tavern did not feature live music, thus attracting passengers who preferred to gather for drinks and conversation. Some voices rose above the others, suggesting they had been there for a while. A vacant round table with four armchairs in one corner caught their attention, so they secured the spot before others noticed its availability.

The server seemed to be overwhelmed, although she did an extraordinary job of maintaining a smile and joking with the patrons. Jake got up and excused himself as he pushed through the overcrowded patrons representing various ages and ethnicities to the bar. He ordered a beer for himself and a glass of white wine for Dani. The bartender asked where they sat and said the server would bring the drinks to them on her next round.

Dani sat with her elbow on her crossed legs and her chin resting on her fist. She appeared to be interested in the crowd, but Jake knew she would be pondering the case. Jake slid into the chair beside her. He said, "The bartender is sending the server with the drinks. I guess that's so she'll receive the tip."

Minutes later, she showed up with a tray laden with drinks. Jake's and Dani's sat on opposite sides of the tray to help balance it. She set the drinks on the table in front of them and picked up Jake's sea pass card from the table. She presented the bill, and Jake added the tip and signed it.

She was a pretty, slight woman in her twenties with curly black hair. Her name was Amoy, according to the plastic tag on her chest. In response to

Dani's question, she said home was in Jamaica. "Do you only work here at the Salty Seagull, Amoy?" Dani asked.

The woman touched her name tag with her free hand. "Oh, you saw my tag." She leaned forward and said softly, "I got in trouble for forgetting my tag this morning. I had to go back to my cabin and get it. We must wear the tag all the time, even if we're off duty." Then, remembering the question, she said, "We are all given different assignments to make things interesting. I work in The Mainmast Grill sometimes or some of the other pubs. We work seven days a week, so they move us around so we won't get bored. My contract is eight months."

"You must miss your family back home," Jake said.

"So much, but the money is good here. I can save a lot and send money back home. It's worth it. I haven't decided how many contracts I'll do. At least one more. Anyway, I'd better go before the natives get restless." Her face lit up in a broad smile. "Nice chatting with you," she said as she hurried off to serve other customers.

The area they sat in was surprisingly quiet, considering everyone in the room seemed to vie for attention. A chest-high panel separated their space from the crowd, offering a small sound barrier. The ship lurched, and Jake and Dani had to grab their drinks to keep them from sliding off the table. A glass shattered on the other side of the bar. A loud woman readjusted her position on a stool at the bar as the motion, and perhaps a drink or two too many, caused her to lose her balance. Jake and Dani smiled at each other in relief. Their drinks might not have reached the edge of the table, but the movement forced them to react.

Dani held her glass and said, "Felton will be here in about forty minutes. What did you learn from your interviews?"

Jake used a napkin to wipe away a ring of water left by condensation from his beer bottle. The bottle might be less likely to slide away with the next sway of the ship if the surface remained less slippery. "You probably noticed Angela Lee has a drinking problem. Her nose looked a little like Rudolph's. She didn't seem that broken up about Gavin Holt's passing. The important thing with her is that she's not pleased with her compensation from the company. She says she's going to leave at the first opportunity. She's in a great position to steal the source code as the lead developer, and she might be disgruntled enough about her pay she would take the risk to earn extra cash."

Dani said, "It's possible. That reminds me, Lonnie should call soon. He'll have checked into the financials of each of the people on the list. Maybe someone on the list needs the money to solve a debt problem. What about the Manager of the Design Division, Raj Patel? He didn't seem that friendly."

Jake said, "I would call that an understatement. Getting information out of him resembled pulling teeth, and he clears his voice before every sentence. Anyway, he worked at a company called Code Fortress before he came to CamGuard. His former company worked on information technology security. He would certainly have the technical knowledge to steal the code. I asked him about animosity or jealousy between the research team and the design team. Would one get more credit than the other? He implied they were all one happy team, but I'm not sure that's true. His mannerisms didn't quite match his words. I hit a nerve when I brought up the subject, but he said he just did his job and didn't care who got credit. If he has a motive other than money, it could be he doesn't think he's getting the credit he deserves for designing the software. He hasn't been at the company long, though." Jake paused to see if Dani had questions. When she didn't, he continued.

"Then there's Brenden Thompson. He shouldn't have access to the source code since he's in the R&D department, but as a senior researcher, he has access to the concept, and if someone stole that, someone else with the technical know-how could develop the software. He started with the company about two months before Patel. He thinks Patel's predecessor was killed in a car accident. We really need more background information on these people. I hope Lonnie comes up with something."

Dani nodded. "I agree. I'll ask him to investigate what happened to Patel's predecessor. You came up with some valuable information, though, Jake."

The ship trembled as it encountered another substantial wave. Jake and Dani once again secured their drinks. Jake observed the dark waves merging with the increasingly threatening sky at the horizon through the window. The ocean was turbulent, with whitecaps contrasting against the low-hanging, progressively darkening clouds. Jake considered whether this disturbance was merely the periphery of the storm predicted by the meteorologists or if they were navigating directly into its centre. Only time would reveal the answer.

Chapter Thirty-One

J ake waved to their server, Amoy, and said to Dani, "How are we going to handle Felton when he shows up?"

"I've been considering that," Dani said. "We need to trust somebody, or we won't get anywhere. Would he sell out his own company? Sure, he could make a lot of money from this transaction, but then what? Retire to an island somewhere? He seems young for that, and the potential for the company is huge. I don't know if these companies only discover something big once, but surely, it's the excitement of chasing the next big thing that drives entrepreneurs. It takes a special breed with a big ego to want to do that, and Felton seems to fit that bill."

Dani's phone rang as Amoy set down their fresh drinks. "It's Lonnie," she said. "Just a minute, Lonnie, I'm putting you on speaker."

Lonnie started to tell them about his findings. "Raj Patel ... financial ... problems ..." Neither Jake nor Dani could understand in the raucous bar, and turning the phone up so everyone nearby could hear was not an option. He might as well have been talking underwater for all the sense the broken bits of conversation made. Even though Jake and Dani leaned forward with their ears almost touching the phone, it was impossible to understand what Lonnie said. Dani took the phone off speaker and shouted. "I'm going to call you back in about an hour, Lonnie. We're in a bar waiting to meet with Zachary Felton, and you're breaking up. It's windy and cold outside, so everyone is inside at the bars." Another shudder of the ship reconfirmed her assessment about the weather.

When she hung up, she said, "It sounded like he tried to tell us something about Raj Patel's financial situation, but who knows?"

Jake shrugged. That's what he understood, too, but he couldn't be certain of anything Lonnie said. He spied Felton surveying the room at the door to the bar. Jake waved to attract his attention, but the CEO didn't see him. He stood and strode toward Felton to guide him through the throng that seemed to increase in size and decibel level.

Felton followed Jake through the masses and bent to put his arms around Dani and kiss her on the cheek. He sat with one leg over the other, while leaning back and beckoning for Amoy to come and take his drink order. The man expected everyone to be at his disposal, apparently. When she didn't rush over, he said, "How long did you wait for a drink in this place? The service seems slow. Maybe we should go elsewhere."

Dani gritted her teeth. "She's one server for all these people. She's run off her feet. Give her a break. I'm sure every bar onboard will be full, the weather the way it is. She'll come when she has a minute. She's been great to us."

Felton drummed his fingers on the table while he waited. Finally, he regarded Jake and asked, "How did you make out with the staff? Did they give you enough to write a positive piece about the company? I'm happy to fill in any blanks."

Jake started to reply, but Dani interrupted. "To be honest, Zachary, we haven't been totally truthful. I'm a detective from Ottawa. It's true that Jake is a retired reporter. A man died on the balcony next to ours the first night of the cruise. He boarded the ship as Alan Brindley, but his real name was Mark Reynolds. He was an investigative reporter researching your company."

Felton's eyes narrowed before he turned to Amoy as she approached the table. "Get me a Vodka martini with a twist of lemon. Make sure it's dry. Be quick. I'm thirsty." He tapped the young woman on the arm and smirked. Amoy hurried off, hiding a look of disdain.

Felton said, "Finally, she showed up. So, you say this Brindley or Reynolds or whatever researched my company. Why? What's to investigate? He could have just asked me like Jake here did. And he died. I guess that's the end of that."

"The situation isn't that simple. He was murdered. Someone must have thought he was getting too close to something. On the day your VP of Human Resources, Gavin Holt, died, we spoke with him. He fed Reynolds information about a plot to steal the source code for your new CCTV software. Reynolds identified four people who might be involved, including you."

"That's preposterous!" Felton exploded. "Holt did *that*? What the hell? Why would I steal my own source code? It makes no sense. Ridiculous! I suppose you're going to tell me somebody murdered Holt, too."

Dani scrutinized Felton's face. His expression suggested this all came as a surprise to him. She sensed eyes and ears surrounding them turn toward their table at the mention of murder. Amoy, who approached the table with Felton's martini, hesitated before coming forward. Jake noticed Felton didn't tip as he thrust the bill and his sea pass at her.

Dani smiled at the surrounding patrons. She leaned toward the closest couple whose mouths hung open in shock. "The Clue game," she said. "It's all fun and games until Colonel Mustard gets murdered in the conservatory with a dagger." That seemed to mollify them as they nodded, smiled with a sincere depth of understanding, and continued their conversation.

To Felton, Dani said, "Please keep your voice down." All three leaned toward the centre of the table. "Yes, we think he was murdered, but it's not only the fact his death wasn't an accident. It's the way both were killed. The murder weapon appears to have been cyanide in both cases. Cyanide is deadly beyond comprehension, and if it ever got into the ventilation system, hundreds of people on the ship might die. Do you understand how serious this is now?"

Felton's expression grew more focused. Though the bar was dimly lit, he looked paler than when he arrived. He took a long swallow of his martini. He coughed as the liquid made its way down his throat. When he recovered, he said, "Why would anyone steal the source code? I guess the obvious reason is money."

Jake nodded. "Money is obviously the ultimate end game. But we need to investigate further. Does anyone hold any grudges against you? Would someone try to embarrass or break your company?"

"The industry is rampant with jealousy, for sure. We're all jostling for space in a hot market, trying to stay one step ahead."

Dani said, "So, if someone stole the source code or even the concept, they could implement the software before you?"

"Yes, but it's proprietary software. We've filed for trademarks. If anyone released the software before us, we could sue them into oblivion. That's not a valid reason to steal the source code."

The ship quivered as another wave hit. Jake marvelled at how water moved something so enormous. He recalled reading about the 2004 Sri Lanka tsunami, which swept a train off its tracks into the trees and houses beside the railway. He refocused on Felton. "Why do you think someone would steal the source code, then?"

Felton appeared perplexed. He gestured toward Amoy, who acknowledged him but showed no urgency to approach the table. Felton took a moment to collect his thoughts, picked up the toothpick skewering a black olive from the glass, and sucked the fruit off, then discarded the pit into a napkin. Amoy sauntered over, balancing a tray full of empty glasses, and asked for their orders. Jake and Dani asked for water while Felton ordered a second martini.

When the server left, Felton said glumly, "The best reason I can come up with is that someone wants to control what the people monitoring the cameras see. Anyone with that control has tremendous power. It could be anything from a bank robbery to a terrorist attack. Someone would pay a lot of money for that power."

Dani said, "What if someone stole the design and changed it enough to avoid trademark issues. Wouldn't that give them a head start and a competitive advantage?"

The table grew quiet again as Amoy arrived with the drinks. Jake sat shocked again as Felton didn't add a tip to his payment. *What a jerk*, he thought. When Amoy left, Felton replied to Dani's question. "Yes, I suppose that could happen."

Dani decided to take him into her confidence. "Okay, I mentioned four people are under investigation, including you. We're going to give you the benefit of the doubt. The others are Angela Lee, your lead developer, Raj Patel, the Manager of the Design Division, and the third is Brendon Thompson, the senior researcher in Research and Development. Is there any reason to believe any of them might be involved?"

Felton gently nudged the olive around the glass with the toothpick. "Not that I can think of. Angela has been with us a long time. Patel is new. I don't really know him that well. Thompson arrived two or three months before Patel."

"Why is there such a turnover in your company? Jake asked.

"The nature of the beast. Every company is looking for the best talent and trying to outbid the others. Everyone signs a Non-Disclosure Agreement. It's standard practice in the industry."

Jake asked another question. "What happened to the previous Design Division Manager? I understand there was an accident."

"Yes, a hit and run. They never caught the driver. Our man crossed the street at a pedestrian crosswalk, and someone ran him over. Didn't even slow down. Just sad."

The drinks and the conversation reached a conclusion. Felton picked up his jacket from the back of the chair and stood. He said, "If there's anything more I can do to help, please contact me." With that, he turned on his heel and pushed through the crowd to the entrance.

Amoy glanced their way, so Jake waved her over. When she arrived at the table, he handed her his sea pass card. Amoy questioned Jake with her expression. "There is no need to do that, sir. You already paid."

"I know," Jake said, "but can you please process a transaction for me? Our friend forgot to tip."

Chapter Thirty-Two

Jake and Dani returned to their cabin to contact Lonnie and deliberate on next steps. They acknowledged Rafael as they walked down the hall to their room. They attributed their unsteady gait to the ship's war with the storm raging outside, rather than any effects from the drinks they consumed. Upon opening the door, an unexpected sight stopped them in their tracks: a colourful blue and white gift bag sat on the dresser, identical to the one in Gavin Holt's room the previous night.

Dani reacted quicker than Jake. "Don't touch that," she said. "Something inside might be laced with cyanide." Jake trailed behind her as they entered the room. Dani pushed back past him to find Rafael in the hall. His cart stood outside a room down the hall. She rushed toward the cart and rapped on the cabin door.

When Rafael opened the door, she demanded, "Where did that gift bag on our dresser come from?"

"I don't know, Ms. Dani. It showed up in front of your door. A tag had your name on it, so I left the bag on the dresser when I cleaned your room."

The news startled Dani. If someone delivered the bag to the door, there had to be security footage. They could see who delivered it. Maybe someone miscalculated. It seemed unlikely given that every CamGuard employee on the ship would be familiar with the fact that closed-circuit television cameras covered nearly every public area on the ship.

"Am I in trouble, ma'am?"

"No, Rafael. You just did your job. If another gift bag shows up, don't touch it. I want you to come to me and let me know. Understand?"

"Yes, ma'am." Rafael turned back to clean the room.

Dani returned to the cabin to find Jake sitting on the end of the bed, staring at the bag. He said, "I didn't touch it, but I peeked inside. There are candy bars and assorted goodies. Any of them could be covered with cyanide. Did Rafael tell you where it came from?"

"He said someone left it in front of our door, which is strange. Unless they disabled the cameras, we should be able to see them. Maybe we caught a break. We'll go up the bridge to check out the camera footage after I speak with Lonnie."

Dani didn't believe the killer made a mistake. The murders so far were too calculated. Too much planning went into them for someone to make a colossal blunder like being caught on a CCTV camera. They were so careful to leave the bag on Rafael's cart in a blind area. They had the foresight to bring cyanide on the ship. They wouldn't make a mistake like this.

She stared at the bag. A handwritten note with their names and cabin number was taped at the top. "This is so frustrating. I could have the handwriting analyzed if we were back home. That is, if we had someone's handwriting to compare it to. It just reminds me how limited we are on the ship." As if that wasn't reminder enough, a thump staggered them as the ship hit yet another gigantic wave. They both looked through the open curtains of the patio door at waves that grew angrier by the hour.

Dani pulled her phone from her pocket and snapped a photo of the note on the bag. Then she retrieved a towel from the bathroom. She wrapped the bag in the towel and asked Jake to open the wall safe. He did, removing their passports and other valuables to make room for the bag, which Dani shoved into the safe, towel and all. "We'll find another place to hide the passports and stuff. We'll notify Security about the bag later," she said as she closed the door to the safe. She slid their valuables from the safe into the side table drawer.

"Let's call Lonnie," Dani said. She dialled the constable, who picked up on the first ring.

Dani was in no mood to exchange pleasantries. She put the phone on speaker and said, "What did you find out?"

"A few things you'll be interested in. Where do you want me to start?"

"Let's start with Angela Lee, the lead developer."

"She has motive. I checked the financials for all of them, and Lee has some debt. She invested sizable sums in a start-up company that went belly up two years ago. Most of her life savings are gone. She's paying off a substantial loan."

Jake mused, "As the lead designer, she's positioned to steal the source code. That might put her at the top of the suspect list."

Lonnie said, "Hold on, Jake. Our next candidate is Raj Patel. He used to work for a company called Code Fortress, where they made him a partner. We contacted their staff, who considered Patel to be upwardly mobile. Everybody liked him and associated him with taking over the company someday. His compensation package included profit sharing, which provided substantial financial benefits. Code Fortress develops software like CamGuard's but also engages in other projects. According to our sources at the firm, his departure was entirely unforeseen and left a significant void in the company. He accepted a considerable pay reduction to join CamGuard. His abrupt departure and pay cut seem fishy. There are no apparent reasons for him leaving."

Dani sat on the end of the bed, leaning forward over crossed legs. She rolled back and forth with the rocking of the ship. "He must have convinced Gavin Holt and Zachary Felton he was the right man for the job, but you're right, it seems fishy. Could he have infiltrated CamGuard to steal the source code or design to gain leverage for Code Fortress?"

"Interesting possibility," said Jake.

Dani nodded. To Lonnie, she said, "You've identified two people with motive. Gavin Holt's suspicions are becoming more probable, and he could have known about all this. This is the kind of information he might have been about to give us. What about Brendon Thompson?"

"Well," Lonnie said. "He might be a third person with motive. Did Brendon Thompson, or should I say Bogdan Tikhonov, speak Russian to you?"

Chapter Thirty-Three

"Come again?" Dani's face normally revealed little about her emotions, but her startled expression disclosed she wanted more details *now*. She reached for the notepad and pen on the dresser and started scribbling.

Lonnie continued. "Brendon Thompson was born Bogdan Tikhonov in Volgograd, Russia, in 1990. Volgograd is on the Volga River and has a population of about a million. He studied engineering at Volgograd State University and emigrated to Canada in 2018. He still has family in Volgograd."

"This might be a dumb question," Jake said, "but does he have contacts in the Russian government? I suspect if he does, you wouldn't find them easily."

"You're correct, Jake. We didn't identify any. He has Russian friends on social media. Any could be a member of the KGB. Running the information down will take time. We're working on it."

Dani chimed in. "Thompson told Jake that Raj Patel's predecessor at CamGuard was killed in a hit and run. Did you discover anything about that?"

"No, that's news to me, but an accident to get rid of his predecessor supports the mole theory. Eliminating the previous senior researcher would present an opportunity for Code Fortress to place their person in CamGuard. I'll check into it as soon as we finish our call."

"What about Thompson's or Tikhonov's, as we now know him, financials? Anything there?" Dani asked.

"Nothing unusual. The salaries at CamGuard aren't great for the industry, though. None of the people we investigated is making much relative to industry standards. Code Fortress seemed to pay much better than CamGuard. Zachary Felton is a bit of a cheapskate."

"We witnessed that firsthand a few minutes ago," Jake exclaimed. "He doesn't believe in tipping either."

Dani asked, "Speaking of Felton, did you uncover anything on him?"

Papers rustled at the other end of the phone as Lonnie checked his notes. "I have the impression he's laser-focused on his work. He has never married. CamGuard has been supplying security software since 2005, and the company seems in decent shape. Felton drives an Audi R8 that clocks in at around $200K. His personal financials revealed nothing unusual, other than he pays himself well enough to afford a high-end vehicle. He lives in a three-million-dollar home on Winding Way in Barrhaven."

Dani said, "Does the salary he's paying himself support that kind of extravagance?"

More paper shuffled before Lonnie answered. "Barely, but possible. There's no sign of extra-large payments into his bank account, and he has a substantial mortgage."

"Okay," Dani said. "Anything else we need to know?"

"That's all so far. How's the cruise going? Have you had time to enjoy it?"

Jake and Dani watched the waves through the patio doors. It was difficult to estimate the size of the swells, but they must be approaching 10 feet. Something creaked in the cabin as the ship rocked. Dani said, "The cruise has been fun, right, Jake?" When Jake said nothing, she continued. "We're experiencing some motion right now. We're supposed to skirt around a storm, but the waves are getting higher. Jake's a little nervous about what's coming, but I'm sure we'll be fine. There's one other thing I would like you to do, Lonnie. A gift bag waited for us when we arrived in the cabin, and I'm convinced a similar bag left for Gavin Holt contained something laced with cyanide. Something he ate. Our gift bag came with a handwritten note with our names and cabin number. I'll send a picture to you, so we can use it for analysis if we need it."

Lonnie agreed and said he would continue investigating. "Cyanide! That would take knowledge to handle a toxin like that safely. I'll investigate if any of our four suspects is trained in handling hazardous chemicals. My understanding is that cyanide is extremely toxic and works so fast that anyone handling it would need to understand the ways exposure can occur and to adhere to all safety practices and protocols. Specialized training is required."

"That's my understanding as well, Lonnie. You're one step ahead of me. Someone might gain enough knowledge to handle cyanide from an internet search, but that would be risky. Check their search history if you haven't done so already."

Lonnie said he would, wished them good luck in the storm, and told Jake with a chuckle he was sure the ship would hold together.

When they disconnected the call, Dani said, "I wonder where Emilie is. Having the time of her life with Leif, I suspect. The storm wouldn't frighten her. As she grew up, we used to stand at the window and watch the lightning. It fascinated her. I dragged her away from the window many times when the storm got close. She would have found the highest hill to view the storm if I let her."

Jake smiled as Dani recounted her daughter's love of storms. He remembered how they always frightened his own daughter, Avery. She would cover her head with a blanket during a storm.

Dani checked her notes. Jake admired how focused she became when immersed in a case. Her dark eyes burned like embers, and tiny creases materialized between her eyebrows. He reached for her hand. Something was coming. A revelation or some sort of insight was forming in Dani's head.

"Something's bothering me, Jake. Thompson and Felton both said stealing the source code would be difficult, if not impossible. Several safeguards are in place, and trademarks have been filed. If someone stole the source code and reproduced something similar, as Felton said, he would sue them into oblivion. Even if the Russians stole the source code, unless they kept it in Russia, Felton would make life miserable for them. Something doesn't add up. I could envision Felton making sure no one uses the code if they stole it. There's more going on than stealing the source code."

Jake hadn't looked at it that way. With Dani's hypothesis, the case became infinitely more complicated. In his mind, riding out the storm and throwing everyone connected with CamGuard off the ship in Seward, as the captain suggested, would be the best solution. Only another few hours remained until they arrived in port. But had he and Dani become the next targets? Did something in his discussions with the possible suspects raise an alarm enough that the murderer would leave cyanide-laced goodies on their desk? Shivers slithered down his spine.

"Earth to Jake." Dani's pen clicked as she jabbed him with it. "You disappeared on me. What are you thinking?"

"We poked the bear, so to speak, if that gift bag contained something covered in cyanide. Someone is worried we'll uncover whatever it is they're doing. Maybe we should stand down. Emilie might be in danger, too."

Dani nodded. "You're right. I'll call her right now."

Jake waited as she dialled and listened for her daughter to pick up. He heaved a sigh of relief when Dani said, "Are you having fun, dear? Where are you?" After a few seconds, she said, "Look toward the front of the ship. A huge storm is coming our way. You and Leif should get ready to head back to your rooms until the storm blows over. With any luck, it won't last long, or we'll get lucky and bypass it, and you can go back to your games. Jake and I will be back in our room soon. There's something we need to attend to first. I'll knock on your door when we get back."

When she disconnected, Dani said, "They're in the arcade. I heard the machines and laughter in the background. She said she would go back to her room soon. Now, before I called Emilie, you said something about standing down. My instinct tells me we need to do the opposite. We have even more reason to investigate further. You're right about the gift bag. We may be backing someone into a corner. If so, they'll make a mistake, and we'll nail them. We need to talk to Eduardo. Time for him and his team to get involved. They need to search some cabins."

Chapter Thirty-Four

"On what grounds? We can't just search someone's cabin for no reason." Before he uttered the statement, the Security Chief's crossed arms foretold his feelings about Dani's suggestion.

"Suspicion of murder," Dani replied. "Look, Eduardo, we can get Captain Svenssen in on this conversation. We're almost certain someone poisoned candy in the gift bag for Gavin Holt. Marc Reynolds was poisoned with cyanide. We just don't know how. Whoever it is might still have leftover gift bags, or they might even have cyanide in a container in their cabin. We need to find out before they dispose of it. Someone also left a gift bag on our desk. At least three people have a motive. We need to get ahead of this."

"I'll need to get the captain's approval."

"Okay," Dani said with a sigh. "Let's go and see her."

Eduardo called the bridge for approval to meet with the captain for a few minutes. The threesome traipsed without a word to the elevator that would take them to Deck Ten. When they reached their destination, Eduardo placed his card in the reader to open the door to the bridge.

The view through the windows surrounding the bridge startled them. A monstrous wall of storm clouds faced the ship like they were about to enter hell's gate. Jake had never seen clouds so dark and heavy with threat. They churned, a tumult of dark and darker, flinging lightning bolts into the sea. Something angered Mother Nature, and the ship headed on course to take the brunt of her wrath. The clouds merged with a horizon misshapen by gigantic, heaving and foaming grey and white ocean waves. The crew on the bridge professionally scrutinized the scene unfolding in front of them without flinching as if they sat in a movie theatre. They obviously respected and trusted their captain deeply.

The pitch and yaw of the ship seemed even more pronounced on the bridge because the drama unfolded right in front of their eyes. As the ship dipped into a trough and climbed the wave on the other side, Captain Svenssen leaned into the motion as any experienced sailor would. Jake's stomach clenched at the sight, but the ship's stabilizers lessened the impact of the manoeuvre. The captain walked toward them with unflinching confidence brought about by years of study, training, and experience on rough seas. She did her job to make sure the journey remained smooth, even when the seas were not. She would scan the horizon, even when off duty, out of habit rather than necessity.

As Jake and Dani peered straight ahead, the captain waved her hand at the windows, the only thing separating them from Armageddon. "As you can see, the weather has changed. Those imposing monsters are cumulonimbus clouds in case you wondered. They're often associated with extreme weather, which we're starting to experience."

"Starting?" Jake murmured.

"Yes," the captain replied as if she were a fisherman in a rowboat discussing an impending summer shower with a friend. "This is Act One. The storm has gathered strength and width and shifted course, which nobody expected. We can't go around it, so we'll go through it. With our advanced weather monitoring systems, we should be able to find the weakest part of the storm, but it'll hit harder before we reach land. We contemplated going back to Juneau, but the safest bet is to continue to Seward since it's closer. The worst of the storm will arrive in about three hours. We'll ride this monster out. But don't worry," she smiled, "the ship has a reinforced hull, and the adjustable stabilizers will keep her as steady as possible. We'll go through severe motion from the waves and wind. We'll batten down the hatches, to use an old sailing term, and make announcements soon, once we have a better idea of what we're in for. We use deadlights on the portholes in the lower cabins and crew areas. They turn outside cabins into inside cabins, but we don't want the ocean breaking the glass and sending water inside, now do we?" The captain chuckled. "The crew will ensure anything loose is tied down, and every precaution will be taken. We'll be fine. You wanted to see me about something?"

The calmness with which the captain approached the gloom ahead astonished Jake, almost like she relished a change from the boredom of sailing in calm seas. Years of experience and training, he guessed. Something he lacked when it came to cruising. The knot in his stomach tightened.

Eduardo looked at Dani with shadowed eyes. He left it to her to explain what he considered a ridiculous idea. She related to the captain that she wanted the security team to search the cabins of Felton, Thompson, Lee, and Patel. She added the grounds were suspicion of murder.

Svenssen nodded. "Three people can enter a cabin. One is obviously the passenger. The second is the cleaning staff, and the third is security personnel if there's a genuine problem that requires the room to be opened. I would call suspicion of murder a genuine problem. Under the circumstances, I'll give the green light to proceed." She turned to Eduardo. "Let's get it done before the storm really gets rolling."

Eduardo began to protest, but the captain held her hand up to end the conversation. She pointed to the front of the ship at the menacing clouds. "If we're finished, I have work to do."

Dani said, "Thank you, Captain. Will everyone be told to stay in their cabin when the storm hits its peak? We'll need to get around on the ship without being stopped."

Eduardo interjected sullenly. "I'll gather my security team and introduce you, so they know who you are. You understand that moving around on the ship during a storm is extremely dangerous and could be life-threatening. You'll be on your own. We'll assume no liability."

Dani nodded. "Of course. We understand, and rest assured; we'll limit our actions to what is necessary. I just wanted to confirm that we'll have the required access to all areas of the ship. Captain, how long until everyone is confined to their cabin?"

"I would estimate two to three hours. Why?"

"It would be an excuse to ensure nothing else happens on the ship. If we find nothing with the search or through our interviews, I might ask you to announce confinement to the cabins a little early and to extend it until we get to Seward. Just putting it out there for now."

Captain Svenssen nodded. "I understand. Please keep me posted." She turned to walk away, but Dani stopped her again.

"We appreciate your time, but there is one more request Jake and I would like to make. Someone delivered a gift bag to our door, and we would like to review the security camera footage again to identify the individual responsible. The bag resembles the one delivered to Gavin Holt."

The captain said, "Sure, go ahead. You know where the monitors are."

Jake snuck one last peek over his shoulder as Eduardo, Dani, and he edged toward the bank of monitors overlooking the bridge.

Dani told the man monitoring the same monitor they looked at before what they wanted this time. He backed up the video to the approximate time they thought the bag arrived at their door. After viewing for several minutes, a female in a bright coloured pant suit carried a gift bag to their door. She set the bag down and turned back toward the direction from which she came. Her face became visible as soon as she turned, and Jake and Dani recognized Angela Lee.

"Well, that raises interesting questions," Dani said. "Eduardo, is the cabin staff allowed to reveal passenger cabin numbers?"

"No, of course not," the Security Chief replied. "They're responsible for the upkeep of the cabins, including cleaning the room and making the beds. Under no circumstances are they allowed to divulge room numbers."

Dani said to no one in particular, "We need to talk to Angela Lee. How did she get our room number? Or did she intend the bag for someone else?" Turning back to Eduardo, she said, "Can you please arrange the cabin searches immediately? We'll interview the suspects while the search is being done."

Suddenly, Eduardo seemed more cooperative. "I can do that. I will need time to brief my team, so they understand what they're looking for. Give me an hour. There's a small boardroom opposite my office. You can use that for your interviews."

The threesome left the bridge with Jake taking one last peek at the sinister sky ahead of them. They had little time to conduct the searches and interrogate the suspects.

As they rode the elevator down to Eduardo's office, Dani said, "The cyanide might be in liquid or powder form and in any kind of container. If in liquid form, look for something pale blue or colourless. My guess would be a small aftershave bottle or something like that. A powder form could be contained in something like a pill container. The FBI agent in Anchorage didn't tell us what form to look for, and I didn't ask. The toxin will be easy to hide because it doesn't take much to do a lot of damage. Both forms will smell like almonds. Eduardo, I suggest your staff confiscate anything that looks suspicious and mark it, so we know which room it came from. We can't test it on the ship. Your port security can send it to Anchorage for testing when we get to Seward. Do you trust your staff to do that? Since we have no jurisdiction on the ship, you or a member of your staff has to sit with us for the interviews."

"Of course. I trust all my staff, but I'll ask my Deputy Security Officer to sit in on the interviews with you. I'll lead the search. She is so qualified, she's in line for promotion. She will be a Chief Security Officer on another ship soon. This will be a wonderful experience for her."

The minute they arrived at Eduardo's office he placed a call on the in-house communication system to all security staff to report to his office. One of them asked, "Is this about the storm, sir?" He replied, "We'll discuss the storm, but I also want to talk about something much more serious than that."

While Eduardo assembled his staff, Dani contacted Lonnie again. She informed him of her suspicion that there might be another issue besides the theft of the source code. She outlined her concerns about the challenges with trademarks and the security surrounding the code. "Most of CamGuard's senior staff are likely on the ship, but please visit their office and speak with the remaining employees. Perhaps a discontented employee will provide more information. Holt and Reynolds were murdered for a reason, and based on what Gavin Holt told us, we've been investigating the source code angle. There could be additional aspects we're overlooking. Maybe something even more significant."

Chapter Thirty-Five

Jake and Dani listened as Eduardo briefed his team. While the team members braced themselves with their feet solidly planted, some with their arms crossed, against the ship's side-to-side motion, Jake and Dani each supported themselves against the wall. The Security Chief discussed the storm and assigned responsibility to members to put away or tie down movable objects on the decks and reinforce windows. He dismissed them to go about their duties and introduced the remaining two as his Deputy Security Officer and Supervisor.

The Deputy Security Officer, Camille Dubois, had chestnut brown hair, warm green eyes, and a naturally radiant complexion. She had a gracefully proportioned and confident posture, and when introduced, her face softened in a gentle, knowing smile. Jake understood why Eduardo spoke highly of her. She would join them in the interviews while Eduardo would lead the searches with his supervisor.

Dani said, "Eduardo, please let Zachary Felton know what we're doing. If he has a problem with it, you can tell him to call me. We don't need to interrogate him right now. Let's start with Brendon Thompson, a.k.a. Bogdan Tikhonov. Again, I have no official capacity on the ship, so Camille, please call him and ask him to join us. Eduardo, you might wish to start with his cabin."

While Eduardo and his supervisor left the office to search Thompson's cabin and Camille called the senior researcher, Dani placed a call to Emilie's phone. She wasn't pleased when her daughter said she and Leif were going for the high score on some game in the arcade and couldn't leave just yet. Emilie described how the ship's rolling complicated their aim, but that made playing more exciting. Dani told her to get the high score but to return to her room within half an hour. She reminded her daughter about the potential strength of the storm and told her the captain would confine everyone to their rooms before the worst hit. When she hung up, she massaged her temples as she listened to Camille argue with the person on the other end of her call.

Camille muttered a string of epithets directed at Thompson after she hung up, and they all moved into a stark room, stripped of any warmth or unnecessary embellishments, where they planned to conduct the interrogations. Cold and utilitarian, the room echoed with the hum of the ship's systems. Overhead lights offered a harsh, white glow. The bulkhead doors, thick and reinforced, sealed the room from the rest of the ship, creating an oppressive atmosphere. Bolts held a single table to the floor in the middle of the room. Camille dragged two chairs from Eduardo's office to supplement the two already there. The only decoration in the room, if it could be called that, was a small clock on the wall.

At first, Thompson refused to come downstairs, but to her credit, Camille advised him he didn't have an option and that if he didn't comply, he would be turned over to local police in Seward. He showed up in the small room next to the security office about ten minutes later. He scowled as he took a seat opposite Jake, Dani, and Camille.

"What's this about?" he demanded. He regarded Jake. "If this has something to do with the article you're writing, it could've waited until we got back to Ottawa." The ship lurched, and everyone's upper torso shifted sideways and back in unison.

Dani answered. "It has nothing to do with that. I'm a homicide investigator from Ottawa, and Camille is the Deputy Security Chief onboard. Jake is a former investigative journalist. We're investigating two murders on the ship: Mark Reynolds, who also worked as an investigative reporter, and the VP of Human Resources at CamGuard, Gavin Holt, whom you're familiar with." Even though Holt's death had not been confirmed as a poisoning, Dani threw it out and waited for the reaction.

The man in front of them remained stoic. The only noticeable acknowledgement at the mention of murder was the bobbing of his Adam's apple as he swallowed. He said nothing.

"You don't seem shocked," Jake said.

"It has nothing to do with me," the man calling himself Brendon Thompson replied.

Dani continued. "We believe someone killed them to cover up stealing the source code for the new software CamGuard is developing. Someone stopped them before they could dig into it further."

Thompson replied, "That's ridiculous! As I told Mr. Scott at the luncheon, stealing the source code would be extremely difficult because of all the surrounding security. It sounds far-fetched to me."

Jake said, "Let's say, for argument's sake, someone figured out a way to do it. Who would benefit most from stealing the source code?"

Thompson leaned his head back and rolled it from side to side while rubbing his neck. He crossed his arms and regarded the ceiling tiles. Without looking at any of his three inquisitors, he said, "I suppose any large organization that wanted to gain an advantage on its competitors, for one. As you said, Mr. Scott, theft of intellectual property is running rampant.

If someone was desperate enough to gain a competitive advantage, stealing the source code would be one way to do it."

Dani said, "What about a foreign government?"

Thompson brought his head forward and caught Dani's eyes with his. "What do you mean?"

"Well, we've discovered Brendon Thompson isn't the name given to you at birth. It appears your real name is Bogdan Tikhonov, and you were born in Russia. There would be some incentive for a foreign government like Russia to get their hands on the source code of the security camera software CamGuard is developing, would there not? They could manipulate the software, so their agents could wander around buildings without anyone knowing. For what? Terrorist attack? Theft? Steal classified information? It's a compelling reason for you to steal the source code. How much is your government paying you to infiltrate CamGuard, Mr. Tikhonov?"

Camille stopped taking notes and sat with a shocked expression on her face. Meanwhile, Thompson/Tikhonov's face grew a crimson colour as Dani posed her question. He took a full minute to regain his composure before responding. "You've got it all wrong. I'm not involved in any theft, and I certainly had nothing to do with any murder. Yes, my name was originally Bogdan Tikhonov, but I changed it so that it would be easier to gain employment in Canada. I was born in Volgograd 1990 and emigrated here with my parents in 2018. Felton was aware of all this when he hired me."

"Where did you learn to speak English? You don't have a hint of an accent." This was from Jake.

"I majored in English at Volgograd University. I have an aptitude for languages. I'm also fluent in French."

Dani said, "Okay, we'll verify everything you've told us. One more question. My investigators tell me that CamGuard doesn't pay well. Why did you choose to work there? Couldn't you make more somewhere else?"

"I probably could, but I liked what CamGuard was doing. Zachary Felton is a visionary in the business, and the company is doing important work. That's why I joined."

Dani thanked him for coming and told him to be careful going back to his room. When he left, she asked Camille to call Raj Patel to the office and then turned to Jake. "What do you think?"

Jake hesitated for a moment before answering. "Stealing the source code for Russia is certainly a motive, but he seemed calm and forthcoming with his answers. We can't eliminate him as a suspect, that's for sure. Let's see what the others say."

Camille told them Patel was even more unhappy about coming than Thompson had been. Dani asked for her perceptions about the interrogation. She seemed happy to be asked. "I agree with Jake that he seemed honest with his answers, but I've been wondering if stealing the source code is something that someone could really do. I took some technology courses, and companies protect the source code with their lives. Maybe you should be looking at the possibility of someone messing with the software instead. Perhaps a virus?"

Dani stared at the young security officer. "Exactly where my mind was going, and who would be in a better position to do that than someone working in the Design Division?"

Chapter Thirty-Six

While they waited for Raj Patel to show up, Jake sought a window in Eduardo's office to check on the storm. Cabin crew had already covered the windows on the lower decks, so he ran up the steps to seek a door on Deck Four. He regretted his decision. Waves slammed against the hull with resonant thuds and leapt from the surface to hit the side of the ship with a thunderous smack. Foaming rivulets of water ran along the outer deck floor. The churning dark clouds and the Ocean Wanderer edged closer to each other on an inevitable collision course. The sight rattled Jake as he turned on his heel and returned to the boardroom, arriving at the same time as the Manager of the Design Division.

At the start of the meeting, Patel was no less sullen than he had been in his discussion at lunch with Jake. Dani explained the investigation of two murders and that his name had come up. She kept the questions about the source code out of the interrogation for now. Patel glared at her through narrowed eyes while she explained the situation.

When she finished, Patel said, "Ahem … how could anyone accuse me of such a thing? I'm new at the company. I wouldn't have had time to steal anything, and I certainly wouldn't murder anyone."

Dani continued to pursue their line of thinking. "That's not the way we see the situation, Raj. Here's our working theory: The company you used to work for, Code Fortress, was not gaining the market share they wanted in the CCTV space. They fell further and further behind, so the only way to catch up was to insert someone into CamGuard to steal the source code. That's where you come in. We think you were the person they inserted. To make matters worse, Code Fortress hired someone to get rid of the previous manager at CamGuard by running him over. Are we warm?"

Patel squirmed in his seat. The question bothered him, but Dani and Jake weren't sure if the scenario Dani painted hit close to the truth, or if Patel just didn't want to listen to such speculation. Only the hum of the air conditioner, the creak of Camille's chair as she shifted in her seat, and the pounding waves outside, interrupted the silence in the room. Patel continued to glare. A hint of men's lotion wafted through the air, reminding Jake and Dani of the cyanide poisoning carried onboard by someone in a small bottle like one that would be used for aftershave.

Finally, Patel said after clearing his throat, "Something at CamGuard gave me my own misgivings. Your suggestion that Code Fortress arranged for me to get the job to steal the source code is completely wrong. Felton hired me legitimately to manage the design of the software. I have no idea what happened to my predecessor other than he was killed. You're right, Code Fortress is a dying company. Their research and development and design teams are too weak to keep pace with companies like CamGuard. I left a sinking ship, so to speak. But when I arrived at CamGuard, I perceived strange anomalies in the software. But nothing to do with the source code. My guess is that someone was building a virus, and I planned to investigate it more when I returned to the office. Now that you tell me two people have been killed over it, I'm not sure I want to continue looking. This is becoming serious."

Jake said, "If you'll continue to cooperate with us, you won't have to investigate further. What's your theory about the virus? Why would anyone insert a virus into the software?"

"The software is scheduled for release soon. If someone built a stealth virus into it, computers belonging to anyone who purchased the software could be infected. A stealth virus is nearly impossible to detect."

Dani said, "You're going to have to explain."

Patel's eyes held hers. More throat clearing. "A stealth virus can take many forms, but its function is to hide undetected inside a computer. Once a computer is infected, the people responsible can operate and gain control over parts of a system or an entire system. They're targeting cryptocurrency now, among other things. A recent example is the StilachiRat that breached cryptocurrency wallets. Someone with the right virus on the right computer could steal hundreds of millions in seconds. The virus could be programmed to destroy itself once the theft occurred, leaving no trace."

Jake leaned forward. "There's no need to steal a source code, then? A stealth virus can accomplish the same thing."

Patel nodded, "In effect, yes."

Jake said, "Do you have suspicions who might be working on such a virus in the company?"

Patel hesitated. "I'm reluctant to give you a name, but I have my suspicions, yes. It's ..."

Dani held her finger in the air to stop Patel as her phone rang. She picked it up and listened. Her mouth turned down in a frown as the person on the other end spoke. The only thing she said was "thank you" as she disconnected.

She looked from Camille to Jake to Patel and back to Jake. "That was Eduardo. He says they found a stash of gift bags in one room. They also found an aftershave bottle with some liquid that smells like almonds."

Everyone waited, observing Dani. Once again, only the sounds of air rushing through the vent and the sporadic thumping of waves against the hull broke the silence. Dani turned to the Deputy Security Chief and said,

"Camille, please detain Raj Patel on suspicion of murder." She turned to Patel. "They found the bags and the bottle in your room, Raj."

Chapter Thirty-Seven

"There has to be some mistake," Patel yelled as he leapt to his feet, slamming his palms on the table. "I know nothing about any gift bags or poisons. You're making a terrible mistake." His thick glasses slid down his nose, and he pushed them back up. A thump as a wave hit the hull, and a sudden lilt of the ship seemed to conspire to emphasize his point.

Camille shot up from the table and rushed to Patel, pulling a set of zip ties from her belt. "Turn around, please, and put your hands behind you," she said as she spun Patel so that she faced his back. As she attached the zip ties, Patel said, "No, no, no, this can't be happening. I'm telling you; you're making a mistake. Someone planted a virus in the software. I had nothing to do with this." He turned to Jake and Dani with pleading eyes. "I'm telling you the truth. Please, you must believe me."

Camille looked quickly at Dani, who waved her hand to take Patel away. As Camille led him out the door and down the hall to the brig, they heard Patel shouting, "This is a frame-up. You're all framing me. I'm innocent. I'll sue your ..." His voice trailed off.

"The man doth protest too much, methinks," Jake declared.

"Oh, you're going to quote a line from *Hamlet* to me now? The actual quote refers to a woman, *me thinks*," Dani replied.

"How do you remember that? It's been so long since we studied Shakespeare. I patted myself on the back for remembering a butchered version of the line."

Dani said, "You didn't butcher it. The quote is right except for the gender." Her face widened in a huge grin before she shoved Jake's shoulder. "And the reason I remember is that I haven't been out of school as long as you."

Jake's mouth formed an 'O' before they both burst into gales of laughter.

They stifled the noise, so Patel didn't hear. Dani gasped for breath. "It seems like forever since we shared a good laugh. It feels good."

Camille rounded the corner into the room with an odd look. Jake said, "Sorry, Camille. This has been the cruise from hell for us. We needed to let off a little steam. Thank you for your cooperation. It's been invaluable. Hopefully, we can enjoy the rest of the cruise with no more surprises."

The ship groaned uncomfortably as the storm intensified. Camille spread her feet for firmer footing, but she didn't grab anything. "He insists on talking to you."

Dani removed her phone from her pocket. "I have to text my daughter first, to make sure she's back in her cabin." Dani's text received a prompt reply. *Yes, I'm just lying here on the bed hanging on with one hand and reading with the other. Where r u?*

Dani replied they would be back in their room soon.

When she finished texting, she turned to Jake. "Okay, let's go and see what more he has to say."

The brig was a functional area distinctly separate from the opulence of the passenger cabins elsewhere on the vessel. It comprised a compact room with metal walls, and it lacked any windows. A bunk bed sat on one side of the room while a sink and toilet occupied the other. Fluorescent lights buzzed overhead, drowning out the hum of the ship and casting a cold glow over the room. The room lacked décor and would feature no entertainment or scrumptious meals. It all combined into a stark reminder that laws and rules must be followed on cruise ships, like anywhere else. Small holes in the walls and ceiling provided ventilation. The solid metal door had no bars. It was not a room that anyone would want to stay in.

Camille followed Jake and Dani to the room. "I left the zip ties on Mr. Patel in case you wanted to talk to him. I'll let you in, but I'll be right outside the door if you need me." She touched the taser on her belt. "I suggest you talk to him from the doorway and not go into the room." She unlocked the door and hauled it open.

Patel sat on the bottom bunk with his hands now tied in front. Fear and anger clouded his face. Jake and Dani expected another laundry list of denials. They stood in the doorway.

Patel's face remained sharp and intense. His narrowed jaw, piercing eyes, and tightly curled lips showed disdain, with a jaw clenched so tight, it looked like it could shatter. Yet, his words trembled. "I suppose I should thank you for coming. This obviously looks bad if you found gift bags and poison in my room."

"Ya think?" Jake asked.

Patel continued. "I'm being set up. Some investigative reporter, uh, Brindle or something like that, asked me a bunch of questions about the source code for the software, and I told him the same thing I told you. So many safeguards exist that stealing the code would be nearly impossible. I did my own digging and found some unusual coding in the software. I didn't have time to find out how advanced it was, but like I told you, it could have been a stealth virus. I planned to investigate more when I returned. The software isn't scheduled for launch for a few weeks."

Dani replied, "The man's name was Brindley. At least that was the name he went by. His real name was Mark Reynolds. You'll have to give us more than you have so far because right now, all the evidence points to you."

Patel nodded. "I understand, but what if I'm right? What if someone is trying to set me up? A murderer would still run around free on the ship. I don't think that's what you want, is it?"

Jake could tell Dani agreed with Patel's point. She said, "Okay, you're not going anywhere until we can verify some truth to what you're saying, but let's say you're telling the truth. Where should we investigate next?"

Patel's shoulders relaxed as he seemed to think he had made some headway. "The one person who has been with the company the longest and who is in the best position to change the software is the lead designer, Angela Lee."

Jake and Dani realized something at the same time. Patel was not clearing his throat anymore. Perhaps he was so confident in what he was saying now that he didn't need time to reset and figure out an answer. Maybe he was telling the truth.

Chapter Thirty-Eight

The announcement came at 7 p.m. Jake and Dani sat in The Mainmast Grill on Deck Eleven rolling with the motion of the ship and eating burgers and fries, when the announcement came, and as usual, they strained to understand the garbled words tumbling from the speakers. The captain announced the storm was about to become more intense, and passengers should remain in their rooms for their own safety until further notice. A server arrived at their table to announce the Grill would close in ten minutes as a tremor shook the ship like a dog shaking a stuffed toy.

The announcement came as no surprise to Jake and Dani, as it seemed inevitable. The ship moved erratically in the heaving waves, with unsettling pitching and yawing. Servers had already removed salt and pepper shakers and napkin holders from the tables. Empty chairs slid back and forth until servers stacked them to secure them in place. Jake and Dani waited to fill their coffee cups until after completing their meals, so they didn't risk them sliding off the table.

Dani had texted Emilie to ask if she wanted to join them, but she said she had already eaten a burger and milkshake. She said she was quite happy watching the waves. She likened the movement of the ship to a ride at the fair. Dani told her to listen for the expected announcement. Despite Emilie's calm demeanour, the announcement was still unnerving to Dani when it came.

Jake and Dani finished their meals and lined up behind five others to pour coffee into paper cups with plastic lids. The stout woman standing in front of Dani wore a pink pantsuit. She turned to Dani and with wide eyes said, "Will we survive the night?" It was an attempt at dark humour, but fear and trepidation swirled beneath the surface.

"I don't know," Dani said, "but if we don't, I'm going to make sure the last thing I have is coffee."

The woman forced a brittle laugh as she reached the front of the line. "Me too."

As Jake and Dani walked along the corridor away from the Grill, the wind shrieked outside, slashing the ship relentlessly, and ripping at any-thing movable on the decks. Walking in the corridor seemed like a chal-lenging journey from a local pub after having consumed a few too many. Lightning split the sky and spit its hot shards into the water as black waves crashed against the hull of the gleaming Ocean Wanderer. A man pulled himself hand-over-hand along the rail outside, his knuckles white and his eyes wide as the ship pitched and rolled. The man made it to the sliding doors, and the wind tossed him inside when they slid open. For a moment, the wind followed him, bellowing like a wounded animal until the doors slid closed again. The man, his hair sticking out in all directions and soaking clothes askew, pulled himself together and grinned at Jake and Dani like a crazed thrill-seeking adrenalin junkie. Jake wondered if this could get worse.

They staggered along the corridor before arriving at the elevator. Wind whistled through a gap in the revolving door leading to The Mainmast Grill veranda. Chairs stood neatly stacked on the veranda, and the win-dows were shuttered. Dani glanced at Jake. "I would like to talk to Felton. Are you comfortable dropping in to chat with him?"

Jake gulped. He wondered, like the woman at the coffee station, if they would make it through the night, but decided he needed something to keep his mind off the wild uproar outside. "Sure, he's only one deck below ours. Why not?"

They chose to take the elevator rather than the stairs because it would be safer, although the swaying of the elevator with the movement of the ship was disconcerting. They arrived at Deck Seven and knocked on Zachary Felton's door. The company president opened it after about a minute. "Come in. I'm glad you dropped in. No one is telling me anything. Have there been any fresh developments?"

Dani brought him up to date on the security team finding gift bags and a liquid smelling like almonds in Raj Patel's room. She told Felton that Patel was now in the brig, but that he protested vehemently, claiming his innocence. "He's convinced Angela Lee is trying to frame him. That would mean that somehow the bags and poison got into his room. Someone would have to sneak them in. We'll review the CCTV video footage to see if anyone went into his room. It can be confirmed easily enough. He claims Lee is in the best position to fiddle with the software, but he said something else that interested us.

"We've been focusing on the possible theft of the source code because that's the direction Gavin Holt pointed us and was what the investigative reporter worked on. Patel suggested something else. He suggested somebody may have inserted a stealth virus into your software to control the computers wherever it was installed. But wouldn't your staff discover that in testing? Could a virus be that good that it became undetectable, even to the people who designed your software?"

The cabinets creaked as the ship lurched again. Jake's stomach lurched with the ship's movement. No doubt about it, the storm was intensifying. A lightning flash lit the room even though the overhead light was on and the drapes closed. A deafening crash, audible even above the sound of the wind, television, and the ship's constant thrumming followed seconds later.

Felton's face turned noticeably pale. It occurred to Jake that the man could be getting seasick, but he had claimed at the captain's dinner to be an experienced sailor, so surely, that wasn't it. Then Felton disclosed the reason for his discomfort.

"I haven't been completely open with all my staff. Because some of my managers are so new, I haven't disclosed everything to them. The system is being tested in a live environment as we speak. A company wanted CCTV cameras to detect unusual activity and deal with it on the spot, so they agreed to allow us to test the software in a live situation. I may have rushed it before it was thoroughly tested by my staff."

"Okay," Dani said, thinking that could be the understatement of the year. "Is it some place that a stealth virus might do some damage? Like theft?"

"Well, yes, it is. It's a company called Nova Trade. A cryptocurrency exchange. With the proper virus, someone could gain access to the exchange's crypto wallet. Hundreds of millions of dollars, even billions, could be susceptible to theft."

Dani asked, "Doesn't most of the action happen in the digital realm in a crypto exchange? I understand the need for firewalls and encryption, and stuff like that, but why security cameras?"

Felton nodded. "Of course, that's all important, but just like anywhere else, physical security is also necessary. CCTV cameras act as a deterrent to prevent unauthorized activity. In the event of a breach or insider threat, cameras can help resolve the issue. They can also protect staff who are handling sensitive files if something goes wrong. My system has its place in a crypto exchange."

Jake said, "Okay, fair enough, but has there actually been a theft of cryptocurrency from an exchange?"

"Yes, hackers stole $1.4 billion from Bybit Exchange in February 2025. They distributed the crypto to a bunch of wallets, but the authorities blocked the thieves so they couldn't convert the crypto into usable cash. They made the mistake of not moving quickly enough. Anyone paying attention would learn from their mistakes and work quicker."

Jake started to figure out where this was going. "Who is to implement the CCTV software at Nova Trade?"

Felton gulped before answering. When he answered, he surprised no one. "Angela Lee."

Chapter Thirty-Nine

The ship now rested firmly in the grips of the storm. As Jake, Dani, and Felton tried to stabilize themselves in Felton's cabin, Jake envisioned the scene outside. The cruise ship, an enormous, streamlined symbol of luxury, was now at the mercy of nature's formidable forces, tossed about like a balloon caught in the wind. The massive stabilizers, the fins extending from the ship's hull and designed to soothe the rolling of the ship, were losing the tug of war with the waves. The thought of the storm overwhelming the ship's advanced technology almost made Jake immobile with fear.

Dani carried on as if nothing unusual was happening, apparently oblivious to the raging storm outside and the lack of stability inside. To Felton, she said, "I suggest at the first opportunity you call someone at Nova Trade and tell them to disable the software."

Felton's face fell until he regained his composure. "I can't do that. I've worked hard to build this company. If word gets out that we built a software package with a virus, CamGuard will be ruined. No one will ever work with us again."

"Zachary, think of the consequences if you don't do this," Jake said. "If there's a virus in the software that's skimming cryptocurrency from Nova Trade's wallet right now, you'll be sued into the Stone Age, and your company will be bankrupt. Weigh the pros and cons. The consequences are far worse if you don't call them. They will look far more favourably on you and your company if you warn them than they would if you let the virus take over. You must contact them."

Felton reluctantly picked up his phone and thumbed through his list of contacts until he found the one he looked for. He dialled the number and repeated himself several times to explain the situation to someone on the other end. The storm played havoc with the phone reception.

While he did that, Dani gestured for Jake to join her in the bathroom. There wasn't room for both in the tiny space, so Jake stood at the doorway while Dani dialled Eduardo. Dani activated the phone's speaker, and the phone rang at the other end, but no one picked up. She disconnected and dialled Camille, Eduardo's Deputy Security Chief. The young woman picked up right away.

Dani asked, "Have you seen Eduardo? I just tried to call him."

"No, I don't know where he is. I haven't seen or heard from him since he went to search the cabins. It's not like him not to call in, but he'll be busy with the storm. Can I help you?"

Dani sucked in a breath as the ship rolled again, and she banged her knee on the toilet. She pushed herself back against the counter and grabbed the top of the shower enclosure for support. "Patel might be telling the truth. Angela Lee has implemented the software at a company called Nova Trade. She might have planted a virus in the software. Can you place her under arrest for suspicion of murder and confine her to her room somehow? I know we're all supposed to be confined to our rooms, but that's not good enough."

"Yes, I can do that. I'll put a guard with a taser outside her door. Some of our staff are well-trained in using nonlethal force and handling tasers. Guns are locked up on the bridge, but my guard will be fine with a taser."

The thought of someone trying to stand outside anyone's door in the middle of a long corridor with the ship rocking the way it was baffled Jake. He was thankful he wasn't assigned to the job. His stomach contents still resisted coming up altogether, but he had been close more than once. He took one of the motion sickness pills Dani had given him earlier.

Camille asked, "What do you want me to do with Patel?"

Dani thought for a moment. "Leave him where he is. He'll be safe there. We'll sort this out with the local police when we reach Seward. Right now, I'm not sure of anything. Thank you for everything. I'm going to call my officer in Ottawa to see if he has uncovered anything more, and then I'm going to hunker down with my daughter and ride out this storm."

Felton poked his head around the corner to announce he had reached the CEO of Nova Trade, and they planned to follow his advice to shut down the new software. Felton said the woman wasn't happy to learn about a potential virus in the software, but she appreciated the phone call. He seemed to be relieved that his company might survive this debacle. The two murders did not seem to factor into the equation for Felton. It occurred to Jake to open the patio door and shove Felton out into the storm, but that would accomplish little except make him feel better.

Dani next called her second in command, Lonnie Davidson, in Ottawa. She inspected her watch. Past midnight Ottawa time. Davidson answered right away, but the transmission broke up. Through broken sentences, Dani understood him to say, "I've been wondering about you. You're all over the news. They are reporting stories about the Ocean Wanderer being caught in the mother of all storms in the Gulf of Alaska. Is it as bad as they say?"

Dani grinned at Jake. "It's a rough ride, but we'll get through it. Jake's a little green around the gills. I'm not sure I'll get him on another ship." Just then, as if to emphasize the point, the ship rolled hard to the left. Jake and Felton bounced off the cabin door and each other while Dani fell into the shower stall, pulling the curtain and the rod it hung on down with her. The closet doors swung back and forth on their squeaky hinges as if alive.

"Are you okay?" Davidson shouted. "All I hear is thumping."

Dani untangled herself from the wet vinyl shower curtain and picked herself up with a groan. "We're fine. The ship is rolling in the rough seas. We need to sit down." She wiped at a wet patch on her pants left by Felton's recent shower and carried the phone to the sofa, sitting beside Jake, who lifted his pant leg to check an angry red welt. Felton sat on a chair.

"Enough about the storm," Dani said. "Have you found out anything more?"

"Yes, I have lots to tell you. I tasked several technology analysts at Cam-Guard with investigating the software since I spoke with you last. I told them to look for a virus, so they narrowed their search. It was like kids looking for candy. One young kid, who shaves about every six months, found something strange in the software. I can't describe what he located because it's too technical for me, but it's a section of the software only Angela Lee had access to. She forbade anyone else from touching it. The technicians said they left the software alone at her direction. They just thought it was 'eyes only' to protect the propriety of the software, but I told them a little white lie. I said Zachary Felton gave them permission to investigate it."

Felton chewed on his bottom lip. A trickle of blood ran down his cheek from a head wound. He made no indication that he disagreed with the decision.

Dani said, "Okay, good work, Lonnie."

"Wait, one other thing. We investigated social media accounts of the people you mentioned. Angela Lee contacted a crew member on your ship before the cruise. Wait, let me get my notes. Here it is."

Just as Lonnie said that a blinding flash lit the room, followed at once by a deep, booming roar from directly above that rattled the cabinets and made the ship tremble. The sudden and unpredictable event left a charge in the room. The threesome flinched, unsure of what would come next. In the brief seconds that followed, Jake, Dani, and Felton held their breath until the next mighty crash occurred. When it arrived seconds later, it pitched the room into blackness and took with it all the communications systems on the ship.

Chapter Forty

The stark glow from Dani's phone flashlight cast jagged shadows across their faces, distorting familiar features into something ghost-like and almost unrecognizable. Every movement turned into something unsettling. Their faces appeared to hang in mid-air, as if detached from their bodies, and the closet door creaked back and forth on hinges needing oil, creating an almost unworldly atmosphere.

As the ship plowed through yet another gigantic wave, a resonating thud flipped Jake's stomach on its edge. He swallowed hard, willing himself not to throw up.

Something in the bathroom tumbled into the sink with a clatter and rolled around on the smooth porcelain like a marble in a bucket before coming to a stop.

A drawer on the desk slid open.

Jake's face drained of colour, and Felton didn't look much better. "What the hell was that?" Jake asked, referring to the crash that plunged the ship into darkness. His voice warbled with a slight tremble.

Felton replied, "My guess is that lightning hit the ship. It sounded like we might have been hit twice. The thunderclap followed immediately after the place lit up. I think we're in the worst of the storm right now. It's right on top of us. If we get through this part, it should be clearer sailing. The lightning could have short-circuited the ship's systems. If the storm didn't knock out the generators, the lights should come back on soon."

About forty-five seconds later, rumbles and shudders from deep inside the bowels of the ship brought the lights back on to a pale yellow. "That must be the backup generator. But at least it kicked in, thank God," Felton said.

Dani shut off her phone's flashlight. "Still no bars on my phone. No signal."

Felton said, "The lightning strike likely hit the radome on the top of the ship. That's the big white ball that contains radar and satellite equipment. If lightning knocked out the radar equipment, our dear captain is going to be navigating manually. The radome is made of fibreglass, so it should be weather-resistant material, but a direct hit could have knocked out the satellite equipment. We could be without communications for a long time if that's the case. It could impact the CCTV cameras, too."

"Great," said Dani. "I need to get back to check on Emilie. I don't think the storm would frighten her but being left in the dark for a few minutes might."

Felton suggested everything would be all right since they had Patel locked up and Angela Lee confined to her room with a guard outside her door. "All the danger has been removed."

Dani shook her head. "I'm not so sure. My constable told me Lee communicated with someone on the ship. We got cut off before he told me who. We don't know if that person is part of this and potentially dangerous. We'll go down to see the Security Chief after I check on Emilie. This ship is so big and without communication… We'll have to walk everywhere, or should I say stumble, to talk to anyone. I wonder if the elevators will work. It's not ideal, that's for sure."

"Anything I can do to help?" Felton asked.

Dani clung to the edge of the desk. "Maybe there is," she suggested. "Speak with Angela Lee. Inform her we're aware of her involvement in the virus's development and that she contacted a crewmember. Advise her that cooperating with law enforcement may bring leniency if she discloses the identity of the individual. If she talks, go to Deck One and tell Eduardo, the Security Chief. Be careful! She may still possess cyanide. Maintain a safe distance by staying at the door and ensure she stays well back. Also, take care navigating the corridors."

Felton nodded gravely. Jake sensed some of the man's cockiness had dissipated when he realized his company was in serious jeopardy. Maybe he accepted his culpability for not paying closer attention.

Jake and Dani stumbled out the door and held both arms out as they tried to roll with the ship. Eventually, they got the hang of it, and walking became easier. They approached the security guard outside Angela's door, who stood with arms crossed, leaning back with one leg braced against the wall for support. "Is everything okay?" Dani asked.

"Fine," the guard responded. "No sound since Camille came up to place Ms. Lee under arrest. I'm just trying to ride out this storm. I've never seen anything like it." Dani considered talking to Angela but decided Felton could handle the job. She wanted to see Emilie. She said to the guard, "Thank you for doing this. Mr. Felton from down the hall will be here shortly to talk to Ms. Lee. Just open the door far enough that they can talk."

The ship rolled again, sending the security guard sliding sideways on the wall and staggering Jake and Dani. The security guard sat down against the wall with his arms around his knees for better support.

Jake and Dani made it to the elevators only to discover they didn't work. "It looks like we're stumbling up the stairs to our room," Jake said. They made their way to the stairs, battling for each step against the wild rocking of the ship. The ship's awkward tilt gave them the sensation of walking on uneven ground.

Wind howled through the corridor.

The ship's structure groaned.

It was another reminder that something manmade held them captive while protecting them from a fierce battle with Mother Nature.

Sick bags to be used by passengers should they be needed lay on the floor in front of doors. The lights flickered and dimmed, throwing the ship into gloomy darkness again for incalculable seconds.

A shriek rose through the semi-darkness. It sounded human, like a scream, and appeared to come from the other side of the shuttered windows.

Jake and Dani looked at each other. They had to check. Jake hurried to the sliding doors, which would only open about a foot and a half. Not enough to squeeze through but enough to allow the monstrous wind to slam him back. Using both hands and applying all his strength, he forced the doors open wide enough for him and Dani to squeeze through. The minute they did, the driving sideways rain almost obscured two huddled shapes on the outer deck. Two teenage girls clung to the railing with both hands, too terrified to move.

The slashing rain mixed with salty ocean spray stabbed at Jake's face like pinpricks. The waves crashed thunderously against the ship as the storm raged above the hissing ocean. Jake and Dani hunched down beneath the glass partition and crawled toward the girls through rivers of water. The girls looked to be around eighteen and petrified. Their hair clung to their heads, and their clothes gripped their bodies, soaked with sea spray. They stared with terrified eyes that resembled white orbs in the dark night. They shivered from intense fear and cold as the wind screeched in fury. Lightning lit the sky at the stern of the ship, and everyone jumped as a stray, unsecured, yellow deck chair slammed into the glass partition feet away from them before gyrating off into the darkness. At least the Ocean Wanderer was still under power. Jake hoped the worst would soon over. The ship lurched forward, slicing through the walls of water, suggesting that Mother Nature still had more to offer.

Jake struggled against the intense wind and thrashing rain, grabbing any handhold he could find until he reached the first girl. He seized her hand while Dani put her arms around the second. Fear glued the girls to the railing. Jake pried the first girl's white knuckles from the slippery wooden guardrail and guided her to safety through the sliding doors, which had stuck open. The shivering girl slipped on the now wet floor and clung to Jake until he found a place for her to sit. He returned outside to help Dani.

The second girl required more coaxing. She didn't want to let go. Jake pried her hand from the railing one finger at a time, and he and Dani crawled with the girl to the door. Once inside, Jake muscled the door closed again. The girls huddled together on a sofa. They wore jeans soaked through to the skin and sodden jackets. Their windswept hair lay in a tangled mess. The sea spray had pasted strands of hair to their foreheads. Dani said, "Okay, what were you girls doing out there? Do you realize you could have been killed?"

Both stared at their sodden shoes. The first girl, a redhead, raised her head. Through trembling, blue lips, she muttered, "We just tried to get a video for social media. We didn't think it was that bad. When we got out, we couldn't get back, and we weren't sure where to go. Then the lights went out, and we couldn't see anything. We found the door, but it wouldn't open. I thought we were going to die. Thank you for saving us."

Jake asked where their parents were, and the girls replied they had their own cabin with their parents in an adjoining room. "You won't tell them, will you?" the second girl asked.

Dani said, "That's up to you. For now, I suggest you go back to your cabin and stay there. Have a warm shower and put on some dry clothes. The captain ordered us to stay in our cabins. Didn't you hear her?"

The girls mumbled they had and thanked Jake and Dani again. When Dani asked where their rooms were, the girls looked down the corridors in both directions to get their bearings. When they spotted the cabin numbers, they confirmed they were not that far down the corridor in the direction of the bow. Dani told them to be careful and watched them go as they lurched toward a door where they let themselves in.

Finally, Jake and Dani made their way back to their room. They removed their wet clothes as soon as they arrived and changed into their pyjamas and bathrobes. Dani suggested to Jake that he should shower first while she checked on Emilie.

"How do you suppose she would handle the storm?" Jake asked as he headed in the direction of the bathroom.

"Storms always mesmerized her. Even when she was little. She would stare silent and wide-eyed. I think adrenalin raced through her veins when a storm hit. She seemed exhilarated by the sheer force of nature. I suspect this is no different. She's not crazy about the dark, though, so she would find it unnerving when the lights went out."

Jake smiled to himself. Quite the pair, Dani and her daughter. It wouldn't surprise him at all if Emilie followed in her mom's footsteps in her career choice.

Jake, Dani, and Emilie agreed at the start of the cruise that the door between the adjoining rooms would remain unlocked, and the occupants could go back and forth with a knock beforehand. That's exactly what Dani did while Jake went to shower. She checked her watch before knocking softly. It was the middle of the night, and she didn't want to waken her sleeping daughter, but she wanted to see her before she went to bed herself.

Jake stood under the shower, trying to warm his shivering body as the water cascaded over him. Suddenly, the door swung open, banging against the wall and startling him. Dani hurried into the bathroom. It seemed unlikely that she intended to join him in the shower, given the exhaustion they felt and the size of the enclosure. Jake pushed aside the wet plastic curtain that clung to him uncomfortably and peered out. Dani didn't need to use the toilet or retrieve anything from the counter. The situation turned out to be much more concerning than that.

Dani shouted above the sounds of the running water and fan, "Jake, Emilie isn't in her room!"

Chapter Forty-One

J ake shut off the water and emerged from the shower, grabbing a towel. "No message, either?" he asked as he towelled himself off. He already knew the answer from the panic in Dani's voice.

"No," Dani replied. "I wonder where she disappeared to this time. That girl is going to be the death of me." She looked at her watch. "It's so late. She wouldn't go out to take pictures like those other two. She's more responsible than that."

Jake dragged his suitcase from under the bed where he stored the clothing he didn't expect to wear and found tan pants and a blue T-shirt. As he pulled them on, he asked Dani what she wanted to do.

She replied, "Em wouldn't wander around on the ship in the storm, and she'd leave a message if she went out to get a closer look. I know my daughter. I don't like to think the worst, but whoever Angela Lee is working with might have something to do with this. That gift bag left for us might have been an attempt to get rid of us. My gut tells me this is connected. We'll look for her, but the ship is too big to tackle it ourselves." She checked her phone. "Dammit! Still no signal. We need to go back to Deck Ten and speak with the captain. I want to see if the CCTV cameras are working. Then we'll speak with Eduardo about getting help. It's so frustrating that we don't have communication. We'll have to run all over the damn ship."

Climbing the rolling stairs again didn't appeal to Jake, but Emilie came first. There was no question he would set aside his trepidation to find the girl, and if she disappeared because someone took her, all the more reason to put on his "big boy" pants and go with Dani. Besides, the ship had settled down some.

Dani changed into a hoodie and jeans, and the two of them set out again on the heaving ship. The combination of the ship coming out the other side of the storm and their experience walking on unsteady surfaces made for a faster journey up the stairs to the 10th deck, although they still gripped the railing. Jake's arthritic knee ached from climbing up and down the stairs and bracing himself against the forces of the storm. Dani's superior shape and anxiousness to get answers helped her travel faster. Jake heard himself breathe as he hauled himself up the stairs.

Dani used her pass to let them onto the bridge. Captain Svenssen glanced at the newcomers on the bridge and walked toward them. Hours of staring at the ocean and distant horizon and fatigue had clouded and reddened her typically bright eyes. Jake thought she should receive a commendation for guiding the monster craft through the storm. The lightning flashed behind the ship now. The moon peeked intermittently through gaps in the heavy cloud cover as if checking to see if it was safe to come out. A halo of diffused light spilled onto the ocean, reflecting off the calming seas. At least, calming seas relative to earlier. The ship still rolled, but to Jake's untrained eye, the swells rose about 10 feet now. While he stared outside, Dani updated the captain on Angela Lee and mentioned that Emilie had disappeared. "Can we see the CCTV footage again?"

"I wish, but a lightning strike knocked them offline. It looks like we won't have the cameras or any type of communication back until we reach Seward. We can't even tell the passengers when it's safe to come out of their cabins. Passengers will come out on their own, anyway, now that the rolling has subsided. I'm so sorry to learn about your daughter. What can I do to help?"

Dani said, "I need to organize a search party. Can we use some of your staff for that?"

The captain agreed they could enlist any available staff for searching but admitted to the difficulty of mustering them without communication. "We're so dependent on technology, even on a cruise ship. Or maybe, especially on a cruise ship. Anyway, ask Eduardo to help you pull a team together."

Jake and Dani thanked the captain and headed to the stairs once again. Jake's arthritic knee screamed at him to stop. But he couldn't. Not now. Now, more than ever, Dani needed him to help find Emilie. They dropped in at their cabin on the way down, hoping to see she had returned, but a silent, empty, haunting room greeted them. Her phone lay on the end table. Her bed covers were pulled back, and her pyjamas lay scrunched up, half hanging off the bed where she tossed them. She had been in bed sometime during the night and got up to put her clothes back on. Dani commented that Emilie never went anywhere without her phone. She was even more convinced that something untoward had happened to her daughter.

They hurried to Deck One, and when they reached the security office, they found Camille at her desk. "Is Eduardo around?" Dani asked.

"I haven't seen him. I don't know where he is. He hasn't shown up since he went upstairs to search the rooms, and the communication system is down, so I can't reach out to him."

A frown creased Dani's forehead, and Jake understood her mind whirled around the same suspicion as his. *Was Eduardo the crewmember Lee communicated with?*

Dani said, "Camille, my constable told me that Angela Lee contacted a member of the crew on the ship, presumably to help her. That person could be involved with the murders. My constable knows the person's identity, but the communication system went down before he told us. It's odd Eduardo hasn't shown up. I don't want to suggest anything, but until we understand more, we need to tread carefully. If Eduardo shows up, I would like to question him but approach him with caution. If he is the one Lee contacted, he could be dangerous. The same goes for anyone else who could be involved. In the meantime, we have another problem."

Dani explained to the shocked Camille that Emilie had disappeared. "We need to organize a search party. Captain Svenssen okayed us using any available resources to help. I'm sure it won't be easy because the communication system is down, but can you organize a group to search?"

Camille said without hesitation, "Of course. I'll talk to the team leaders and ask them to contact their team members. That everyone has been confined to their cabin helps. The team leaders can find them. Some will be assigned to repair damage to the ship and help ill passengers, of course, but we'll do what we can."

They needed a better understanding of where to search, even though Jake feared the answer. "If someone took her daughter, where are the hiding spots on a cruise ship?"

Camille's face darkened. After a moment's hesitation, she started rhyming off the places someone could hide or be hidden. "I can come up with countless places on short notice, such as the crew quarters or storage rooms. If someone really wanted to hide someone, they could do so behind fake walls or removable panels, in the luggage area or a less trafficked area like the engine room. Perhaps in a covered lifeboat or tender. Maintenance tunnels or void spaces. A hidden compartment, although that would take detailed knowledge of the ship."

Every mention of a new hiding place hit Jake and Dani with the weight of a punch to the gut. Finding Emilie seemed like an insurmountable task.

Chapter Forty-Two

Camille gathered a team of sleepy-eyed housekeeping, maintenance, theatre, and administrative staff to join available security personnel to search the ship. She used the term "Alpha" to summon personnel, which she said was the code for an emergency. Everything was done old school-by word of mouth. It was an impressive display of management given the lack of communication technology. The crew enthusiastically accepted the challenge when Camille told them the reason for bringing them together. Within an hour, she divided the gathering into groups to search each floor of the ship from front to back.

And still no sign of Eduardo.

Dani's hand tightened in Jake's when someone asked the chances of Emilie being swept overboard during the storm. Before Camille responded, Dani said loudly enough for the crowd to hear, "I'll answer that. I one hundred per cent believe that didn't happen. She left her cellphone in her room, and if she got out of bed to watch the storm, she would have taken it with her to take pictures. She's on the ship somewhere." A sleepy-eyed Amoy, their server at the bar, cast a sympathetic look over her shoulder at Dani and Jake.

Camille wrapped up the briefing by saying that housekeeping would clean all occupied rooms when they reached Seward, so they didn't have to do a room-to-room search. Jake and Dani spoke in whispers before joining the search team. The time was now 5:25 in the morning. If the ship maintained its schedule, it would arrive at Seward in just over three hours. Dani sensed they had to find Emilie before they arrived. She wasn't sure why, but that nagging feeling tugged at her brain and wouldn't let go. There must be a reason Emilie disappeared, and her intuition suggested it had to do with the ship docking. When she expressed her concern to Jake, he agreed. There had to be a reason.

The team dispersed and started the search. The theatre crew searched every nook and cranny behind the stage. Kitchen staff searched hiding places in the galley while the security staff looked under tarps in lifeboats. Since the storm moved away, Camille asked some of the hospitality crew out of Jake and Dani's earshot to check the outside deck on every floor for potential clues, like pieces of clothing or scratches on the railing suggesting a scuffle. She warned everyone not to approach Eduardo if they found him. Camille assigned herself to check Eduardo's cabin. She carried a taser. Dani joined the group searching the crew area on Deck One while Jake headed to Deck Four. Their random decision allowed them to satisfy themselves about every deck of the ship. Each planned to work their way up from their starting point.

As they searched, they came across damage caused by the storm. Chairs overturned, shattered glass, water damage … The crew made notes as they exhaustively searched. The commotion caught the attention of some passengers, tired of being confined to their rooms, or others who spent the night fighting sea sickness. Word spread, and passengers joined the search. Soon, hundreds of people combed the ship looking for Emilie. Shouts of "Emilie" echoed throughout the corridors, which attracted more people. It was like everyone took it personally, as if Emilie were one of their own.

But after an hour of searching, people reported back with no sign of the teenager. Camille didn't find Eduardo either. So far, it had been an exercise in futility. Dani became frustrated at the herculean task of searching every nook and cranny on the ship. If only the CCTV cameras worked. They didn't, and nothing could be done about that.

A crew member raced down the hall toward Dani, carrying a soaked jacket. "Is this Emilie's?" she asked breathlessly. Dani couldn't hide her shock. She grabbed the blue jacket and saw Emilie's high school logo on the arm. The odour of wet cloth stung her nostrils. Dani turned the label outward to confirm the jacket as Emilie's size. The near-zero likelihood of other jackets on the ship of the same size and from the same school sent a jolt through her. "Yes," she cried. "Where did you find it?"

The crewmember hesitated for a beat until she finally said quietly, "Wound around the railing on Deck Eight."

"That's the deck we're staying on. She must have left the jacket outside before the storm started, and the wind wrapped it around the railing. That's the only explanation."

The crewmember looked sad and with skepticism at Dani. To her, the explanation didn't seem right. Emilie had somehow gone overboard. Dani realized the woman thought she was making excuses. She rejected it outright. "We have to keep looking," was all she said.

Meanwhile, Jake continued his search on Deck Four. The deck was home to the lower part of the dining room, a room for cards and games, a bar, the shore excursion desk, and several cabins. Jake relied on the crew to search nooks and crannies and hidden compartments. Only the public spaces were familiar to him, and few of those. He wandered through the empty dining room and the galley behind, calling out Emilie's name but feeling pretty much useless.

He passed an area in the middle of the ship where the sun gleamed through the windows and the ocean appeared calm, as if nothing had happened during the night. The sight didn't give him much of a lift. The exhaustion of being up all night, walking miles on the cruise ship, his sore knee, and fear for Emilie's safety dragged him down. He realized his shoulders sagged. His body and his arthritic knee screamed at him to lie down. The worry consumed him, and every passing minute weighed like an anvil on his chest. As he trudged along, his thoughts ran through the possibilities. *Could we have done more to prevent this? Is she safe? Is she even alive?* He shoved the thoughts from his mind as much as possible as he carried on.

After exiting the dining room, he wandered down a corridor past several staterooms. A woman with a dog wearing a vest approached from the other direction. "Are you looking for that poor girl?" the woman asked.

"Yes, she's my girlfriend's daughter. We're worried sick. We just don't know what happened." Happy for a brief respite from the search, he said, "That's a beautiful dog. Is he working?"

"Yes," the woman answered. "I worked in the military and received post-traumatic stress disorder as my reward, so Tommy keeps me company." She added, "I'm not complaining. I enjoyed the experience in the military." The dog sat obediently by his master, looking up at the mention of his name.

Jake said, "I'm sure he's splendid company. Incredible that all the people and noises on the ship don't sidetrack him. He must be extremely well trained."

The woman tugged on Tommy's leash. "He hardly ever barks, and people don't excite him. He ignores them. If he hears an unusual sound that he perceives as a potential threat to me, he'll make a noise or get between me and whatever is bothering him. Anyway, I won't keep you. Good luck finding the girl."

Jake continued walking along the corridor when a sound stopped him in his tracks. Contrary to what the woman just said, Tommy whined and barked. Jake whirled around to see the dog straining at his leash. Tommy's master asked what the problem was, but the dog continued to whine and stand between his master and the door of an inside cabin. Jake turned on his heel to investigate.

When Jake approached, the woman said, "This is so unusual. Tommy never does this."

Her comment from their conversation echoed in Jake's head and sent shivers squirming down his spine. *"...if he thinks there might be a threat to me..."* were the woman's words just a few seconds ago. Jake placed his ear against the door to identify what troubled Tommy. He knocked and thought he heard a thumping sound, but that was it. At this stage, anything had to be worth investigating.

Chapter Forty-Three

Jake banged on the door again with his ear resting against it. He thought he heard a muffled sound again but couldn't be sure. He tried his passkey in the door, but no luck. He supposed the key the captain gave them only provided access to the bridge. *What's so special behind this door?* He said to the woman, "Why would Tommy react to this cabin and not every cabin on the ship? He must hear noises coming from every cabin he passes. What attracted his attention?"

The woman gave Tommy a little more leash, and the dog turned his head up toward his master before staring at the door again. "I don't know what's behind the door, but I'm sure you're familiar with dogs' special hearing. It's not only high frequencies, as most people assume. Dogs are also attracted by low frequencies that humans can't hear. Tommy must have heard a sound in the room that bothered him. A sound that we can't hear."

Jake said, "We need to get into the room to find out what's going on. Wait here while I find someone with a key."

He checked the cabin number and rushed down the hall to find a house-keeper helping with the search. She jumped when he tapped her on the shoulder. When she turned, he said, "My name's Jake Scott. The missing girl, Emilie, is my girlfriend's daughter. A room down the hall attracted the attention of a woman's service dog. Emilie could be in the room." The words tumbled from his mouth.

"What room number, sir?"

"Number 4019 at the end of the corridor."

The woman pulled out her cellphone. "Let me check, sir." She scanned room numbers on her phone. "Oh, that room has been sealed. The room is scheduled for maintenance when we return to Vancouver. No one is in there. It's a restricted area."

The hair on the back of Jake's neck stood at attention as he considered the possibility. It would be an excellent place to hide someone, especially if no one was allowed in until they got back to Vancouver.

Then, the housekeeper said, "This is strange, though. Only a toilet replacement is required." She scrolled on her phone. "The work should have been completed before we left Vancouver. Or maintenance could have done it while we travelled or at any of the ports along the way. This doesn't seem right."

Jake's radar zeroed in even more. "Do you have a key to the room?"

"Yes, my key should work."

Jake led her down the hall to room 4019 where the woman still stood beside Tommy. The dog remained agitated. The housekeeper knocked first and, hearing nothing, shoved her key card into the reader beside the door. Nothing happened. She tried again. Still nothing. "That's strange. My card should work unless someone has done something to the reader. My card won't go in all the way." She tried a third time, trying to force the card, but the door didn't unlock.

Jake insisted. "We have to get into that room."

"Let me find someone from maintenance," the housekeeper said over her shoulder as she rushed off.

Tommy's handler said she had to go; that the dog would be looking for food and water soon. "I'm praying you find Emilie and that she's okay."

Jake thanked her and waited by the door for the longest ten minutes of his life until a maintenance man showed up in coveralls. Tools rattled in a bag hanging from his right shoulder. He examined the key card reader and inserted his card, only to agree it wouldn't go all the way in. Something had been jammed inside the slot to prevent a card from activating the latch. He said, "These things are battery operated. I wondered if someone removed the batteries, but they are designed so people inside can get out. Somebody disabled this lock so nobody can get in." He rifled through his toolbox, tossing tools aside.

Dani showed up while the maintenance man worked on the door. Word spread throughout the ship with the speed of one of the previous night's lightning bolts that Emilie may have been found. A crewmember was dispatched to Deck One to find Dani. As she approached, her eyelids drooped from fatigue, and her expression seemed unfocused to Jake. Her voice sounded low and strained, like she was running on empty. Her chest heaved from running up the stairs from the first deck, and sweat glistened on her forehead.

From 10 feet away, she asked Jake, "Is Emilie in that room?"

"We don't know yet, Dani. This man is trying to open the door." Jake relayed the story of Tommy becoming agitated at something behind the door and how he thought a thumping noise came from inside the room. "It could have been anything," he said, not wishing to raise Dani's hopes. At the same time, he prayed they had found Emilie and that she was okay.

The maintenance man set sections of the card reader on the carpet and removed a folded piece of cardboard, preventing the pass from going in all the way at the bottom of the slot. His screwdriver whirled as he reassembled the reader and tried his master key card. The lock whirred and unlatched the door. He stepped aside to let Jake and Dani in.

At first, they didn't see her in the pitch-black room. They couldn't see their hands in front of their faces. Dani switched on the light to find a cabin identical to the one she and Jake occupied but with no balcony or porthole. They found Emilie bound and gagged in the far corner at the foot of the bed. She had her eyes closed to block the sudden light. She sat leaning against the bed. Marks on the wall showed where she kicked it, explaining the thumping noise Jake heard. Her feet and hands were tied with zip ties, and a scarf had been wrapped around her face and tied at the back of her head, gagging her mouth. She opened her eyes to slits, but at the sight of Jake, they sprung wide. She had obviously expected someone else. Jake pulled the scarf from her mouth and asked the maintenance man for something to cut the ties. The man removed a box cutter from his bag and handed it to Jake, who released Emilie's hands. The ties were nearly worn through. Jake handed the box cutter back and lifted the mattress at the end of the bed. He smiled when he discovered Emilie had been rubbing the plastic tie on the frame to release herself.

Dani leaned down and hugged her daughter. "Are you okay, sweetheart? We should get you to the Medical Centre for a checkup."

Emilie said, "Yes, I'm fine. I'm thirsty, though. I don't need to go to the Medical Centre, but I need to go to the bathroom so bad." They helped her up and waited a few seconds while she regained circulation in her feet. Unable to wait, Jake and Dani each took an arm and helped the teenager walk to the bathroom.

Dani exhaled with a deep breath. Jake sensed the tension release from her shoulders, as tightness in his neck loosened and the heaviness from his chest lifted. Dani's relief manifested itself in a few tears she swiped away, hoping no one noticed. Someone brought a bottle of water from a nearby fridge for her daughter and handed it to Dani. She said to Jake as Emilie opened the bathroom door, "We're going to hunt Eduardo down. Anyone who would do this to my daughter is going to pay. Only a monster would do this."

Emilie's circulation returned as she walked with a steadier gait back to sit on the bed. "Mom, if you're talking about the man who brought me here, you're wrong about Eduardo."

Chapter Forty-Four

"Are you certain it wasn't Eduardo who put you here?" Dani inquired as she removed the cap and handed the water bottle to Emilie. Dani's expression reflected anger, relief, and surprise simultaneously. Jake sat taken aback, given that Eduardo's disappearance cast the suspicion directly upon him.

Jake and Dani waited for an answer as Emilie drank deeply from the water bottle before turning her weary eyes toward them. With a hoarse voice, she said, "Oh, I'm sure. I was asleep in bed in my cabin when the phone rang. Just before the power went out. He said you had been knocked down and injured when the ship rocked from side to side, and you were being treated on the 4th deck. He said you were searching for clues to the murders in the cabins. I couldn't figure out why they wouldn't take you to the Medical Centre, but he told me you needed treatment before they moved you. It didn't sound good. I was so worried, but I was stupid. I believed him. He said because the ship was rolling so badly, he would come and help me reach you. I got dressed and waited for him. When he showed up, he hurried me out the door before I grabbed my cellphone and brought me to this room, where he hit me over the head enough to stun me. I still put a scratch on his face. He tied me up and left me here. He said he would tell you where I was after we reached Vancouver."

Dani's thoughts whirled. She rose to check the back of Emilie's head to see a lump surrounded by dried blood. Emilie needed to get to the Medical Centre for assessment for a possible concussion. The idea of Emilie being tied up in this dark room for two more days without food or water or the ability to reach the bathroom sickened Dani. She draped her arm around her daughter and said, "Come on, Jake, let's get her to the Medical Centre and then to bed."

Emilie got up gingerly, but her head swam as she did. She sat down again for a minute before she tried again. As Jake and Dani led her to the door, Dani said, "Do you know the man who brought you here, Em?"

Emilie nodded. "Of course I do, Mom. Rafael, the man who made the towel animals for us."

Jake and Dani stopped before the doorway, pulling Emilie to an abrupt halt. Dani held her daughter's eyes with hers. "Rafael? Are you sure?" For the second time in a matter of minutes, Dani questioned her daughter's recollection of events, and her tired daughter had had enough.

Emilie rubbed her bruised wrists. "Yes, Mom, I couldn't be surer about anything. He called me. He identified himself as Rafael. That's why I believed him. Rafael brought me to this room. He hit me over the head with something and tied me up, and he has a big scratch on his face. Not only that, but he was nervous as hell. He sweated like a pig, and his hands shook when he put the zip ties on me. He was so nervous, I smelled him a mile away. I almost broke the zip ties before you showed up. I would have been ready for him if he came back."

Jake didn't doubt for a minute that Emilie would have been ready for Rafael, but he was glad it didn't come to that. If Rafael helped Angela Lee commit murder, who knows what he was capable of? They reached the doorway to the cabin and turned into the corridor where people lined up to the end. Crew and passengers stood side-by-side from the cabin all the way to the elevator. Dani caught sight of Zachary Felton and smiled. Grinning and relieved faces clapped and cheered as the threesome walked by, and the sound grew with each step they took until it became a thunderous roar. Emilie, not used to such attention, smiled with her head down, and offered a small wave as a crimson tide rose from her neck into her cheeks. Jake and Dani mouthed "thank you" to the crowd as they made their way to the elevator. Jake felt sorry for anyone on the deck who still tried to catch up on sleep lost during the night.

Thankfully, the elevators worked again. Passengers squeezed to the back to create enough room for the three of them. On the way down, passengers compared notes about things they saw or rumours they heard.

"I heard the pool overflowed and flooded the deck below."

"I pushed the bed against the wall and lay between that and a suitcase to keep from being thrown on the floor."

"You slept!? I puked all night. I can't wait to get off this God damned menace of a ship."

"Glass is lying all over on Deck Six."

"I wonder if they'll ever get the damn internet working again. I'm going to ask for a refund. This is ridiculous."

Dani checked her phone and confirmed no signal. They rode the elevator to Deck One, and Jake and Dani supported Emilie down the hall to the Medical Centre. She walked much steadier and seemed in good shape, except that she was nearly asleep on her feet. Still, Dani wanted to have her checked to make sure. Jake still limped.

Six people lined up in the corridor to get into the Centre. A nurse removed a blood-soaked cloth from a woman's head wound to check on the severity of a cut. Another nurse helped a man into the Centre who held one arm with the other. His wrist hung at an odd angle, and his face was the colour of snow. Others had assorted cuts and bruises. Jake, Dani, and Emilie stood at the back of the line, but when word spread that the "kidnapped girl" waited to see the doctor, most passengers insisted she move to the front of the line. All except one elderly, grey-haired lady who was hobbling. She said she didn't care if the King of England stood in line. It was her spot in line, and she planned to keep it.

Finally, they got in to see the doctor. An antiseptic odour greeted them at the door. Fluorescent lights lit the pale green room. Glass-covered cabinets held a selection of pills, gauzes, and other supplies. Various machines hung from the walls or sat on cabinets with multiple drawers. It could have been a more compact version of any clinic on land. While the doctor examined Emilie, Jake scanned the room at the beds occupied by the most serious of the injured passengers. Drapes hid most of them, but a nurse spoke to a man in the bed farthest from the door. Because of his exhaustion, he blinked twice to verify the identity of the person. Jake tried not to stare, but his eyes kept drawing back to the man who lay covered from chin to toe in a sheet. When certain, he pulled his head back, catching Dani's attention. He pointed his chin toward the man lying on the bed. When she looked in the direction Jake pointed, she nodded and smiled the smallest of smiles.

Eduardo lay on the bed with his head wrapped in a white bandage. After the nurse left the Security Chief's side, Jake said to the doctor, "Is it okay if we talk to Eduardo?"

The doctor continued to hold up fingers for Emilie to count and separated strands of her hair to get a better look at her wound, but he nodded without saying a word. He was hooking up an IV machine to hydrate Emilie when Jake and Dani wandered to Eduardo's side.

"How are you doing, Eduardo?" Jake asked.

Eduardo turned his bloodshot eyes toward Jake and Dani. His slow movement elicited a groan. "It sounded like you from your voices. Aside from a splitting headache, I'll be fine. I feel guilty taking up this bed. A parade of people came in with various bumps and bruises. Some with seasickness. The doc says I should stay here for a couple more hours of observation. I have a concussion."

"We've been wondering about you," Dani said. She wasn't about to tell him she would have happily throttled him when she initially held him responsible for Emilie's disappearance. "What happened?"

Eduardo closed his eyes as if trying to recall. "I don't remember much. I sent my Security Supervisor ahead. I remember coming down the stairs after searching Raj Patel's room. We found the gift bags and a bottle of aftershave that smelled like almonds. The ship lurched, and I must have lost my footing. Luckily, I wasn't carrying the evidence. We sealed it in the room. My head must have hit the railing and then the wall. A crewmember found me unconscious at the bottom of the stairs. The maintenance guys will probably have to fix the dent in the wall." His chuckle was accompanied by another groan. "I guess Patel is in jail now."

Jake and Dani exchanged glances. Neither expected Eduardo would absorb everything that took place overnight in his condition. It would only make his headache worse. Dani said, "Uh, yes, he is. But a lot has happened in the last few hours. Get some rest, and either Jake and I or Camille will fill you in when you're up to it."

Eduardo's eyes closed as they turned to leave, but he mumbled, "Rumour has it your daughter disappeared. Is she okay?"

Dani withheld a smile, thinking about what she had been prepared to do to him. "She's fine."

"Thank God," Eduardo said as he drifted off to sleep.

Chapter Forty-Five

The doctor removed Emilie from the IV and, after prescribing rest and lots of fluids, said she would be fine. Jake and Dani felt immediate and immeasurable relief. As they started to leave, the doctor said, "Do you want me to check out your leg?" Jake realized he had been limping from his arthritic knee. That and the bruise he received in Felton's room. "No thanks. It's just arthritis. Everyone here is worse off than me."

All three were exhausted, so they told Camille about Rafael and headed back to their rooms. Dani insisted on sleeping on the sofa in Emilie's room, and her daughter didn't resist. Dani said, "Make sure you wake me if you need anything." She kissed Jake and shut the door between the two rooms before flopping onto the sofa without undressing.

Jake opened the drapes in his room enough to peek through and see the Port of Seward. Snow-topped mountains surrounded the port. He remembered all three had booked an excursion to visit the Kanai Fjords, hoping to observe sea lions and whales. He had been looking forward to the excursion, but right now he looked forward more to a few hours' sleep.

Jake went to the bathroom when suddenly, his world shifted like someone had flipped a switch. A deep and pervasive fatigue of mind and body hit him. An overwhelming weariness manifested as heavy limbs, sluggish movements, and a complete lack of energy. The last thing that occurred to him as he returned from the bathroom and dropped onto the bed was that he was glad he wasn't doing anything requiring judgment or quick thinking.

Around 10:30, a commotion outside the door awakened him. The sudden noise startled Jake, and he shot up from the bed. His head spun for a moment as he checked the bedside clock. He groaned and slumped back down on the bed, but in his semi-conscious state, someone in the corridor yelled something about Rafael.

Jake rolled out of bed and stumbled wearily to the door. Dani must have heard the same thing, as she already stood at the hallway door of the adjoining room. She asked what was going on. A passenger said, "Someone's in the water on the opposite side of the ship to the gangplank side, and the rumour is it's Rafael, our steward. Apparently, he jumped off the ship into the water."

Jake admitted to himself he hadn't given a second thought to where Rafael might be on the ship, although he realized now the cabin steward could still possess some of the cyanide. It sounded like Rafael was making a run for it. He wouldn't get far if he had been spotted in the frigid water.

"Let's go and see if we can help," Dani said. Jake marvelled at her energy level after a few hours of sleep. He still felt sluggish and lacking motivation. Dani returned inside the room to see Emilie still asleep. She scribbled a note, which she left on Emilie's dresser.

Jake and Dani each grabbed a jacket and hustled down the corridor to the elevators. Deck Eight featured rooms from one end of the ship to the other with no outer deck, so they needed to go lower or higher to see what was going on. They descended all the way to Deck One to catch up to Camille.

They found her in the security office. She said, "I didn't expect we would see you two for a few more hours. You must have heard about what's going on. The Coast Guard just fished Rafael out of the water. I guess he realized there was no other way off. He would have to show his sea pass to leave the ship, and we posted security guards at the demarcation gate. We would have nabbed him as soon as he tried to leave."

"Is he alive?" Jake asked. "The water must be freezing."

"Yes, they'll take him to the local police station for questioning. He tried to swim to the marina. I'll talk to the port security team. They might want to speak with you as well. You're under no obligation, of course. This is not your jurisdiction."

Dani agreed. "Of course we'll be there. No, this isn't our jurisdiction, but I've been outside my jurisdiction all along. We just happened to be in the right place at the right time." She glanced at Jake. "Some would say the wrong place at the right time." That elicited a chuckle from Camille. Dani asked, "I imagine you released Raj Patel by now?"

"Yes," said Camille. "We released him with our apologies. There is some other news, though. You asked Zachary Felton to speak with Angela Lee in her room. When the guard let him into the room, he found her lying on the bed. She was dead. The body has been removed and is in the morgue, but the room has been sealed until we reach Vancouver. She held a small bottle in her hand, and the doctor said she exhibited the same symptoms of cyanide poisoning as the others. She left a note addressed to her family in a sealed envelope on the dresser. The FBI will investigate, and I imagine they'll open the note, even though it was most likely suicide."

Dani understood, but she said, "It's even more reason why I would like to sit in on the interrogation of Rafael at the police station. Three people are dead, and Rafael seems to be complicit. We may not learn all the details, but I would like to understand the motivation for them conspiring to commit murder."

Chapter Forty-Six

Jake and Dani disembarked from the ship to encounter a group of reporters standing on the pier. Vehicles representing local and state radio and TV stations lined the streets, and journalists, equipped with television cameras, mobile phones, and notepads, engaged with passengers. Jake and Dani skirted around them without hindrance. As they walked by, they overheard enthusiastic passengers recounting their experiences during the storm. One mentioned the circulation of a rumour regarding a murder and kidnapping, which would undoubtedly capture the reporters' attention.

Light jackets and casual clothes were the outfits of choice. The brilliant Alaska sun made the temperature seem warmer than the 60 degrees Fahrenheit displayed on a post at the port. Jake converted it to Celsius in his head. *About 15 degrees. Still cool.*

Boats in the marina had sustained visible damage during the storm. A fishing boat was pushed on top of a pleasure craft. One boat seemed to be orphaned in the water, floating alone several yards from the marina. Others had smashed windows, and a crew worked to remove a broken sailboat mast that sheared off and crashed down on neighbouring craft.

Debris washed up by the pounding surf littered the shoreline. Jake commented to Dani that while the damage appeared to be significant, the storm must have subsided before hitting land. He expected the damage to be much worse.

Dani checked her phone, and her face lit up when she discovered a signal. She said to Jake, "You might want to check your messages."

Jake retrieved his phone from his pocket and was astonished at the number of text and call messages waiting for him. Many came from his daughter, Avery. At least one came from each member of the breakfast group, and another from Janice Richardson, his friend and former colleague at the Ottawa newspaper office. When he stopped to think about it, he understood their concern since the ship had floated unreachable for several hours during the storm.

"You should call Avery first," Dani said. "Put her mind at ease."

Jake agreed, and they found a bright yellow park bench to sit where Jake dialled his daughter and put the call on speaker. She picked up right away.

"Is everybody okay? The media have been all over the story. Nobody could reach the ship. An airplane flew into the storm and reported you were still afloat, but the waves were really high. They showed video and said you could evacuate. I don't understand how that could be possible. Surviving in a small lifeboat in those waves doesn't seem possible. They also said the ship had some technology to keep it level. It must have been awful. I just can't imagine."

Jake tried to calm his daughter and downplayed the storm. Dani also assured Avery that everything was fine. "It was like a ride at the fair. That's how Emilie described it." Jake told Avery about the ship's stabilizers but said nothing about the murders or Emilie's kidnapping. "I'll tell you more when we see you. How are Ava and Nick?"

Avery replied, "Ava loves the stuffed toy you gave her. She's sleeping with it right now. Nick's doing well. Always busy. I know you're not telling me everything that happened on the ship, Dad. We've been down this road before. I hope the rest of your cruise is uneventful. Will the internet be working on the way back?"

"That's a good question, sweetie. They'll be fixing it while we're in port, but a couple of lightning strikes hit the system. With any luck, we'll be back online. If not, I'll phone you when we arrive back in Vancouver, but we'll be fine. I promise I'll contact you as soon as possible."

Avery said, "Okay, I'll hold you to that. Love to all of you."

"We're sending love back," Jake said. When he hung up, he said, "I'll text the others. They'll ask all kinds of questions that would be more easily answered when we see them." He chuckled. "It's easier to sidestep the questions by text."

Dani laughed. "I'll call Lonnie, and then we should get to the police station." She dialled the constable in Ottawa, and he also picked up right away with comparable questions to Avery's. Dani brushed them off with the same technique Jake used. Then, she said, "You were about to say something when we got cut off."

"Yes," Lonnie said. "I wanted to tell you when we checked Angela Lee's social media, we found she communicated with a crewmember on the Ocean Wanderer named Rafael. She asked about his itinerary. It just seemed to be too much of a coincidence. It may have been nothing or a romance or something. I just wanted to give you a heads-up."

Dani smiled at Jake. "Oh, your instinct was correct. I'll fill you in when we get home, but Rafael helped Angela with the murders. We're trying to understand how much he knew about what he was involved in. We'll interview him soon. We're going to the police station to sit in on the interrogation, at least if we get there soon enough. We'd better get going."

When Dani hung up, they asked a man for directions to the police station and slipped around fallen tree limbs on the twenty-minute walk. Store owners removed plywood barriers from their window fronts. A bar owner who failed to board up his windows as others had done swept up glass from the sidewalks in front of his place.

"I may have underestimated the damage," Jake said.

Chapter Forty-Seven

They arrived at the two-storey, rectangular Seward Police Department building on Adams Street a few minutes later. A blue sign beside a set of seven concrete steps announced that the police department and other city services occupied the main and second floors of the building. One set of steps led up to the police department, while another led down to the Alaska Court Magistrate.

Jake and Dani entered the building and walked to the receptionist desk. Dani showed her credentials and asked to see someone in charge. A few minutes later, a man and a woman emerged from the back of the building. Dani introduced herself to the man, who turned out to be the Deputy Chief of Police. He introduced Sloane Parker, the FBI agent from Anchorage whom Dani spoke to earlier. While it seemed like weeks ago, it was only a couple of days.

The Deputy Police Chief apologized that the Chief was unavailable. "We're fortunate the power is still on in this part of town. There are outages all over the city, and the Chief is investigating a serious car accident at an intersection on the west side. The storm played havoc all over the city, so it's a busy morning."

Dani said she understood. "We're happy to meet you both. Agent Parker and I spoke on the phone, so it's nice to put a face to a name."

Parker was a striking woman in her thirties. The soft waves of her golden blonde hair framed her face. Her hazel eyes were full of depth, and she carried herself with grace in a tailored outfit. Her smile was engaging. "I'm delighted to meet you, too. And this must be Jake." She shook hands with both and said, "I contacted the police department here and they told me your ship was docking this morning, so I drove from Anchorage to meet you. You've been through quite the ordeal with murders and the storm. I understand your daughter was kidnapped, too.

"When I arrived, I found out our friends here had taken someone into custody. A cabin steward named Rafael, I believe?"

Dani nodded. "Yes, if we can go somewhere quiet, Jake and I will fill you in. The story is kind of involved."

The Deputy Chief led them into a room in the back, not unlike the one on the ship where they interrogated Patel and Thompson. He brought in extra chairs, so they could sit across from each other at the table. He excused himself when his phone rang. When he returned, he said, "If you don't need me, I'll leave you to it. Some teenagers are looting a jewellery store that wasn't secured properly during the storm. The teenagers think they can take everything they want since the front window was shattered." He didn't wait for an answer and disappeared on the run down the hall.

Jake and Dani filled Parker in as best they could. "There are still gaps only Rafael can help us sort out. It's your jurisdiction, but do you mind if we sit in on the interrogation?"

Parker said, "I have no problem with you sitting in as the officer who uncovered the plot. In fact, you should take the lead questioning the suspect. It stretches protocol for Jake to be in the room, but what the hell? You've been involved the whole time, so you might as well sit in as an observer, Jake."

Dani decided she liked this woman a lot.

Parker left the room and asked an officer to bring in Rafael. While they waited, Dani rearranged the chairs so that Rafael would sit opposite her and Parker while Jake would be behind them in a corner, so he could observe without being obvious. When the officer returned with Rafael in tow, Jake was shocked. Many criminals crossed his path during his time as an investigative reporter, but he had trouble reconciling this pathetic-looking man with their friendly cabin steward of a few hours earlier.

Rafael wore a T-shirt and jeans provided by the police station. The clothes hung off his shoulders, and the pant cuffs had been rolled up. The crotch hung almost to his knees. The clothes had to be two sizes too big. His shoulders hunched, and his gaze directed downward in either an unfocused or possibly embarrassed manner. Dark circles rimmed his eyes. A deep red scratch angled from the tip of his nose across his eye onto his forehead. *Emilie's handiwork.* For a moment, Jake felt pity for Rafael, but that dissipated just as fast when he recalled the steward had kidnapped Emilie, struck her on the head, and left her abandoned. He doubted Dani would be lenient with him.

Rafael sat, and Dani started the interrogation. A red light on a camera at the ceiling in the corner indicated it would capture every word and movement. She asked him to state his name for the record. Silence. She asked again but still no response. Rafael stared at a dark patch in the woodgrain of the table, saying nothing. He blinked often, his left eye watering from the wound Emilie inflicted.

Dani said, "Look, Rafael, we know Angela Lee contacted you on social media. We think she contacted you to help her carry out two murders onboard the ship. I'm sure you received a lot of money for doing that. We think you delivered gift bags with poisoned food in them to Mark Reynolds and Gavin Holt. At the least, you are an accessory to two murders. You also set a gift bag inside our room, which we will probably find out contained poisoned items for us to consume. That would add attempted murder to the charges against you. We're just waiting for confirmation. People don't jump off a cruise ship into freezing water and try to swim to a marina if they're innocent. You look very guilty, my friend." Rafael's eyes shifted slightly, but he continued to say nothing.

Jake, Dani, and Parker sat in impotent silence until Dani slammed her palms on the table and scraped her chair back. The move startled Rafael, but he still said nothing. "Okay," Dani said, "we'll leave the room and let you mull it over. You're going away for a long time, my friend, but it might be for murders you didn't commit. Angela Lee is dead, so we'll assume you did everything. When we come back, we want answers."

Jake, Dani, and Sloane Parker got up to leave. Dani hoped he would stop them, but he just sat immobile, staring at the table. His demeanour changed at the news Angela was dead. He gulped and continued to blink. The skin tone on his face paled.

But he said nothing.

They stood outside the room, and Dani said, "Let's give him fifteen minutes. If he still won't talk, I have an idea. While we wait, do they have coffee here?"

Chapter Forty-Eight

The small interrogation room seemed warm and crowded to Jake. Four people occupied the room again. Rafael wrapped himself in an invisible haze of defeat, but a spark of defiance hovered behind the hollow expression. He remained silent.

Dani asked if he was ready to talk. Rafael's swollen eyes drifted to Dani, but his lips remained sealed, his jaw firm.

"Look, Rafael, we get it. You think if you don't say anything, we won't be able to prove your involvement. Since Angela Lee is dead, you think no one will testify against you. There is no video. But here's how this is going to work, my friend. We're holding proof you killed Angela Lee. A witness saw you entering her room. You're in big trouble, but here's the thing. I'm prepared to offer you a deal. If you talk, I'll go easy on you."

Jake tried not to show any emotion, but his surprise betrayed him. He just hoped he didn't utter something out loud. Adrenalin zipped through him as he waited for Rafael's answer, if he answered at all. Rafael didn't kill Angela Lee. *How could he*? A guard remained at Lee's door the entire time after her arrest. He saw from the corner of his eye Parker turn toward Dani with a surprised look. He leaned forward with anticipation, his elbows resting on his knees, his hands clasped, waiting to see if Rafael would say something.

Rafael saw none of the reactions. He blurted, "I didn't kill Angela Lee. I didn't kill anyone. I'll talk if you promise me a deal so the courts will go easier on me."

Dani leaned back in her chair and said, "Let's start with your full name and where you're from."

"My name is Rafael Miguel Santos, and I live at 3777 Mabini Street, Makati City, in the Philippines."

Dani walked Rafael through his teenage years to the point when he joined the cruise line and, specifically, the Ocean Wanderer. Rafael's shoulders relaxed, and his voice became stronger while his confidence grew with the comfortable questions. The tension lifted in the room, but the questions were about to become more difficult.

Dani said, "Tell us how you met Angela Lee."

Rafael drew a deep breath. His distinctive mahogany brown eyes sought Dani's, almost pleading, yet resigned to talking about something he would rather not discuss. "I met her on a cruise in the Caribbean. I worked on the ship, and her cabin was on the deck assigned to me. We got to know each other, and she tipped me well. Better than most passengers. She talked about her family and showed me pictures on social media. My mother lives in the Philippines, and I showed her pictures of her and my home, and we exchanged social media contact information.

"A few months later, she contacted me by direct message on social media and said she would give me money if I would reveal my itinerary for my next contract. She said she was helping her boss organize a cruise for their company executives, and it would be great if we met again; that she wanted to see me again. Things all came together, and she said she would pay me $2,000 to do extra things for her on the ship. I agreed, but I made a big mistake. I understood she meant arranging for spa treatments, getting her exclusive deals in the shops, or dining reservations. She said she would pay me more when the cruise ended. I never dreamed she meant murder."

Dani prompted Rafael to continue. "Did she give you the money, and what sort of things did she want you to do?"

"Yes, she boarded the Ocean Wanderer in the first group early in the afternoon. She had given me her cabin number, so I visited her as soon as she arrived. She gave me $2,000 in cash and a gift bag to deliver to Mr. Alan Brindley's room. I should have known by the amount of money that she wanted me to do more than the simple services I expected. She set me up and paid me for my silence. It shocked me when Security showed up at Mr. Brindley's room and then the doctor came, but I assumed he died of natural causes. You must understand, the earnings from this contract and the money from Ms. Lee would buy a new house for my mother."

Jake leaned back in his chair as another brief twinge of pity for Rafael shot through him, but his thoughts kept returning to the fact this man wasn't so innocent. He kidnapped Emilie.

Dani's laser eyes zeroed in on Rafael's. "Brindley's real name was Mark Reynolds. You knew Reynolds died. That must've raised suspicions about the contents of the bag, yet you delivered a second and third bag. The second one to Gavin Holt and the third to our room. Holt died from eating candy from the bag. We haven't confirmed the contents of the bag you set inside our room. Why would you keep handing out bags if you were suspicious about their contents?"

Only the breathing of the four occupants and the creak of Rafael's chair as he fidgeted filtered through the room. "Yes, it made me suspicious. I asked Ms. Lee, and she said I shouldn't be concerned. She told me to make sure the second bag was delivered to Mr. Holt's room. She went even further. She reminded me how much money she gave me and how she would shift all the blame to me if I didn't do what she asked. She became a different woman from the one I met in the Caribbean. She terrified me."

Rafael's pupils dilated, a sign to Dani that this conversation bothered him. The excessive hand movements revealed even more. Recent studies indicated that hand gestures alone cannot determine if someone is lying but combined with the pupil dilation and the sweat popping on Rafael's brow, Dani wondered if his involvement with Angela Lee bothered him as much as he let on. She saw a pattern. Rafael may have been a reluctant participant, but now he was doing everything he could to protect himself. He deserved whatever he got for this.

"What about the gift bag left in our state room? What did Lee say about that?"

"Nothing. She just said to put it inside your room. That's what I did. She had a list of all the people onboard who worked for CamGuard Solutions and the rooms they occupied. I swear I knew nothing about the contents of the bags."

Dani leaned forward, her palms flat on the table. "How did the gift bags and the bottle with the poison get into Raj Patel's room?" Her voice rose. "You tried to set him up."

More sweat on Rafael's brow. "No, I swear, it was Ms. Lee's idea. She threatened me again. Because I had the master key to the rooms, I could slip in and out easily. She gave me a small bottle that looked like aftershave and a bunch of empty gift bags and told me to stash them in Mr. Patel's room. The CCTV cameras were offline, so it was easy to do."

Dani studied the clock on the wall. She and Jake needed to return to the ship soon if they wanted to make the trip back to Vancouver. She would be delighted to hand the whole mess over to the FBI, but she had one more question. She leaned back in her chair, her lips barely moving, her voice low.

"Why did you kidnap my daughter, Emilie Perez? You left her bound and gagged in a dark room without food and water. She would have been there for the entire trip back to Vancouver if we hadn't found her. We're lucky we found her. Otherwise, she might have died."

Rafael lifted his eyes. He whimpered, "I didn't want her to die. I wanted nothing more to do with Angela Lee, so I planned to disembark at Seward, hitch a ride to Anchorage, and disappear back to the Philippines. It became obvious my part in this would be uncovered and Security would want to see me, so I realized I couldn't just walk off the ship at Seward. I needed a diversion so I could swim away. Everyone on the ship would be preoccupied looking for your daughter. Once the ship set sail for Vancouver, I planned to call from a burner phone to tell you your daughter's location. I just hoped the communication system would be working."

Dani sat back in disgust. She glared at Rafael with one hand on her chin and the fingernail of the index finger on her other hand beating a steady drumbeat on the table. How naïve of Rafael to think he had a solid plan. Had he successfully disappeared from the ship, she would have organized a manhunt to beat all manhunts to track him down and bring him to justice. He said he made a mistake by taking Angela Lee's money. His bigger mistake was messing with Dani's daughter. She had not one shred of pity for him.

She said to Parker, who remained silent for the entire interrogation, "Have you heard enough for now?"

"Yes," Parker said. "We'll conduct a more thorough interrogation when we get him to Anchorage." She laid out preliminary charges to Rafael and read him his rights as she handcuffed him.

Rafael cooperated by putting his hands behind his back, but he said, "Wait a minute. Shouldn't I be signing something confirming the deal?"

Sloane replied, "I didn't make any deal." She gestured toward Dani. "She did. But she has no jurisdiction here."

Chapter Forty-Nine

The voyage back to Vancouver and then to Ottawa came and went without incident. The ship left Seward two hours late but made up most of the time on the way. The weather became clear and bright and warm enough that Jake and Dani spent time with a raucous crowd around the pool. Two free drinks for each passenger courtesy of the Ocean Wanderer combined with the euphoria of escaping a life-threatening storm and having a story to tell turned up the decibel level at the pool. They dined with Emilie in the Swordfish Restaurant the last night on board, thanks to Eduardo's earlier gift. Emilie exhibited the healing power of youth and spent her time sleeping and playing video games and mini putt with her new friend, Leif. She hid any aftereffects of her ordeal well, but Dani resolved to have her attend sessions with a counsellor when they returned to Ottawa.

The ship just seemed to be a happier place since the internet worked again. Except for broken chairs, boarded-up, shattered windows, and sealed cabins belonging to Mark Reynolds, Gavin Holt, and Angela Lee, it was like nothing had happened. The steward who shared a cabin with Rafael was delighted to claim the extra space for himself.

Zachary Felton joined Jake and Dani for drinks after the theatre production on the last night of the cruise and expressed his sincere gratitude. He still didn't tip the server.

The captain invited Jake, Dani, and Emilie to visit the bridge. Emilie's wide-eyed tour from one side to the other behind the expansive glass on the bridge thrilled Dani. The brilliant sun beat down on the smooth-as-glass azure ocean as if its brilliant reflection was leading them back to their starting point. Once again, the immense ship moved effortlessly through the water. Captain Ingrid Svenssen showed Emilie all the gadgets on the bridge, enthralling the teenager. Jake whispered to Dani, "I could have sworn she would follow in your footsteps, but she might aim to work on a ship."

Dani regarded Jake before replying. "I guess working on a cruise ship wouldn't be a terrible thing. I mean, what could go wrong on a cruise ship, right?"

The captain advised Jake and Dani that the helicopter Parker ordered couldn't land, so Holt's body would be delivered for autopsy in Seward. She called Dani over before they left and handed her an envelope. Jake didn't notice the exchange, but he heard them share a laugh. "What was that about?" he asked.

"Ah, nothing," Dani replied. "Just a joke between women."

When they disembarked, crewmembers directed them to a warehouse where hundreds of suitcases sat side-by side, most of them black. They searched for theirs among the myriads of choices, and a strange, slimy feeling slithered down Dani's back. She scanned the room to identify the source, and her eyes landed on a man she recognized staring at her. His wife and daughter stood by his side. Dani was stunned when the man's lips turned up in a crooked smile, and he raised a gloved, misshapen hand in her direction. She brushed the interaction off by telling herself the man was simply saluting Emilie's safe return from her kidnapping. Still, the self-confident gesture from the man they originally suspected of poisoning Reynolds bothered her over the following months.

Sloane Parker called Dani to tell her she read Angela Lee's suicide note, in which the woman admitted everything. Desperate to resolve her financial difficulties, Lee installed the virus in CamGuard's software to steal money from the crypto company. Lee learned Holt had blown the whistle and Reynolds was investigating, so she thought she had to do something about it. Unfortunately for Rafael, she dragged him into her plot.

Parker also confirmed Dani's suspicions that the chocolate bar in Holt's room had been contaminated, but not the candy in the bag left for Dani and Jake. They concluded it must have been an attempt by Angela Lee to distract them from their investigation. Lonnie uncovered search history on Lee's computer related to handling cyanide.

Lonnie also informed Dani that the driver of the hit-and-run vehicle, who created an opening for Raj Patel to join CamGuard Solutions, had not been found. The stolen vehicle was located a few blocks from the scene. Investigators satisfied themselves that Patel spoke the truth. His motivation for leaving a higher paying job was the opportunity to work on leading edge technology. They attributed his sullenness to a distrust of law enforcement and media, which was unlikely to change following his experience on the ship.

Avery and Ava surprised Jake by waiting for them at the Ottawa airport. Avery drove up from Toronto with her daughter to visit. At least, she used that as the thinly veiled pretext of her visit. Everyone understood the real reason was to grill her dad on exactly what happened on the ship and to admonish him for getting himself in trouble yet again. She knew it would do no good. Her dad and Dani made a great couple, and he obviously loved Emilie. Deep down inside, she respected that her dad was born to investigate, and as a retired reporter, he just couldn't turn down a good mystery. There would probably be more adventures in his future with his beloved Dani, the homicide detective.

Jake got to spend a week reacquainting himself with his new granddaughter. Oliver, his temperamental cat, punished Jake for leaving him behind by spending all his time with anybody else who happened to be in the house. He did allow Jake to feed him.

A few days after returning, Jake called Janice Richardson, his friend at the newspaper, and gave her an exclusive first-person account of their experience in a terrifying storm on a cruise ship. Typically, he downplayed the story and said nothing about the murders. He didn't intend to be the first to bring the story up. He felt bad about not telling Janice about Emilie's kidnapping. Word would soon be out, and when it was, he would talk to Janice again.

Avery insisted on leaving Saturday, but Jake and Dani convinced her to join them for breakfast with their friends. Emilie, always happy to listen to the stories and bantering that occurred at breakfast, eagerly tagged along. When they arrived at Brew and Buns, their friends Ryan Cambridge, Eric Jacobson, and Pierre Chevrier had already commandeered an extra table and chairs for the guests, including a highchair for Ava.

Pierre, whose mind rarely lifted from the gutter, said to Jake and Dani, "So, I guess you guys spent a lot of time, uh, cuddling during the storm. That must have been a wild ride."

Emilie said, "Ewww!"

Jake had been waiting for the opportunity. He smiled and said, "Well, you could say the storm was an afterclap to the slight breeze preceding it."

Everyone around the table burst out laughing, except Pierre, who sat dumbfounded once again. Jake mentally patted himself on the back and thanked Alexa, his home electronic assistant, for finding yet another word to throw out when the opportunity arose. He wasn't going to tell Chevrier it meant an unexpected subsequent event.

The friends spent time discussing storms, laughing at jokes that weren't really that funny, and enjoying a leisurely breakfast. At the end of the meal, Dani pulled an envelope from her jacket and announced she and Jake had helped the captain with a minor problem onboard the ship, and she rewarded them with a token of appreciation from the cruise line. "I've kept it a secret until now. There's no better time to show Jake."

With a flourish, she handed the unopened envelope to Jake. He slid his finger under the sealed flap. Everyone at the table will swear to this day that Jake turned several shades of green at the contents of the envelope.

It was a complimentary fourteen-day cruise for three.

Thank you for reading *Shadows of Truth*. If you like what you read, please consider leaving a review at your favorite online book retailer.

DISCUSSION QUESTIONS

1. Describe the personalities and motivations of the main characters in *Shadows of Truth*. Did you find them to be fully developed?

2. How would you react if you were on a cruise ship in a storm like the one experienced by Jake, Dani, and Emilie?

3. Did you identify any hidden clues?

4. Did the author try to throw you off track and if so, how?

5. Did the twists and turns enhance the story and add to the suspense?

6. At what point did the suspense start to build?

7. Is the conclusion probable and believable?

8. Were there any questions left unresolved in the story?

9. Did you feel any sympathy for Rafael, the cabin steward?

10. Have you read the other books in the series? How does *Shadows of Truth* compare?

ABOUT THE AUTHOR

Barry Finlay is an accomplished and award-winning author known for works such as the travel adventure *Kilimanjaro and Beyond – A Life-Changing Journey* (co-authored with his son Chris), the humorous memoir *I Guess We Missed the Boat*, and the motivational title *Just Keep Climbing*. He has also authored five bestselling and award-winning thrillers within The Marcie Kane Thriller Collection: *The Vanishing Wife, A Perilous Question, Remote Access, Never So Alone,* and *The Burden of Darkness*.

His recent work includes the Jake Scott Mystery Series, beginning with *Searching for Truth, The Guardians of Truth,* and *The Secret Truth*, followed by his latest release, *Shadows of Truth*. Barry was recognized in the 2012-13 Authors Show's edition of "50 Great Writers You Should Be Reading" and has received the Queen Elizabeth Diamond Jubilee Medal for his efforts in raising funds to support children in Tanzania. He currently resides in Ottawa, Canada, with his wife, Evelyn.

Contact Barry Finlay

Author Website: https://www,barry-finlay.com

Facebook Page: https://www.facebook.com/AuthorBarryFinlay

Instagram: https://www.instagram.com/barry_finlay_author

BOOKS BY BARRY FINLAY

THE JAKE SCOTT MYSTERY SERIES

Searching For Truth: A Jake Scott Mystery (Book 1)

The Guardians of Truth: A Jake Scott Mystery (Book 2)

The Secret Truth: A Jake Scott Mystery (Book 3)

Shadows of Truth: A Jake Scott Mystery (Book 4)

THE MARCIE KANE THRILLER COLLECTION

The Vanishing Wife: An Action-Packed Crime Thriller (Marcie Kane Book 1)

A Perilous Question: An International Thriller & Crime Novel (Marcie Kane Book 2)

Remote Access: An International Political Thriller (Marcie Kane Book 3)

Never So Alone (Prequel novella to the Marcie Kane Thriller Collection Book 4)

The Burden of Darkness: A Marcie Kane and Nathan Harris Thriller (Marcie Kane Book 5)

NON-FICTION TITLES

Kilimanjaro and Beyond: A Life-Changing Journey

I Guess We Missed the Boat

Just Keep Climbing: Inspirational Stories for Overcoming Challenges and
Living Life

My Limitless Life: Karen Meades

READ THE FIRST THREE BOOKS IN THE EXCITING JAKE SCOTT MYSTERY SERIES

SEARCHING FOR TRUTH

Former journalist Jake Scott relies on his weekly breakfast gatherings with friends and a temperamental tabby cat named Oliver to keep his spirits up. He has lost his wife, retired from his job, and watched his daughter move to Toronto with her boyfriend.

Things change when one of the breakfast attendees, a beautiful and tenacious police detective with a troubled teenage daughter, suggests Jake should write a book. When he takes her advice and researches a convicted murderer's case, he finds out something is terribly wrong. Could a member of the breakfast group be hiding a secret deadly enough to commit murder?

Jake follows leads that uncover a mysterious and disturbing rollercoaster ride of clues, all while his attraction for the detective grows. An attempt to force the true murderer out of hiding results in a terrifying ordeal on the coldest night of the year.

THE GUARDIANS OF TRUTH

The affable and shrewd, yet old-fashioned, Jake is hot on the trail of a case when a body discovered in a bog and three suspects lead him to the doorstep of The Guardians of Truth, a shady organization with an opportunistic and charismatic leader. While the organization purports to offer everlasting support to its followers, Jake discovers just the opposite is true. Now Jake and an insider, Cassie Wright, want to expose the leader and protect his followers from financial ruin or worse. Their harrowing quest isn't without peril, as one will disappear and the other will be forced to fight for survival.

If you like your heroes to be, well, like you and me, the second book in the Jake Scott Mystery Series will draw you in and have you wishing you could dive in to help.

THE SECRET TRUTH

Retired investigative journalist Jake Scott narrowly avoids a collision with a speeding car on his way to a Bed and Breakfast where he plans to spend the night. Moments before his arrival, the peaceful atmosphere at the B&B is shattered by a devastating explosion, claiming the lives of everyone there. While authorities initially chalk it up to a tragic gas leak, seasoned homicide detective Dani Perez can't shake her suspicions. Given her overloaded schedule, she enlists Jake's expertise to delve into the backgrounds of the deceased. As Jake pursues the investigation, he unearths a web of secrets hinting at a darker truth lurking beneath the surface of the seemingly idyllic B&B.

FIND THEM ONLINE OR AT YOUR FAVORITE BOOK STORE OR LIBRARY

www.barry-finlay.com